Evidence

Lynn Clarke 1/16/14

AND

Judgment

Lynn Clarke, J.D.

ANA PHORA

Anaphora Literary Press
Anna Faktorovich: Director, Designer, Editor
104 Banff Dr., Apt. 101, Edinboro, PA 16412
(814) 273-0004
pennsylvaniajournal@gmail.com
http://sites.google.som/site/anaphoraliterarypress

Published in 2010 by Anaphora Literary Press

Evidence and Judgment

Lynn Clarke, J.D..—1st edition.

ISBN-13: 978-1-456-50116-7
ISBN-10: 1-456-50116-X

With thanks to my family, Greg, Rachel and Anna

CONTENTS

CHAPTER ONE

"When thou buildest a new house, then thou shalt make a battlement for thy roof, that thou bring not blood upon thine house, if any man fall from thence."

—*Deuteronomy* 23:8, King James Version

*M*ay I help you?" The receptionist at the law firm of Hantler Vintberg was too new to recognize Jeff Rogers, ex-husband of Jane Sidley. Jane was a junior non-equity partner at the firm.

"Yeah, sure. Jeff Rogers, here to see Jane Sidley."

"Do you have an appointment?"

Jeff leaned across the curved counter of the polished teak reception desk. His straight black hair nearly covered his eyes but the receptionist could still see him look down her blouse and then glance at the phone in front of her. She glared at him for a moment and punched in Jane's extension.

"There's a Jeff Rogers here to see you."

Jeff? Jane tucked her shoulder length hair behind one ear. She glanced at her schedule on her computer screen and sighed.

"Send him up to nine."

Jane hadn't seen Jeff for at least a year since the divorce was final. Would parenthood and domestic life with Cassie, the shipping clerk he'd met at an industrial parts manufacturer where he was failing in the sales department, have cost Jeff his looks? Would he have a gut? And what about that hair? Jeff had quite a head of thick black straight hair. Maybe he'd have a receding hair line now or even a bald spot.

When the elevator doors opened Jane could see nothing had changed. Jeff still had the lean, wiry physique she had liked. No, in the year and a half since he'd left her, Jeff hadn't gained an ounce of fat or lost even an ounce of muscle. And his hair wasn't thinning even a little. Not even in his mid-thirties.

"Baby, you look good." He leaned in for a kiss and Jane turned away. She heard the clicking of keyboards stop in the surrounding cubicles. The messenger in the hallway slowed his rolling cart.

"My office is this way now." Jane started down the hallway.

When they reached her office, Jeff settled into one of the two client chairs she'd arranged around a small glass topped table to the side of her massive mahogany desk. Jane looked at the high backed chair behind her desk but then slid into the other client chair, facing Jeff across the small glass table.

"What's going on? Why did you come to see me?" Once Jeff married Cassie, Jane no longer had to pay alimony, so it couldn't be about that.

"I miss you. Sure baby, I do. We were good together, right?" He reached for her hand, Jane pulled it away. "I know you're not seeing anybody."

"I really don't have time for this. Is there an actual legitimate reason you came to see me?"

"Our house is empty right now babe, am I right? Why not take the afternoon off?"

Jane moved to the chair behind her big desk. "If that's why you came to see me, you're absolutely wasting your time. I mean, for heaven's sake, you betrayed me. And divorced me. And got married, to the mother of your child, who is someone other than me." Jane wanted to shout at him, but was afraid her voice would carry even with the door shut. "You ruined us. Do you want to ruin everything with Cassie too? Do you want her to raise that baby alone?"

"I wasn't exactly planning on telling her, sweetheart."

Jane stood up behind her desk. "Get out."

"Wait, calm down, baby. Sit down. I'm just messing with you. I'm really here because I need a loan. Seriously. Cassie hasn't gone back to work and my commissions, babe, getting started here is murder. It takes time. To make contacts. Personal contacts. Personal contacts are what it's about in this business. And I know you're mad about the divorce, but you got a good deal on the house, you know you did. You just paid me for half what we had in it and nothing for the potential upside, all that you might get from it someday down the road. If you ever sell, I get nothing for that. So you owe me. Anyway, I just need a couple thousand. It would really help me out."

"Unbelievable." Jane walked around the desk and reached for the brass handle on her office door. "Absolutely unbelievable. No loan. Not now. Not ever."

"Hey, look." Jeff leaned forward in his chair and looked up at Jane. "Sorry for hitting on you. I thought maybe you'd expect it, like a compliment, and now you're sore. I thought you'd want me to say I still think you're hot, which I do. I really do. But baby, honest, I need the loan. And you got money. You always made money easy."

Did she? Jane tilted her head to one side and frowned. She'd worked hard for her law degree. Now she worked hard at her law practice. OK, it wasn't hard physical labor, like breaking rocks or farm work in the hot sun, but it was complicating and took a lot of time. She worked five days a week and a lot of evenings and most Saturdays, so really six days a week, sometimes even seven. That wasn't easy. Her work paid fairly well, but did that mean she made easy money? Other people might work harder for less money. A person in a third world country might work really hard and make a whole lot less. It still seemed like a lot of hard work to earn it. And that wasn't really the point, was it?

"No way." Jane said. She opened her office door. "Not ever. On both counts. No afternoon off and no loan."

"You always were a real ball breaker, you know that?"

"The elevators. They're down the hall. Get on them. Ride them straight to the bottom and get out and don't come back. Ever."

As infuriating as Jeff could be, Jane still wished her marriage hadn't turned out so badly. She hadn't meant to be living alone, with multiple cats, at thirty-one. A husband to shovel the walk in the winter and keep her warm. And babies. Husband or not, a baby was what Jane really wanted. She wanted a baby so much.

Jane slumped in her desk chair, listening to Jeff striding towards the elevator.

She'd gone to college about four hundred miles away, in a bigger city. About a third of her high school class went to college out of town, with the rest going to one of the colleges near-

by or straight to work at Integrated Products or one of the dwin-
dling number of companies that hadn't yet moved overseas. A
few of her high school classmates had gone into the military.

Jane was very smart and occasionally funny. She was tall,
thin and pretty. In college, she had long straight brown hair. It
was shoulder length now and still thick and shiny, striking with
her big blue eyes. She had lots of friends at college and did well
in her classes. She majored in English Literature with a minor in
Economics. Her senior paper was on the influence of colonial-
ism on British novels in the late nineteenth century. "Well re-
searched and well written, if somewhat unoriginal," were the
comments her professor wrote on the paper. She gave Jane a B.

Then law school. Jane applied to several but chose one in
the same city as her college. She knew her mother was lonely,
since her dad died in Jane's senior year of college. But Jane was-
n't ready to move back to her hometown. She missed her mother, but she was having trouble dealing with her own grief and
thought she and her mother would both drown in mutual grief if
she moved back home just then. She lived during law school in a
small studio apartment near the campus. Jane studied long hours
and got reasonably good grades. She liked her classes, especially
contracts and corporations. Jane didn't think she wanted to be a
courtroom lawyer. She wanted her work to be more positive, less
adversarial. Building up businesses or helping people somehow.
She took some tax courses, a course on insurance law and one
on estate planning as electives in law school.

She didn't meet her ex-husband at a party or in her law
school classes. Jeff was a salesman at an insurance company just
a short ride on the subway from Jane's apartment. Jane clerked
there in the legal department during the summer after her first
year of law school.

She'd barely noticed him until there he was, leaning on his
elbows on the stacks of file folders on her desk, grinning and
looking into her eyes with a few glances at her chest. "Baby, you
and me. Dinner and a movie this Friday," he'd said. "How about
it?"

"The firm's sexual harassment policy restricts socializing
with persons under direct supervision," or something along those
lines, was what Jane said. "While I'm not your superior, techni-

cally speaking, I am assisting with the pending litigation defense of several complaints filed in regard to transactions in which you participated. I will be part of the team preparing you for your deposition and testimony. Accordingly, I believe outside social contact between us is inadvisable at this time."

Jeff had just leaned in closer and Jane remembered how she liked the clean smell of his hair. "Do you good. You'll see."

Jane didn't sleep with Jeff until about halfway through the summer. She was glad she waited, but not too long. His energy was amazing. It was almost like a drug. And Jeff was a talker. The few boys she dated and actually slept with in college would either want to leave right away after sex or, if they had a dorm room or a bedroom in an apartment to themselves, they would drop right off to sleep after sex. Not Jeff. They'd lean back against the pillows and he would tell her his latest ideas for new sales pitches.

"Hey, how about this? Say you've been thinking about insurance or maybe you haven't, but here's the deal. I tell you no one gets out of this alive. And dead people don't get paychecks. Yeah, that's it. No paychecks and no unemployment checks, not any, if you're dead. No looking for a better job either. No, you're just dead."

"Ok."

"I mean dead is what the average dickhead worries about, right, baby? So that makes it real. If I mention no paychecks and no unemployment, death seems like something that might happen to anybody, because paychecks and unemployment checks are what you see everyday. You get what I'm saying?"

"Sure, but maybe say something about the premiums too? I mean even if everybody needs life insurance, nobody's going to buy something if it's not affordable."

"You're sure wrong about that, baby. People buy stuff they can't afford all the time. And if I talk enough about dying without a paycheck, the stuff they'll buy is life insurance from me. This is my ticket. I can do this. I know how to talk to Mr. and Mrs. Dickhead. You watch."

Jane sighed. Never mind the past. She needed to get back to work right here and now in the present. She looked at the open documents on her computer screen. Unfinished wills, drafts of trusts, estate inventories, tax returns, and a few prenups. She could also picture the faces of the impatient clients waiting for her to finish each of those open documents. Daydreaming and moping wasn't going to help with that or with meeting her billable hours target for the week.

Henry "Ted" Willingham, the firm's managing partner, appeared in her doorway. "How are we doing with Max Bowden's estate? I've got Oliver and Adelaide calling me every five minutes to complain that you're holding up the estate. I'm sure I don't need to remind you the estate holds a majority share of the stock of our very good client Integrated Products."

"I'm not holding it up. A taxable estate with stock in a family business takes time. Getting a proper value for the stock just doesn't happen overnight. And there's no rushing the IRS."

"Are we having a communication problem here?"

"No, we're not. I hear you loud and clear. It won't make the estate filings go any faster but how about if I start calling Adelaide every week? I've been sending written status reports every few weeks, but I don't know if Adelaide reads her mail. So I could call her. And I can send weekly updates by e-mail to Oliver and his sister Nora. How's that? Should keep them from calling you so often."

"Ah, yes. Glad we understand each other. Good, good. Every week, yes, that should keep them happy." Ted fished a ticket out of his jacket pocket. "The Risterian Club is having a woman speaker at some charity fundraiser over at the Liberty Express Inn tonight. I have a ticket I can't use. I don't know what she's talking about, empowerment or juggling kids or whatever you're calling it these days. Not my cup of tea." He held out the ticket.

"Tonight? Sorry, I can't make it. I'm volunteering Wednesday nights as a tutor in an adult literacy program at the Justice Community Center."

"The Justice Center? Where is that, for Pete's sake, Stockdon Heights? Didn't you hear that speaker we brought in from the Metcalf Group at the firm retreat, on what did he call it, 'Doing Well by Doing Good?' How we all need to give back to the community, but we don't have to wear hair shirts to do it. I belong to the Risterians and we help the poor, or what are you supposed to say, the underprivileged, we help them. But I still get to meet and greet. I just played in a foursome at their annual golf event with the CEO's of three of our largest clients. And that raised, well I don't know how much, but I'm sure it was a lot, for some charity. Are we on the same page here?"

Are we on the same page? Are we even in the same book? "I understand, but I just can't go tonight. I can't cancel last minute, my student in the literacy program doesn't have a phone."

"Pick up the pace on the Bowden estate, alright?"

"Got it. I'm on it."

After her tutoring session, Jane headed down the hall at the community center toward the door to the parking lot.

"Jane, wait up, Jane." It was John Hauser, a stockbroker she'd met a few times through her clients. Hauser had sent some of his investment clients to her for help with drafting a will or the administration of an estate. "Glad I ran into you." He held out his hand. "You here drumming up business with a seminar on wills or estates? I've done great with seminars to seniors about investment strategies, but I'd love to send some clients to hear if you're doing something on wills or trusts. Or insurance. That would be great. You got something on that?"

"I'm not here doing a seminar. I'm here as a literacy volunteer. There's a program on Wednesday nights. I just finished my tutoring session."

"No kidding. Literacy. That's terrific. Just great. If you're done with your tutoring for tonight how about grabbing a cup of coffee with me or a bite to eat?"

Jane did that sort of thing all the time. She went for coffee or lunch or even dinner with brokers who had clients who needed wills. And, in turn, she had clients who needed stockbrokers. It was a good way to establish a rapport with people her firm called business referral sources. Like bankers. They invited her to lunch or she invited them to lunch, and soon they were sending their clients to her to draw up trusts, and the clients were right back to them for bank trust services. Insurance agents, accountants, even the people who ran some of the major community funds and charities in her city, they were all on her calendar. Jane lunched with them, dined with them and they sent their clients back and forth to each other. Just part of the job. So why did she feel so uneasy about Hauser?

Some of her business referral sources were men and some were women. Jane prided herself on gender equality. A broker was a broker, not a male broker or a female one. Same with bankers, insurance agents, accountants and most of all attorneys. She didn't want to be a female attorney, she wanted to be an attorney. Period. So she didn't want to think of Hauser as a male stockbroker, or even the pudgy, male, middle aged, married stockbroker that he was. She wanted to think of him as a businessperson. And it would show Ted he was wrong. She could too spend time doing the kind of volunteering in the community that she liked, instead of only joining the clubs he liked, and still make connections that brought in business. But something felt wrong.

"Sorry John," Jane said. "I just don't have time tonight." Jane continued down the hall, with Hauser trailing after her.

"You gotta eat," Hauser said. "And I've got these clients who were asking about paying for nursing home care. Could I just pick your brain for a few minutes?"

Was Jeff's crude proposition making her suspicious of everybody? Why not just go get some coffee and answer Hauser's questions? "I'm really in a hurry tonight. Already have other plans. But I can try to answer your questions as we walk."

"They were asking about the something they called the Medicaid spend down. I've heard about it at company seminars, but I'm not sure I know how it works. Do both the husband and wife have to be over sixty-five or just the one going into the nursing home?"

"No," Jane said. "Sixty-five is for Medicare. Medicare is health insurance. Medicaid is based on need and it pays for long term nursing home care for the poor. The spend down is using up assets to get to be poor enough and that's for Medicaid eligibility. Sixty-five is for Medicare eligibility."

"I know several of the attorneys at your firm personally," Hauser said. "I've sent them quite a lot of business over the years. Worked with you on one or two as I recall. Sure you don't have time even for a quick cup of coffee?"

Besides the remote possibility that this pudgy, balding man, who could barely keep up with her brisk, long-legged strides, was asking for more than a little time over coffee, what exactly did he mean by mentioning his past business referrals just now? Was he implying that she owed him something, more than just doing good legal work, if he sent clients her way? Or was there some kind of implication that she needed to make nice with him because he had influence with big clients and some of the big shots at her firm? If he was going to get free legal advice over coffee, it would be because she felt like it was worth it. In terms of building a relationship, a business relationship, over the long term, with someone who could provide services her clients might need, and who in turn might have clients who needed her help. Not because she owed him anything for sending her one or two small matters over the past few years, or because he introduced one or two of the firm's more senior partners to some bigwig CEOs on the golf course.

Maybe she was just mad at the world after seeing Jeff earlier that day. Maybe she was reading things into Hauser's invitation to go for coffee or a bite to eat, that really weren't there. Probably best to just call it a day.

"Sorry, gotta run," Jane said. "Feel free to send an e-mail if you have more questions about Medicaid or Medicare eligibility." Jane lengthened her stride and outpaced him as she headed across the parking lot to her car.

"Hey, hold up." Hauser was nearly running to catch up.

"Is that man bothering you?" A man sitting in a van parked near Jane's car spoke to her through his open driver's side window. Jane nearly jumped out of her skin and then looked around for Hauser. A moment ago she was trying to reach her car ahead of him but now she was really glad to see him catch up.

"No, no," she said. She shook her head at the man in the van and made a mental note of the lettering on the side of the van. Jane always parked near lights in a parking lot if she could. She could see 'Hi-Grade Window Clean' on the side of the van. She reached her car and almost dropped her keys opening her car door. The van started up and pulled away. Hauser caught her car door before she could get it closed.

"Did you know that guy?"

"No. Look, I really have to go."

"Just coffee. Twenty minutes, I promise, no more than that."

"Some other time. Really, gotta run." Jane pulled the door

shut and waved to Hauser, watching him retreat as she drove off. What was with the guy in the van? That had been way too scary. Jane always had her keys out when she walked across a parking lot. Maybe she should take out her pepper spray too. She scanned the traffic around her, checking for the window cleaning van.

And what about Hauser? She'd kind of treated him like some stalker in a creepy van too. Maybe she really was being an idiot about him. Aren't personal connections over coffee or a meal how business is done? Personal contacts. That was what Jeff was always saying about how to get ahead. Personal contacts.

Traffic was light as Jane drove home. She decided to take the freeway across town instead of a route she knew through back streets, just in case the van was following her at a distance, where she couldn't spot him. With more cars, the freeway felt safer. She had her cell phone in case of a breakdown, not to mention her pepper spray. Even though there was slush on the road, Jane trusted her Sierratti. It was practically new and had all wheel drive and enough horse power to pull a boat or trailer. If Jane had a boat or a trailer, which she didn't. She mentally inventoried the contents of her purse and the back of her Serratti. Just in case other items besides her phone and pepper spray might be useful if the van was following her and bumped her off the road. Not that she thought he would, but you never know. Along with the pepper spray and a rape whistle, her purse held her wallet, checkbook, hair brush, cell phone, business card case, tissues, hand sanitizer, pain relievers, cold medicines, vitamins, granola bars, herbal tea bags and backup paper calendar and address book. In the back of the Sierratti, Jane had a tire iron and a small shovel, those might be useful. There were also flares, cat litter, salt, a flashlight, extra batteries, blankets and a first aid kit.

There was no sign of the van. Jane exited the freeway onto familiar streets close to her house. So was Hauser on the level? Or was he trying to start something out of line by getting her to go eat with him? Wasn't there some Bible story she'd read in a women's studies course she took in college where a man offers food to a woman thinking she's a prostitute when she's not? Judah and Tamar, in Genesis, that was it. Judah thinks Tamar is a prostitute and he offers to send around a goat from his flock for her if she'll have sex with him. Was Hauser's offer of coffee or a meal, an offer to make a business connection? Why did it feel like an offer of a goat? Was Hauser offering a goat because he thought, like Judah thought about Tamar, that Jane traded sex for food or a little attention? Like Jeff thought. Maybe that unexpected visit from Jeff really was throwing her off her game. It all seemed doubly unfair because, like Tamar, she wasn't in the business of trading sex for goats. And what Jane wanted was the same as what Tamar wanted. Jane wanted a baby. Not with Hauser, that was for sure, but Jane wanted a baby. Which was what Jeff didn't want, at least not with Jane.

By the time Jane got home it was almost nine o'clock, but still not too late to call her mother. She hit the button for her mother on her speed dial as she put a frozen dinner in the microwave.

"Hi Mom, how are you?"

Jane's mother still lived in the two bedroom suburban house where Jane had grown up and just a few blocks from the house Jane lived in now. Her mother lived alone since Jane's father died just over ten years ago, when Jane was still in college. Patricia Sidley was tall and thin, like Jane, and in good health at seventy. Other than a few female cousins she kept up with more or less, Jane's mother had no family except Jane.

"Good, good, I'm good. I wish the weather would let up so I could see you more. Oh, and Laura, you know, from across the street, she called and said our mailman fell yesterday, just three houses down from here, on icy steps, and sprained his ankle. Lucky he didn't break his neck. Good thing you cleaned my steps on Sunday. So he wouldn't fall. Of course he did fall, but you know what I mean."

"You be careful, Mom. Just stay in until it warms up. Should just be a few more days. If you need anything, call me and I'll get it. Don't go outside."

"I know. He could have broken his neck."

CHAPTER TWO

*T*hursday morning Jane walked down slushy front steps, holding the railing. Jane had spread salt and cat litter, as planned, before breakfast. Now with the sun coming up, the steps were covered in a melting slush. If her mailman fell, it wouldn't be here, not today anyway. Jane had salted her steps.

Jane took the freeway downtown toward her office. The sun was out at last, after days of intermittent snow and sleet. The morning traffic was erratic, slow then fast, then suddenly slow, but still moving. It snows here every year and people still don't know how to drive in winter. All wheel drive, for starters, that's how. And slow enough to avoid sliding on any black ice. And looking and thinking ahead instead of playing with the radio or worse, talking on a cell phone or texting. Jane saw a small dog dart out onto the interstate in front of her car. She was able to brake in time for the dog to run past, but she heard the squeal of brakes and crunch of metal in the oncoming lanes.

Jane plodded down the hall to her office. She pulled off her boots and put on one of the two pairs of shoes, the black ones this time, not the brown ones, she kept in her bottom desk drawer. Her first clients were scheduled for 9 a.m., but Jane knew she had to get to her office by 8:30. Elderly clients were always early.

"The Thompsons are here." Jane looked up to see her assistant Helene in the doorway. "I put them in Conference Room Q. I'll bring in coffee."

"Yes, good, thanks Helene. Tell them I'll be right in." A will signing for a couple that had been married to each other forever and had one grown child with no horrible spending habits, drug habits, mental, physical or emotional impairments. Should be easy. Except of course it never was. Not with Jane's clients. She hoped there were other attorneys in other firms who could sit down for a will signing, with all the papers drafted and ready, and have it take less than half a day, but in her six and a half years with the firm, Jane hadn't been able to manage it.

Jane sat down at the conference room table with Jim and Barbara Thompson. She went page by page through the originals of their wills that were ready for signature, explaining each paragraph.

"Did we mention that Barbara isn't a U.S. citizen?" Jim Thompson said.

"No," Jane said, "I guess not. I thought we went over this at our first meeting, but maybe not."

Jane pulled her client intake questionnaire out of the file. Had they skipped that question at the initial interview? There it was, in writing on the form. U.S. Citizenship, yes or no? She'd checked yes for Jim and yes for Barbara. Did they not understand the question when she asked it? Did they think she was just asking about Jim and not Barbara? Or maybe that she was asking about residency instead of citizenship? Did they have a hearing problem?

No point in arguing with clients. Jane crossed out 'yes' and made a note in the margin of the form that Barbara was not a U.S citizen. She added today's date by the marginal note on the form. She'd ask Helene to scan the form with her handwritten note into the computer file for the Thompson's estate plan.

And they hadn't mentioned that Barbara, a Canadian citizen, owned real estate in Ontario. One lot in her own name and one that they might have put in both names, unless that was the one they sold a few years ago. They hadn't mentioned that their son Mark was actually Jim's son and Barbara's stepson. Or that Barbara had decided to leave some bequests to charity.

By 11:30 Jane had sorted it all out, revised the documents and everyone had signed. Just enough time to finish up a draft of a pre-nup she needed for her 1 p.m. client. She headed to her office and heard her phone ring as she stepped through the doorway. The caller id screen showed the receptionist calling. Jane leaned over and picked up the receiver.

"There's a Mr. Bennett here to see you. He says his appointment was for 1 p.m. but he's here a little early and wondered if you could see him now. Should I send him up to nine?"

By late Friday afternoon Jane had billed more than enough

hours to meet her weekly goal, which was her annual billable hours target divided by fifty, not fifty-two, even though Jane rarely took any vacation. Jane would spend most of Saturday at her desk, and then Sunday in Church and visiting her mother, but it still seemed like she had a free weekend ahead of her.

"Clearfield Community Bank, Personal Banking, Sherri Winger speaking. How may I help you?"

"Sherri, it's Jane. Want to catch a movie tonight?"

Sherri was Jane's best friend since kindergarten and maid of honor at Jane's wedding. She worked as a loan officer in a bank just a few blocks from Jane's law firm. "There's a party for Roy Adams' birthday tonight we could crash. It's at Arthur and Mindy Ogden's house. Should be a lot of people. Roy is turning 40. I haven't exactly been invited but I know Arthur and Mindy and I know the drummer in the band they hired. I think if we just show up it'll be ok. It doesn't start until 10, so we could still catch a movie."

"I don't know about crashing a birthday party where I don't even know the person having the birthday," Jane said. "I mean who is Roy Adams?"

"His sister Anita was in school with us. Roy is what, maybe nine years older, so you probably don't remember him."

"I don't think I even remember any Anita Adams," Jane said.

"Remember your gym uniform disappeared in eighth grade gym class?" Sherri said. "I think she took it. You could see where the initials 'JS' your mom had sewn on it were torn off. I think somebody stole her uniform and she stole yours. So they owe you and you can crash Roy's party."

"You remember that? From eighth grade? Even so, I don't think it works that way, but ok, I'm in. There's a chick flick at 7:40 at East Cinema. I know you eat dinner at your parents' house most Fridays, and if you're having dinner with them tonight, how about if I pick you up there at 7?"

Jane had another low calorie frozen dinner from the microwave. She tried on 15 outfits and carefully returned 14 of them to the closet. Shirts lined up with other shirts in the shirt section, pants with pants, jackets and blazers on the upper double bar and sweaters on shelves. Jeff had been annoyed about that. He thought she should be more spontaneous, less organized. Hardly mattered now that he didn't live there anymore. On her way out the door, even though most of the snow was gone, Jane made a mental note to get more salt and cat litter when she did her grocery shopping Saturday afternoon. Always good to have some in the car in case she slid off the road.

When she turned down the street where Sherri's parents lived, she saw Sherri standing at the curb halfway down the block. She looked like she was freezing in a short coat and even shorter skirt.

"What are you, twelve years old?" Jane said. "Sneaking out of your parents' house? You're thirty-one. No way your parents care if you go out on a Friday night to a movie and a birthday party with a girlfriend."

"No, trust me, it's not that. If you came inside we'd never get to the movie on time. It would be at least an hour of 'have some pie' and worse yet, 'when are you getting back together with Jeff?' I'm sure you don't need that. I told them I was meeting you at the movies and had to park a few doors down when I got here before dinner. Then I said goodbye five minutes ago and waited out here. My car's on the next block. You should thank me. Really."

When was Jane getting back together with Jeff? She could see him sitting in her office, his fidgety charm turning mean when she refused his advances and the loan. She'd seen a picture of the new Mrs. Rogers and their baby boy in an adorable sailor suit onesie. Somehow the word never seemed inadequate. Double never. Never squared. Never to the nth degree.

"I really do appreciate being spared that question," Jane said, "especially tonight. Jeff showed up at my office on Wednesday and it wasn't pretty."

"Oh no," Sherri said. "What did he want now?"

"Quickie afternoon sex and a loan of a couple thousand dollars."

"Oh, ick. In your office?"

"What? No, he suggested going to my house. He even called it 'our' house. Then he said he just asked for sex as a favor to me. That I'd think it was a compliment. Can you believe I actually married that guy and then cried when he left?"

"You didn't give him the loan, right?"

"No loan, no sex. I wanted to tell him to go to Hell, but instead I told him to get on the elevators, ride them to the bottom, and get out of the building and my life. And never come back."

"So are you ok?"

"I don't know, I guess," Jane said. "I'm kind of paranoid maybe lately. I ran into this guy, after I finished my volunteer work at the Justice Community Center Wednesday night. He was there to give some kind of seminar to a seniors' group. And he's this pudgy, middle aged stockbroker. So, long story short, he asks me to go grab a bite somewhere with him because he said he had some questions he wanted to pick my brain about, something to do with Medicaid eligibility. Then he drops some hints about business referrals. I do that kind of thing all the time. I have half a dozen bankers, accountants, brokers and insurance agents I go to lunch with all the time. Men, women, it doesn't matter. It's social but it's a way of trading business referrals. But this time, all I can think is that he's hitting on me. That he wants to start some kind of affair or something. So I said I was too busy and rushed to my car and practically drove over him to get away from him. I mean all this guy says is what people in my business say to other professionals all the time, asking if we can talk a little business over coffee or lunch or something, and all of a sudden I'm worried that I can't tell if he's hitting on me. I never ask myself that when somebody wants a business meeting over coffee or lunch, but all of a sudden I'm conflicted about it. Do you think it was because of Jeff suddenly showing up and hitting on me? Am I just losing it? Is this whole bad marriage and ugly divorce thing turning me into some kind of paranoid nutcase who's afraid to get out there and drum up business connections? I mean here's this guy, and he's a stockbroker, and he probably really did have some questions. Medicaid eligibility is complicated. He's got elderly clients. And what would he know about legal matters like that?. But as soon as he mentioned the business referrals all I could think was that he was like some cave man offering me a pelt from a hunt as a play for sex."

"Offering a what?" Sherri said.

"A pelt," Jane said. "An animal skin."

"Maybe you are a little off your game because of seeing

Jeff. Or maybe there was something funny about the way this guy asked for some time with you. Like you said, it's possible this guy really has business to send to you. He does have clients who need wills and trusts and you draft them for a living, I mean, after all. But on the other hand, maybe not. Maybe something about the way he asked, maybe his tone of voice or the way he was looking at you, maybe something tipped you off that his real motive here was, how did you put it, to offer coffee or food or business referrals like a cave man might offer some kind of animal pelt? In exchange for sex. But either way, if he was legit or not, so what if you said you were busy and brushed him off? I mean you're not on 24/7. It's ok if he thinks you're busy. I mean you are busy."

"I guess I'm just worried that the nonsense with Jeff has undermined my instincts," Jane said. "You know, my intuition about people. Some ordinary guy asks me to go for a perfectly ordinary bite to eat to ask for some free legal advice and maybe establish a business connection and I'm a mess thinking 'how do you tell?' Was he offering to spend some time so we could exchange business information and clients or was he angling for sex? Was he trying to figure out whether time and interest was enough, or if he would have to give up a goat from his herd?"

"A whole goat this time?" Sherri said. "Not just a goat pelt?"

"Pelt, goat, that's not the point. The point is that I'm not like this. This should be no big deal and I'm still upset about it, days later."

"You've been through a bad time," Sherri said. "You were expecting to be married for life. To not have to worry about dating or pelts or goats or even frogs that might turn into princes. Now things are different. And Jeff shows up and it all gets even more confusing. But I think the important question here is, if a man is offering something, some time or coffee or ok, even a pelt, let's just say, not for sex, but maybe for some of your time and a chance maybe someday at something more, and I'm not saying that's what happened here, but let's just look at the possibility, is that necessarily a bad thing? Are we far enough post-divorce here, I mean it's been a year, that interest from a pudgy, middle aged man who is actually employed might be a good thing?"

"He's married. He has two little girls. It would be a bad thing. Really bad."

"Ok," Sherri said, "but let's say interest from a hypothetical, unmarried pudgy middle aged stockbroker. How about that? But let's lose the pudgy. Say he's got washboard abs and he's six feet tall. He likes children, puppies and walks on the beach."

"I don't know, I'm not really looking. I mean ok, maybe I am. I guess I would like to meet someone."

"And old movies," Sherri said. "This tall guy with the great abs likes classics, like Casablanca."

The movie let out a little before ten. Navigating the crowded parking garage, Jane drove very slowly, staying under the 5 mile an hour speed limit. Jane came to a complete stop to let an elderly driver, hunched over the wheel, into the line for the cashier's booth. The elderly driver turned to wave to her and stalled his car. He ground the clutch and Jane and three other drivers behind her eased around him.

The party at the Ogdens' house was crowded. People were milling around a kind of open floor plan living room/dining room that was adjacent to a large kitchen. The party spilled over into a family room toward the back of the house, leading to an attached garage where, from the sounds of it, the band was already getting the party started. Most of the guests looked like they were thirty-somethings, with a few newly minted forty-somethings, including the birthday boy.

"Are you sure it's ok to just crash like this?" Jane said.

"I told you," Sherri said, "we went to school with his baby sister Anita. I might even have met him once. And I know the drummer in the band. That counts as invited. And we're girls. Everyone wants more girls at a party."

"We're not strippers or pole dancers. We're just ordinary women. I'm not sure everyone wants that these days." Jeff didn't, apparently.

"Oh just shut up and try to have a good time," Sherri said. "I'll introduce you to Roy and you can wish him a Happy Birthday."

"Which reminds me, shouldn't we have brought a gift? People are putting gifts on that table."

"Roy, Roy! Over here. I want you to meet somebody." Sherri was waving at tall man. His receding hairline made him look his age, but his T-shirt, crew neck sweater and jeans hung loosely on what looked like a trim, solid frame. Jane liked his deep brown eyes. They seemed kind.

"I don't think he recognizes you," Jane said.

"Roy, it's Sherri. Sherri Winger. I went to school with your sister Anita. I met you one time when Anita did the prom decorations and your mom made you drive us to school, with a paper mache pyramid, in your dad's truck."

"Hunh, I must have been home from college, maybe for a long weekend. That was a long time ago." He was looking at Jane.

"This is my friend, Jane. She went to school with Anita too, but she didn't help with the prom decorations. Too busy with the debate team."

"Hi Jane," Roy said. "Who went to school with Anita and was on the debate team. Very nice to meet you."

"Hi Roy," Jane said. "Happy Birthday. Good party."

"Thanks," Roy said. "Don't miss the sandwiches. My mom made them and sent them over. And there's drinks. Beer in kegs and people brought a few bottles of wine if you like that. And soft drinks in the coolers over by the sandwiches."

"C'mon, we gotta hear the band. My friend Ansel is the drummer." Sherri pulled Jane across the living room, through the kitchen and the family room and into a heated attached three car garage where the band had set up. Jane had listened to a lot of bands before choosing one for her wedding reception. She'd hadn't heard this one, but they were playing a lot of the same music. Danceable covers, some slow, mostly up beat. Her wedding seemed so recent, but really, it was over five years ago now. She still had some of the napkins. Jeffrey and Jane. She should probably throw them out, but they were perfectly good napkins. She didn't know if she could actually still bring herself to use them, but throwing them out seemed so wasteful.

"Jane! Earth to Jane!" Sherri was shouting over the music. "We can dance to this one."

Jane was happy to dance with Sherri. When did that happen that she could just dance and have a good time with her friends instead of standing around waiting for a boy to ask? Somewhere between junior high and thirty-one.

"C'mon, sing with me!" Sherri was dancing with Jane, then with anybody anywhere near her. "Sing with me! And I'm falling in love something, something, love, love, falling something."

"What's your story, Jane?" It was Roy. Jane had left the dance floor to try out the sandwiches and he walked up to her there. The sandwiches did look good. Crusty rolls, interesting cheeses and actual roast turkey and beef tenderloin. Not processed cheese food and grocery case packaged lunch meat slices. Jane had just taken a big bite. She knew Scarlett O'Hara in Gone With the Wind, would eat before parties so she would appear to have a lady-like small appetite. Not Jane. Not since the Exit of Jeff. Jane would eat what she liked, but really, just now it would be easier to chat if she wasn't chewing. Roy didn't seem to mind waiting.

"Your mom did a great job with the sandwiches," Jane said. "Great rolls. And beef tenderloin. Yum."

"I'll tell her. She'll probably remember you if you were in school with Anita. Mom knows everybody."

The lead singer announced that the band would be taking a break and people started streaming in from the garage toward the food. One lurched into Jane. She steadied him, preventing him from overturning the sandwich table.

"Good save," Roy said.

"Almost, anyway," Jane said. They watched as the man she had just steadied fell over the coolers into the dessert table, scattering pies, cookies and fruit. Apples rolled across the floor of the dining room area.

"That's Arthur," Roy said. "You may already know him as he's our gracious host this evening. Great guy. Good friend, noted local amateur actor. Maybe you've seen him in some of the plays done by the Adderton Players?"

"No, I haven't. I'm on an Arts Board that funds the Adderton Players, but somehow I never manage to get to the plays."

"Arthur's done a terrific Othello and he's been Reverend Parris in The Crucible. He told me he's looking into some new local theater group that does original, local works. Plays that no one has seen before, written by local writers. Could be great, could be terrible. But Arthur doesn't handle booze all that well. I'd better go see if he's ok and try to keep him away from the table with my birthday cake." Roy turned toward a group that had gathered near Arthur and were placing him in a chair. Then he looked back at Jane. "Could I call you sometime?"

Jane looked up from staring at the wrecked desserts. "Call me? Sometime? Well yeah, I guess."

"Would Anita have your number?"

Eighth grade gym class was a long time ago.

"Uh, no. Probably not." Jane pulled her phone out of her jeans pocket. "Here, call your phone. Then you'll have the number." Roy dialed and hung up, handing the phone back to Jane. He headed toward Arthur.

Jane went to look for Sherri. She was with the band. They were standing around a keg, filling plastic cups with beer during their break.

"Jane!" Sherri said. "This is Ansel. Like Ansel Adams, the famous photographer, only it's Ansel Kaminski, the really good drummer. Ansel, this is Jane."

Ansel had olive skin and light brown eyes, set in a face with an angular bone structure and a straight nose. His hair was dark brown, very wavy and a little unkempt. He was tall and lanky. He leaned forward a little and bent down to talk, close to Jane's ear, so she could hear him in the crowded room.

"Just Jane?"

Jane looked up at Ansel. "Jane Sidley."

"So how do you know Sherri?"

"Since kindergarten," Jane said. "Our sneaker cubbies were next to each other. Jimmy Johnson was going to put his gum on Sherri's sneakers and I stopped him. He said he didn't want to put his gum on Sherri's old sneakers anyway, but thought they were mine. Then Jimmy saved his milk from lunch the next day and poured it in my sneakers. Sherri and I swore to protect each other from Jimmy Johnson and we've been friends ever since."

"Gotta go do another set. Jimmy Johnson probably liked you."

Sunday morning after Church, Jane went to a Children's Christian Formation Committee meeting. The meeting was in the small, overheated classroom used for Sunday School for children in the second and third grades. The committee members were seated precariously, on child sized chairs around a table strewn with crayons and coloring pages depicting Jesus' presentation at the Temple. Jane read the lines below the picture of the 'Holy Family with Simeon and Anna' that the children were supposed to color. The last line said that to this day, we still present each baby to the Church. If Jeff had agreed to start a family with Jane, instead of getting Cassie pregnant, she might have done that already, maybe more than once.

Even though it was only February the Committee was already discussing Easter. Jane usually volunteered to help with the Easter egg hunt. For several years, she had helped put pennies and little candies in plastic eggs and then taped the center seam shut. She would hide the colorful eggs around the Church garden. She was careful to leave most of them almost in plain sight, for the littlest ones to find. Jane had hoped that by now she would have a little one of her own, old enough to toddle around the Church garden at the Easter egg hunt. She'd planned, by now, to be one of those parents who gave a lot of hints and then went nuts with praise if their little darling found an egg.

"I've been worried the pennies might be a choking hazard," Jane said.

"Parents are watching. And the children tend to bring the eggs right to their parents." one of the other committee members said.

"A small child might get an egg open before their parents see them," Jane said. "There's a lot of commotion. A child could put the pennies in his mouth and choke in an instant, before anyone even saw."

"Wouldn't the child just swallow the penny? Would a child actually choke? On a penny?"

"Swallowing pennies isn't a good thing either," Jane said. "And yes, I think a child could choke on a penny. Why take the chance?"

"What fun is it if all they get are plastic eggs and no treats?"

"We could have them hunt for empty eggs and then serve safe treats, like cookies and cupcakes, indoors on a table," Jane said. "They could sit down and eat. That would be safer than eating candy, and maybe pennies, while they are distracted looking for eggs."

"If we serve cupcakes and cookies, we're going to have complaints from parents who are going to Easter brunches after Church," one of the more senior, veteran members of the committee said. "I mean a few candies in an egg is one thing, but serving cookies and cupcakes is going to get us complaints, I'm sure of it."

"Ok, we could just hand out some candies then," Jane said.

"How is that different from putting treats in the eggs?" This was from one of the newer members, and Jane was surprised she spoke up on this particular topic. Jane didn't think she'd ever even been to the Easter egg hunt, after all.

"If an adult hands out a candy," Jane said, "that's different than having an overlooked child in a corner of the garden stuffing candies and pennies in his mouth. I just think it's safer."

After the meeting, Jane called her mother from her cell phone. Jane's mother hadn't made it to Church that morning because the weather was still very cold, even if there was no snow. Jane didn't call while driving. She called while still parked in the Church parking lot, before she put her keys in the ignition. While she was waiting for the call to go through, Jane saw a man standing near the side door to the Church, engaged in what looked like a heated argument with the pastor. The man was waving his arms, pointing up at the stained glass windows. The pastor was shaking her head, shivering without a coat as she stood in the parking lot. Jane recognized the Hi-Grade Window Clean van, parked at the edge of the lot. With a tile roof and stained glass windows, Jane knew the Church had special and expensive arrangements for window cleaning. And it was still winter. No way could anyone get anywhere near those windows without breaking their neck in the winter. What was the man thinking? She felt sorry for her pastor, shivering and patiently listening as the man towered over her, his face turning red, from anger or maybe just from the cold air and wind. I guess that's part of the job. Listening to nut cases. At least Jane could bill for it in her line of work. Her mother answered on the third ring.

"I thought I'd come see you this afternoon. The weather is getting a little better. It's still cold, but the day is warming up some."

"I haven't been able to get to the store, but I can make egg salad." The shouting stopped and Jane looked up to see the man turn from her pastor and look right at her car.

"Egg salad. Great. I'm hanging up now. I'll be right there." Jane put the key in the ignition and drove out of the lot, not even pausing to turn on the GPS.

Back at the office on Monday, Jane's morning was once again a harried mess. Another will signing and, of course, another round of last minute complicated changes. Why clients couldn't call her assistant or her paralegal in advance and let Jane get the changes made ahead of time was always a mystery. Jane would send drafts for the clients to read ahead of time. Even the people who actually read them would still come in and say that when they read them they noticed that some changes were needed. So why wait until then to say so? Jane could never understand that. Why did clients wait until everyone was sitting around the conference room table, with originals printed and ready for signature, to tell her they wanted changes? Did clients enjoy sitting there waiting while Jane ran back and forth to her computer trying to make the changes quickly without any mistakes? But it was always like that, and today was no different. When Jane got into the conference room with the clients, hoping that this time things would be different and everything would go smoothly, the clients immediately began pointing out last minute changes needed in the documents.

It was early afternoon before Jane got everything signed and everyone safely packed off into the elevator. Her assistant Helene, bless her, had ordered in a salad and knew without asking to get one for Jane too. She had a half hour before her next client's appointment. Jane rinsed her coffee mug and filled it with water from the sink in the employee lounge. She headed back to her desk where she unwrapped the salad and dug the plastic fork out of the bottom of the bag. Jane even managed to get the top off the little container of dressing before the phone rang. She looked at the caller id screen. Wendell Insurance. She'd met Gordon Wendell at a seminar. Could be a good source of new business.

"Jane Sidley."

"Jane, it's Gordon Wendell. I'm an agent over in the Shuley Building. We met at the Fall Retirement Round Up."

"Sure," Jane said. "I remember."

"Are you still doing estate planning?"

"Oh yes. Wills, trusts, all that. Keeps me out of trouble I guess."

"Insurance trusts?"

"Sometimes," Jane said. "If it's needed, sure."

"I have clients who need insurance trusts and I'm always looking for good people to send them to," Wendell said.

"Great. Glad to help if I can. Thanks very much."

This was going well. Here she was talking business with an insurance broker with no problem. Maybe there was a valid reason she got upset last Wednesday when she saw John Hauser at the Community Center. Maybe something had been wrong with the way Hauser talked to her, and it wasn't that she was paranoid as part of the fallout from her divorce. If she wasn't comfortable with the way Hauser talked to her, it didn't mean she was too cautious to make her way in the business world. It didn't mean she was seeing Jeff under every rock. Here she was today doing business like usual. Maybe she should ask Wendell if he wanted to meet for lunch. She could give him some brochures about her firm's estate planning services. For sure, she's got her business referral groove back.

"What do you charge?" Wendell said.

"$105 an hour. But insurance trusts generally run about fifteen hundred dollars. That's not a flat rate, just an estimate. If the situation is complicated, a second marriage with two or three sets of children or a child with special needs, the charges can be higher. But even then I try to give a good estimate up front so nobody gets sticker shock."

"What about commissions?" Wendell said.

Jane sighed. She guessed this wasn't going to go so well after all. But not because she thought every man over thirty was hitting on her. No, this was about to go down the drain because Wendell was about to ask her to take money on the side. Money she wouldn't take because it would impair her ability to represent her clients. She knew some attorneys took that kind of money. Some got licensed as insurance agents in addition to being attorneys. Or just took a piece of the insurance agent's commission even without that. She knew they got involved in the financial side of things somehow and made good money from blurring the lines between lawyer and insurance agent. She didn't even fully understand how it all worked, and didn't want to. She also knew in her state there were no rulings on this sort of shenanigans. Not from the state bar, the state attorney general's office, state insurance commissioner, the state courts or the state anything. But just because the state bureaucracy was comatose about these under the table dealings right now didn't mean they always would be. Someday somebody might wake up and realize these guys had their fingers in too many pies. And even if they didn't, it was still wrong. Wouldn't clients get hurt if their lawyers were steering them to buy a certain policy or investment because the lawyer was taking money on the side from the insurance agent? How could that possibly not be wrong?

"No, sorry," Jane said, "I don't split commissions if that's what you're asking. I don't want any extra fee."

"Honey," Wendell said, "we're not talking any $1500. These commissions can run $20,000 just in the first year. And I give the attorneys half. These are good products. I've got Regents Mark and Livistar. They're top of the line. What's the problem? There's no law against it. I've got lots of attorney who do this."

"I'm sure you do have other attorneys who do this," Jane said. "And you're right, there's no law on it in this state. But if you send me a client, then I represent them, not you. If they want a Regents Mark policy or a Livistar policy, I won't steer them away from it unless I see something really wrong. But if I do see something wrong, I'll say so. And I'll tell them it's a good idea to look around and compare policies. And nobody pays me but them." And don't call me honey.

"But I don't see why," Wendell said. "If it's perfectly legal and I've got other attorneys who think it's ok, what's the problem? I could have you talk to them. They don't think it's wrong."

"No, no thanks," Jane said. "I'm not saying it's right or wrong. It's just not what I do."

"Don't you want $10,000 or even 20,000?" Wendell said. "I'll just give the money to someone else."

"That's fine with me if you do give it to someone else," Jane said. "I just want my regular fee. That's all I want." And my salad. She looked at the time on her computer screen. If her next client was early, which she probably would be, Jane wasn't going to get even two bites if she couldn't get Wendell off her phone. And she would be missing out on her salad for no reason if he wouldn't send her any business because she didn't want to take ten times her usual fee under the table in exchange for brow beating elderly clients into choosing his company's policies. Great. And it had the croutons she liked. Would it be rude if she put him on speaker and started eating while still on the phone? Croutons would crunch pretty loud. Did she care? Maybe she could use the phone's mute button.

Helene leaned in the doorway. "Ms. Linley is here."

Jane nodded at Helene. "I'm sorry, my two o'clock is here already. I appreciate your calling, really I do. But I have to run."

CHAPTER THREE

*T*he weather for Easter Sunday was just as everyone hoped. Warm spring breezes blew and all the congregants gathering for Church were bathed in sunshine. Jane was wearing a new dress. It was a light blue cotton print with small yellow flowers. She wasn't wearing an Easter hat or gloves, but she had on high heeled sandals she'd found on sale, that almost exactly matched the blue in the dress. Jane's mother always said blue looked nice with her eyes.

Jane hid the empty plastic eggs around the Church garden and handed little bags of candies and Easter themed stickers to the parents. Putting the candies in bags and giving them to the parents to hand out or save for later was a compromise reached by the Children's Christian Formation Committee after several months of meeting after Church services every other Sunday. The meetings were tedious, but Jane liked seeing the leftover materials from the Sunday School lessons on the table in the room where the Committee met. Sometimes the explanations on the children's coloring pages for their lessons seemed a whole lot clearer to Jane than the readings or the sermon the adults heard during the Church service.

A majority of the Children's Christian Formation Committee voted in favor of the use of stickers as a safer alternative to pennies for treats to hand out during the Easter egg hunt. The Committee also thought the use of stickers, rather than pennies, was a better choice because it put less emphasis on money and materialism. The Committee members were nearly unanimous in thinking that stickers, as opposed to pennies, would send a more spiritual message to the children participating in the Easter egg hunt. One Committee member, fairly new to the Church, had voted in favor of the use of the stickers not as a safety issue or a spiritual issue, but because in her opinion, no one, not even toddlers, and certainly not their parents, really wanted pennies anymore.

Jane looked at the babies and toddlers in their Easter clothes. All the spring colors. Pinks, purple, yellows and greens. She hoped she'd get to hold a baby. Jeff had rarely gone to Church with Jane, but sometimes she could get him to go on a holiday like Christmas or Easter. Thank goodness she hadn't seen him at her Church, even for holidays, since the divorce. Somewhere across town was Cassie cajoling Jeff into putting on a suit jacket and going to an Easter service, with their son in a little Easter outfit?

Jane moved further out into the Church garden among the excited children. Some were too young to understand. Others dashed from egg to egg. There was lots of squealing and some pushing and shoving, but not too much. Bonnets and frilly dresses on the girls. Little suits and bow ties with belts or suspenders on the boys. Shiny shoes all around. Jane spent so much time at work with elderly people, facing death and trying to get their affairs in order. Writing wills. Last wills. Last testaments. Last everything. Here it was the first of everything. First green leaves of spring on the trees. First flowers. All new little faces, bright and smiling. And none of them choking on a penny.

Jane sat with her mother during the service. She liked the sermon. About Easter people. About new people, leaving behind our shells and emerging brand new. Maybe she could be a new person. Not Mrs. Ex-Jeff, not some person getting over her husband starting a family with someone else. Not someone moving on after a divorce. Not that person, but a new one. Someone in spring clothes. A person in a new dress, light blue with yellow flowers. A person who might run around in the sunshine chasing something silly, like colored eggs. That sort of person. Why not?

After Church they drove over to her mother's house.

"Is chicken all right?" Jane's mother said. "I got a rotisserie chicken yesterday at the grocery store and we can warm it up. And I have a bag of salad. We can cut up some tomato and cucumber and put a little sliced onion with it. I got some dinner rolls and half a chocolate cake."

"Great Mom. I brought blueberries and raspberries. And I cut up some fresh pineapple. Where's that serving bowl you have with the kiwis printed on it?"

"Did you hear that Emily Ainsley's little girl almost choked to death at the Easter egg hunt?"

"What?" Jane said. "No! How did that happen?"

"Emily said Brittany had a penny in her mouth. I've said for years they should stop putting pennies in those plastic eggs. A child could choke on a penny. Not every child will give the egg to a parent to open, you know. Some can pry them open even as toddlers. I know. I've seen it. And they put everything in their mouths. Only a matter of time until some poor child chokes to death. Aren't you on the committee that handles the Easter egg hunt? Why don't you say something about it when you're planning the Easter egg hunt for next year?"

"I did say something," Jane said. "We hid empty plastic eggs this year. I insisted on it."

"I'm telling you, Brittany Ainsley almost choked to death. If her mother hadn't been watching, and heaven knows parents don't watch these days like they should, I don't even want to think about what could have happened."

"Mom, the plastic eggs were empty this year. She must have found a penny on the ground. Maybe from last year. Or maybe she found an egg that was still hidden and hadn't been found from last year with pennies in it. But we hid empty plastic eggs and gave little bags of candy and stickers to the parents to hand out. Really."

"I suppose she might have just swallowed it and not choked," Jane's mother said. "But then wouldn't they need to go to the emergency room? Pennies for little children is just not a good idea. Or carrots or peanuts for that matter."

"Right," Jane said. "I agree completely."

"Well you might say something about it when you're planning for next year."

"Right. Got it, Mom."

"I heard you went out with the older brother of that girl who took your gym uniform when she was in your gym class in eighth grade, Anita something or other."

"Sherri thinks that too," Jane said. "That it was Anita who took my gym uniform. How would either of you know something like that? And for that matter, how would you remember it all these years later?"

"Never mind that," Jane's mother said. "The point is I think it's time you did go out on dates. Have some fun. Get over Jeff. Move on. Meet people."

"Ok," Jane said. "I did go out with Anita Adams' older brother Roy. He's a contractor and he does some carpentry. He builds out custom kitchens, additions on houses, decks, that sort of thing. I actually met him this past winter at his birthday party. Sherri knew the people hosting the party and she knew the drummer in the band."

"You met him in the winter? So what took him so long to go out with you?"

"I don't know really," Jane said. "He called a few weeks ago. It had been so long since the party I'd forgotten he'd even asked for my phone number. He did say he meant to call sooner but he was busy with work for some demanding clients. I can understand that. That's for sure. And anyway, I'm glad he took this long. I don't think I was really ready to go out with anybody until now."

"So?" Jane's mother said.

"So what?" Jane shot back.

"So the date, Jane. So how was the date?"

"I don't know. Ok, I guess. No big deal."

"Movie? Long walk? Bowling?"

"Bowling?" Jane said. "Who goes bowling on a first date?"

"Did you?"

"No," Jane said. "We had dinner at the Kirwood Restaurant. I had ravioli with the house marinara. I didn't want to try to cope with spaghetti on a first date."

"And the house salad? Garlic toast?"

"Yes on the salad," Jane said. "No on the toast. Didn't want to reek of garlic."

"It's ok if you both have garlic breath."

"Thanks, Mom. Good to know."

"So are you going to see him again?"

"I'm going to see him Saturday," Jane said, "but it's not a second date or anything. When he told me he was a contractor, I told him about building a house with Jeff. About how Jeff wanted a flat roof over the bonus room on the first floor."

"Which you never finished."

"I did have it finished, Mom. The flat roof is finished. And the French doors in my bedroom leading out to the roof of bonus room. I had them finished too."

"But it's not a proper deck. There's no railing. You could fall and break your neck out there. Tell me you keep those doors locked and don't go out there with no railing."

"Ok, Mom, sure. Whatever. Do you want to hear about Roy or not?"

"Of course, sweetheart."

"When I told him about the flat roof over the bonus room, he wanted to see it. He said even if it was reinforced enough to be a deck, strong enough so I could put some chairs and a table out there, it still needed some kind of extra roofing layers to keep it from rotting or leaking. That's because it's flat, not pitched. You know, not slanted at an angle like a usual roof. He said water doesn't run off a flat roof as easily. It can rot if extra steps aren't taken to protect it in the process of putting it together. So he's coming by early Saturday to look at the roof, before he has to get to a job he's finishing up at someone's house near mine."

Jane put down the spoon she was using to mix the fruit salad. She'd said "mine" not "the house I built with my ex" or "the new house." She wanted to remember, every time she mentioned the house, to say "my house."

When Roy came to see the roof on Saturday she wouldn't say 'the flat roof Jeff had the builders put over the bonus room.' No, it was just the flat roof that was there now, on part of her house. Her flat roof on her house. Not the roof that was Jeff's idea. Just the roof on the bonus room on her house. The flat roof that might get made into a deck, that would be her deck, on her house, if she decided to finish out the roof by building a deck on it. If she decided to do that she would hire builders, who would then be her builders, to build her deck. Her choice, her deck, her roof, her house. Not because of Jeff or his ideas. He was gone and his ideas were gone with him. They didn't live on in parts of the house. Her house. And her deck, if that's what she wanted. If that was the choice she made.

"Doesn't sound very romantic," Jane's mother said. "Seeing him to discuss a roof."

"I didn't really want him to look at it," Jane said. That was true. Even though Jane considered, off and on, talking to a con-tractor about building out a deck with a railing on the flat roof, she hadn't made up her mind. She didn't know if she wanted to bother with it or not. And even if she had been ready to take on a project like that, she was dating Roy. She didn't want to him to think she was showing him the roof on Saturday as a hint that she wanted him to work on it as a favor because they were da-ting. And even if he was the one who asked to come over, if she let him look at the roof, and give her advice about it, was even that, even if he didn't do any actual work on the roof, accepting a favor? Accepting favors from someone she was newly dating, that had to be a mistake. It would make the situation more com-plicated. And then there was the 'never hire someone you can't fire' rule. If she hired Roy while dating him, and then he did a lousy job, she couldn't fire him without breaking up with him, right? And even though Roy just wanted to take a look at the roof, and wasn't asking to be hired, what if he did look at the roof, and then Jane hired someone else? Wouldn't Roy be upset that she didn't hire him? So why had she agreed to let him come over on Saturday morning to look at the roof?

"But he said that it could rot really fast if it wasn't done right," Jane said, "and he really seemed to want to take a look at it, that's all. I guess I have been thinking about hiring someone to turn it into a real deck, not just a flat roof, with actual deck flooring, some built in seating and a sturdy railing. And Roy said I should let him figure out if it needs something better on it, to waterproof it, before I do anything like that. So I said ok, I'd appreciate him taking a look, I guess."

Jane's mother gave Jane a look. Jane didn't need the warn-ing it carried. She already knew. So maybe she could avoid the whole problem if she just left the roof alone. That way, no mat-ter what Roy said about the condition of the roof on Saturday, or even if he wanted to do the work to build out a deck up there, Jane could just say she wasn't planning on doing anything. She could say she'd made up her mind to leave the roof as it is. No deck would mean no hiring Roy. And no upsetting him by hiring someone else. Problem solved.

But was it solved? It had been Jeff who said they didn't need to bother with deck flooring or a railing, back when the house was being built, and didn't she want to make her own decision about it now? Jeff had said with a flat roof they could go out there and get some sun once in a while but why bother with a railing if it wouldn't be that good for parties because the french doors to the roof are in the second floor master bedroom. If they were going to be the only ones up there, why spend the money to put in a railing?

Jane picked up the spoon and took the bowl of fruit salad to the table. I should have known. It should have been a tip off that he wasn't ever planning to raise a family with me in that house. If we had children, a railing would be really important. You couldn't just tell children not to go out there, or only to go out there with a parent. They'd never listen to that. Doors leading to a roof would be irresistible for children. Anyone could see that, even Jeff. So he must have been thinking all along he would never have children with me in our house.

My house. Who cares what Jeff thought or what memories went with what house parts, right? Not anymore. No more sad thoughts every time someone mentions the house. My house. And why not make it my own? Maybe the deck is a good idea. My new deck. Just mine. A positive change. A step forward.

"If Roy sees something that is a problem I'll be taking care of it before it gets worse," Jane said. "Can't argue with that." Jane's mother gave her another look.

No surprise if Roy does find drainage problems with the roof. Everything Jeff touched meant a problem, so why not the flat roof too? No, no more of that. New thinking. Positive thoughts. New person. I'm a new Easter person. The divorce has been over for more than a year. I'm even done with writing checks for alimony payments. New start. New.

"But you did like him?" Jane's mother said.

"I guess I liked him," Jane said. "He was polite and not pushy or anything. He picked up the check. And he had on a clean shirt."

"Jane, honey," Jane's mother said, "I just want you to be happy. You deserve to be happy. You did nothing wrong with Jeff, that idiot."

"I know, Mom. But that's all in the past, so let's leave it there, ok?"

"Of course, dear."

By Wednesday there three more voicemail messages, for a total of six so far, including three she'd already deleted, on her office phone from John Hauser. The pudgy stockbroker who asked her to go for coffee back in January. She hadn't heard anything from him or seen him since then, until last Friday. Jane had picked up a salad to go at a sandwich place two blocks from her office. Hauser came through the door with two other people just as she was leaving. He tried to stop her to talk, but she waved, pointed at her watch and kept walking out the door and down the block.

And then, first thing Monday morning, the calls started. Her own fault, for being in that sandwich shop at noon on Good Friday, instead of going to the Good Friday service they had at her Church. It was possible he just wanted to send some business her way. If he would just say that on the voicemail messages, she might even call him back. Or if he didn't leave so many messages, or sound so, well, how to describe it, awkward or emotional or something. "It's John Hauser. Call me. I need to talk to you" or "Give me a call, Jane. Didn't you get my messages?" The messages were short and to the point, but they set off all kinds of warning bells in Jane's head.

I mean, couldn't he at least say what it's about? Even if it's something too confidential to leave in a voicemail message, he could still say something general, like 'call me about a new client' or 'call me, I need a new will.' And if he wants to send me a new client, why doesn't he give up when I don't return his calls? Who wants to send a client to a lawyer who doesn't return phone calls? Jane deleted the three new messages.

She had an assortment of trust documents that she needed to finish so she could get drafts in the mail, (or by e-mail to those of her elderly clients who actually used e-mail,) no later than the following Monday. Even if she met that deadline, she knew some of her elderly, cranky clients would still be on the phone complaining. They would tell her they've been waiting and checking the mail every day, as soon as it arrived. She believed them. She was sure they were doing just that, even now, every day, even though the Monday deadline was still almost a week away.

She opened a draft of one of the unfinished trust documents on her computer. The trust was particularly complicated, and Jane needed to do some research on income tax law before she could finish drafting it. She knew she should use one of the new associate attorneys at the firm for the research. A new associate would have a lower billable rate than Jane's billable rate. In theory, if she used an associate for her routine research, Jane's clients would get smaller bills for her firm's services on their behalf. That was the theory, anyway. The reality was that Jane, with her experience, could find the answer to her tax research questions in a few minutes. If she could just find a few minutes to look for the answer, that is. And if she asked an associate to do the research, it would take time to explain to the associate what she wanted. And the explanation to the associate, she also knew from experience, would have to be in writing for Jane to have any hope that the associate would research the right question. And then she would have to wait a week at least for the associate to send her a lengthy memorandum summarizing the associate's research and conclusions about her question. And the lengthy memorandum would most likely miss the point. Leaving Jane, now a week or so later, to try to find a few minutes to do the research, while wishing that she'd just done it herself in the first place.

Jane knew she needed to delegate tasks to the newer associate attorneys in her firm anyway, even if it seemed to waste time at first. It was the only way the associates could get trained and someday stop missing the point. It was the only chance for Jane ever to get some Saturdays off.

Jane opened a browser and went to a tax research website. An e-mail came through to her inbox from a client, asking about one of her other unfinished trust documents. She opened the e-mail, but didn't draft a reply, instead going back to the tax research. Her phone rang. Distracted, she made the rookie mistake of reaching over and picking it up, without looking up from her research to check the caller id.

"Jane Sidley."

"Well hello at last Jane Sidley. It's John Hauser. You know, the guy whose phone calls you don't return."

"Sorry about that," Jane said. "Really busy. Did you have

more questions about Medicaid?"

"Some about Medicaid," Hauser said, "and a few other questions besides. I was still wondering if we could get together for coffee sometime or maybe lunch."

Going for coffee or lunch with stockbrokers, many of them men, was no big deal. Jane did that all the time. But she disliked Hauser's tone now even more than the tone of voice he used back when he first suggested going out for coffee in January. Add the sarcastic tone of his voice to the sheer number of his voicemail messages, and throw in the creepy feeling she had last Friday at the sandwich shop, and it was just not right. If it's just a casual cup of coffee, why call six times, and this call made it seven times, in one week? And why be so nasty about her taking a while to return a phone call? It had only been three days. How would he know if she was even in town? For all he knew she could have gone on vacation and just forgotten to say so on her voicemail greeting. That happened to people sometimes. Not to Jane ever, but it could.

"Are you still there?" Hauser said.

"Oh. I'm still here," Jane said. "Things are just so busy right now. You understand. Seems like clients want everything yesterday. I just don't have a free minute these days."

"You can't be too busy for coffee," Hauser said. "Or lunch. You gotta eat."

"Listen," Jane said, "is there some business you need to discuss with me? If you have brochures or something you'd like me to read so I can put you on my list to recommend to clients who need investment advice, I'm glad to do that. Just send them to my office."

"Indulge me here," Hauser said. "You probably go to lunch every day. So have lunch with me. What's the big deal?"

"Look, I'm sorry I didn't return your calls right away," Jane said, "but I really have to run just now."

"Hold on, hold on," Hauser said. "How about this? We've got this new investor wealth strategy resources program. It gives clients access to the best wealth managers in the big cities, right from here. I've got brochures on that. We can look at those over lunch. Come on, it'll take what, an hour? You've got an hour sometime in the next week or so. You know you do."

"That sounds very interesting," Jane said, "but I really don't have an hour to spare these days. If you want to send me the brochures, or a link to your new investment program, I'll take a look. That's all I can manage right now. Sorry."

"Oh come on," Hauser said, "I happen to know you're not seeing anybody."

Did he really just say that? She had known, intuitively, that it was coming, but she was still surprised.

"Excuse me?" Jane said. "What did you just say to me?"

"Wait," Hauser said, "don't get all mad at me. Maybe I shouldn't of said that. But I'd like to spend some time with you. I'll admit it. You have, you know, you have a positive attitude. So I'd like to see you. And, don't take this the wrong way, I don't mean to say you can't get a date or anything, I'm sure you can, you're nice looking, but as long as you're not seeing anyone else, why not go to lunch with me?"

"I don't know what I might have said or done that may have given you the wrong impression. Whether or not I'm seeing anyone, I don't want to be seeing anyone married, if that's what you're asking here." Especially not married with two young children, she thought. That was doubly despicable. Didn't Hauser care about his family? Besides the fact that Hauser had a comb over, no way Jane wanted to hurt innocent people, which always happened with affairs. She knew that much from Jeff and Cassie's affair. And she especially didn't want to hurt Hauser's little girls. She'd seen them when he brought his family with him last year, to stay at the resort hotel for the Retirement Round Up. For pity's sake, who would want to mess up the home of those two little angels?

"It's just lunch, for Chrissakes," Hauser said. "You got a lot of nerve, you know that?"

Does that work? Jane wanted to ask. Does bullying get some women to change their minds? Were there women who turned down the flattery and the cajoling and then turned around and said yes if the guy turned mean? Or is it like playing the slot machines? Keep dropping in the coins and see what comes up? Try a little flattery and if that doesn't work try insults and see what happens? Lemons the first few tries but then cherries are sure to come up eventually? And what about Hauser saying 'I know you're not seeing anyone?' Is that the only excuse allowed? Another man? If she had no man in the picture is she supposed to be available to any man who pays her a compliment or bares his teeth?

Hauser had hung up. Jane looked at the screen on her office phone that recorded the time for phone calls. Nine minutes. Rats. Jane's firm billed in six minute units. If she could have gotten him to hang up in six minutes she would have to leave out only one billing unit from the time she was recording for the client whose trust she'd been revising when he called. Now she'd have to leave out two billing units, or twelve minutes, even though the call only took nine minutes. It didn't seem fair to round down, taking way from her calculations only six minutes, when the call had lasted for nine. Why should her trust client pay for any part of her time in getting rid of Hauser, that horse's ass? Jane really wanted to bill a full eight hours today. With bathroom breaks, lunch and now another twelve minutes blown on that stupid nine minute phone call, she would be lucky to get out of the office by six or seven at night.

If she thought about it much longer she'd go past twelve minutes and have to leave out three billing units, or eighteen minutes, from the trust client's time record. But she'd been right about Hauser, hadn't she? She wasn't paranoid because of the problems with Jeff. Her intuition was dead on. She could tell when bankers or brokers wanted to meet for lunch to discuss business referrals and when she needed to avoid a slimy confrontation with someone like Hauser. Her intuition was just fine. She looked at the time again. Focus, I've got to focus. She tapped out a new section of a marital trust on the computer keyboard.

Early Saturday morning, as promised, Roy appeared at her front door. He was here to look at the flat roof Jeff had wanted over the bonus room at the back of their house. No, not 'their house.' She would not mess up the pronouns this morning. And she wouldn't say 'the roof that Jeff wanted.' Jane was determined not to slip up. She was going to say 'my roof' and 'my house' to Roy.

"Hi Roy," Jane said. "Thanks for coming by."

"No problem," Roy said. "I like these sorts of projects. And

I don't mind seeing you. I had a nice time the other night."

"Me too. I had a nice time too. The roof is over the bonus room in the back. I have french doors in an upstairs bedroom that lead out onto the roof." Jane wasn't happy about even mentioning her bedroom, let alone having to take Roy up there, but the french doors in her bedroom were the only way to get to the bonus room roof. Even if it was just to give him access to the roof, it was still sending the wrong message. This was getting complicated. And it was only 8 in the morning. Jane wished she hadn't agreed to let Roy come by to look at the roof over the bonus room, but it was too late to back out now.

"I'll get my ladder. " Roy walked to his truck and pulled an extension ladder off the side of it. "I'll need to go up on the ladder to get a good look at the flashings from underneath."

Roy disappeared onto the roof. Jane looked up at the sky. It was a beautiful morning. The day would likely be much warmer later on, but just then it was still cool and a little foggy. There was dew on the grass in the yard. Birds were chirping. Jane was glad to have an excuse not to go into the office right away. And she could give a favorable report to her mother. Roy showed up on time and was wearing another clean shirt.

"How's it look?" Jane stood in the driveway, looking up at Roy standing on the flat roof above the bonus room. The fog was dissipating and she squinted to see him up there, framed by the late spring sunshine shining in patches through the overhanging trees.

"C'mon up," Roy said.

"Up the ladder?"

"Why not?" Roy said. "I'll steady it from the top."

Jane could go inside and get to the roof through the french doors, but she didn't want to call attention to her bedroom. On balance, the ladder seemed like the better choice. Roy reached for her when she was near the top. He had a firm grip on her upper arm as he helped her from the ladder to the roof. And he didn't let go right away.

"Are you okay with heights?" Roy said.

"Yeah, I'm fine." He let go of her arm.

"Let me show you what's up with this roof," Roy said. "Look here, under this shingle. The builder put in the extra liners needed. This was done well. From what I can see from the side, it looks like there are extra beams supporting the roof. So that's good news. You could leave it as it is, and you should get some good years out of it with no leaks. Just keep the trees pruned back enough so the leaves don't touch the roof or the gutters and flashings. Air needs to circulate, or even the best roof will rot. The other choice is that you could go ahead with a deck with wood flooring, some seating and a sturdy railing. My recommendation is to complete the deck, especially with the doors there. You're going to want to come out here with doors like that right there. You're going to have people up here. It's not a good idea to have an outdoor space like this that's so inviting and up high, without a strong railing."

"It is pretty up here," Jane said. "I hadn't realized how nice it is." There was a slight breeze and Jane could see the patterns of the shadows from the new, fresh green leaves on the trees. The shadows were moving on the roof, interspersed with sunshine. This would be a great place to have her morning coffee, except of course, in winter. Building out the deck was a very appealing idea. She could sit out here with her cats and have coffee. The cats already spent a lot of time prowling around out here looking for birds and squirrels.

A wave of sorrow hit unexpectedly, like a sucker punch to the stomach. Jane had promised herself she wouldn't think about Jeff, but there it was. The sadness just washed through her. Jane might have had her morning coffee with Jeff, not just with her cats. There might have been mornings with Jeff out here. With morning coffee, after sex. Or even sex at night out here. Or maybe she would have sat out here in the middle of the night and looked at the stars while holding a baby, their baby, who needed a midnight lullaby under the stars to get back to sleep. How many hopes were still tied up in this house, especially on this roof that Jeff wanted to use like an upper porch? It was so nice out here. She hadn't realized. And now that she did, even with all her resolve to move on and not dwell on what might have been, with Jeff, in this house, the feelings of loss were still so intense.

"Are you ok?" Roy said. "Are you sure you're ok with heights?"

"Oh sure," Jane said. "I just got lost in thought imagining what the deck might look like. Maybe I could have some planters out here with flowers or herbs or something."

"Sure, why not? You could do something like that up here."

"Do you have time for coffee?"

"Sounds good."

Jane went in through the French doors. There was no way she could get a tray of coffee mugs up the ladder on the way back to roof so she might as well go into the house through the bedroom. Roy seemed more interested in the roof shingles anyway. She came back with a tray and two mugs of coffee, a pitcher of cream, a sugar bowl, an assortment of packets of sugar substitutes, two spoons and a couple of bialys she'd bought the day before. If she heated them a little in the microwave, they were still pretty good second day.

They sat on the roof with their backs pressed against the side of the second story of the house. About half the deck was in shade from the old trees in the yard, but they sat in the part that had dappled sunshine, as the morning was still cool. Jane felt better after she had a sip of coffee and a bite of bialy. The past receded and the pain faded. She was having a nice morning, right then. What might have been was nothing really. This nice day, right here, that was what mattered.

"If you wouldn't mind waiting," Roy said, "I could do this for you just for the materials cost, no charge for labor. I have a couple of jobs going on, but I could work on this around those, in my spare time. It would take longer than if you got a crew in here, because it would just be me, but it would really keep your costs to a minimum. I like this kind of project. And besides, I'd have an excuse to see you."

Jane didn't know about that. This was just the kind of complicated arrangement she'd been worried about. She didn't like taking a favor this big from a guy she wasn't even sure she wanted to keep dating. What if things didn't work out? Would she have an unfinished deck, or worse yet, an angry man to deal with, when she got home from work? And would it be like trading sex for work on the deck if things did work out between them? And she wanted him to have to make an effort to see her. An excuse to see her was definitely not a good thing for him to have. Would he bother to ask her out again if he could see her by stopping by to work on the deck? And then there were all the dashed hopes tied up in this roof. All the pain she just felt pass through her. With all that, did she really even want to put in a deck?

"I don't know Roy. Let me think about it, ok?"

"Sure. Just let me know if you decide to go ahead with this." One of Jane's cats strolled by and Roy stroked its back. "So how's your mom?"

"She's good," Jane said. "I went to Church with her on Sunday for Easter and then I was over to see her Thursday evening."

"Yeah we had a big family get-together for Easter," Roy said. "Usually my mom cooks up a storm, but she's been a little unsteady lately so this year Anita stepped up to the plate, so to speak. She had everybody over to her place. Kids everywhere. And all kinds of food. I'll bet Anita's still serving the leftovers even though she sent everybody home with all they could carry."

"Sounds nice. Must be great to have so much family near by. It's pretty much just my mom and me."

"You must be pretty close."

"I phone my mom just about every day," Jane said. "And I go with her to Church on Sundays if she's feeling up to it and then I try to stop in at least once more during the week. Just to see if she needs anything."

"You like Church or do you just go for your mom?"

"I guess I like it. I go by myself a lot of Sundays even if Mom's not going. I like the singing and seeing people I know. I don't mind a good sermon. Something optimistic."

"You think Jesus really did rise from the dead?" Roy said. "Walked around like you and me after being dead for three days?"

"Actually, I do think that."

Roy looked out at the trees. "And what about Judas? It always kind of bothered me that he got such a bad rep for doing something that was supposed to be all part of God's plan. I mean if Jesus was supposed to die for our sins, and Judas turning Jesus in to the authorities brought that about, are we really giving Judas a fair shake if we condemn him for it? He was just playing his part in something that was supposed to happen, right? So why is he a bad guy?"

"Believe it or not," Jane said, "I've heard that argument before. From my mom even, and more than once, oddly enough.
And, no, I don't agree with it. I mean I heard a good sermon on
Judas where the preacher said that said a big part of why we see
him so negatively has to do with the way early Christianity became a Gentile movement and how the Gospels were interpreted
for centuries with a lot of anti-Judaism. She said Judas was closer to Jesus and more of a complex person than the caricature we
learn about in Sunday School. That part's not fair. And the terrible sin Christians committed for centuries in blaming Jews and
Judaism for Jesus' death, that was horribly wrong, and it's something all Christians need to guard against and remember to speak
out against. But holding Judas individually accountable, as one
person, for his choice in helping the authorities to arrest Jesus,
that's fair, in my view."

"But if the Crucifixion was supposed to happen," Roy said,
"then why is it wrong for Judas to do what he did? If it helped
bring it about?"

"Because Jesus was on route to death and Resurrection before time itself," Jane said, "that's why. He didn't need Judas to
help get him arrested. Judas had free will and could have stepped
aside from the betrayal. Jesus would have made it to the Cross
some other way. Even if Pilate and the Roman authorities were-
n't a bunch of cowardly, murderous bastards. Still would have
happened. We're each accountable for our choices no matter
what God's plans are, or how things turn out."

"Well ok, Jane." Roy turned toward her and smiled. "I guess
you've got an opinion on that one."

"That a problem?" Jane said.

"No," Roy said. "No problem." He drank some more coffee.
They were both silent for a few moments. "I'd like to see you
again. I've got tickets to a play next weekend for Friday night.
At the Shore Theater. Remember Arthur and Mindy Ogden from
my party? Arthur's in the play. It was written by somebody local, but Arthur says whoever it is has gotten good reviews for his
plays in the past. So it shouldn't be too terrible. Would you
come with me?"

"This coming Friday?" Jane said. "I've got afternoon meetings that might run late. What time is the play? I could meet you at the theater."

"I'd like to pick you up and go together," Roy said. "The play doesn't start until 8. Just call me on my cell when your meetings finish. You should have the number from when I called you. If we have time we can get a quick dinner. Otherwise we can eat after the play."

"Ok," Jane said. "I'll call as soon as I finish up on Friday. With luck, it shouldn't go much past 6, but I never can tell when I'll run into a problem and have a meeting go until late. But this should work, if you don't mind the possibility of eating after the play if I do run into a problem. Sounds good."

Roy nodded and got up, handing her his coffee mug and heading to the ladder. Jane watched him carry the ladder down the driveway. Good shoulders. He looked sturdy and tall. She couldn't get a good look at his arms in his workshirt, but he carried the ladder easily. He put the ladder on the truck and had it secured in no time. And he was gone. Hadn't even tried for a kiss. Maybe that's how he got to forty without ever being married.

CHAPTER FOUR

*M*onday at work, the morning flew past. At lunchtime Jane thought about picking up another salad from the place a few blocks away and then bringing it back to eat at her desk. It was a little late to call anyplace for delivery. Corinne Eberly, also one of the younger junior non-equity partners at the firm, stopped Jane in the hall.

"Got lunch plans?" Corinne said. "Have time to go get lunch someplace close?"

Jane hardly ever went to lunch with her law partners. On the days when she didn't have to eat at her desk because a client meeting ran over, or because she was behind on a project, Jane was too busy running errands or trying to cram a visit to the gym into a lunch hour. And then there were the days when she need-ed to have lunch with a client or someone referring a client. There was always something else scheduled or going on and she never seemed to get around to having lunch with any of her part-ners. She didn't dislike them, exactly. They were ok, most of them. A few she even liked enough to think of as friends. But not close enough friends to go to lunch with, at least not very often, if she could do something else instead.

Jane had been warned by the consultants the firm hired that her lunch habits weren't helping her. Those arrogant, annoying consultants the firm hired, what a waste. The overhead just keeps going up every year with more costs for employees and supplies and computers and the senior partners on the Productiv-ity Committee go and hire a bunch of expensive consultants. How hard do they think they can push the new associates to bill more hours and make more money to cover the cost of that kind of nonsense, really? But one thing the consultants said to Jane, that she had to admit made a lot of sense, was that she would do better as a junior partner if she spent more time socializing with people in the firm.

Like going to lunch with Corinne, for example. Like maybe now. But Corinne? Everyone knew about her affair, presumably everyone except Corinne's husband and the wife of her paramour. Is that the word? What's the word for a male mistress? Not gigolo. The guy was one of the senior equity partners in the biggest firm in town. He probably made at least two or three times as much, and probably a lot more than that even, as Corinne did as a junior non-equity partner at Jane's firm, and wasn't a gigolo a man who had affairs with rich women for their money? If he was having an affair with Corinne, it wasn't for her money, not with all that he must be getting from the big cases his firm handled. So not gigolo. Or fancy man. No, not that. Not a Sugar Daddy. Jane didn't know the exact dollar amount of Corinne's income, as a junior non-equity partner, but it was probably somewhere close to what Jane made, at least it should be, even given the often inscrutable logic of the Compensation Committee when it came to setting partner compensation. And that level of income was more than you'd think of a woman having, if she needed a Sugar Daddy.

And even if Jane couldn't think of the right word, so what? Who cares what Corinne does in her spare time? Jane didn't want to be so judgmental. We're all sinners, right? The whole thing about ignoring the plank in own her eye while getting on her high horse about a speck in Corinne's. She shouldn't be that way, judging others, right? But what a speck. Corinne and her husband had a little boy in kindergarten. The paramour and his wife had two in junior high. Why didn't they just take up playing with dynamite as a hobby instead?

"Jane. Hello Jane," Corrine said. "I'm still standing here. Can you do lunch?"

"What? Oh yeah, sure, great, let's go."

They walked the few blocks to a chain restaurant nearby. Corinne sent text messages even as they crossed the street. Were the messages about work or the affair? Imagine being defined like that. Did Corinne know everyone was thinking about her affair when they saw her? Jane supposed plenty of people thought about Jeff's affair and Jane's divorce when they saw Jane. But even just walking with a colleague to a restaurant for lunch, did Corinne think other people were thinking about her affair? Or did other people not think about it? Was it something Jane was just prone to obsess about, since finding out that Jeff was having an affair? At least she hoped that with Jeff it was an affair, not affairs. Guess that didn't matter anymore.

"Two for lunch?" The hostess was standing just inside the door to the restaurant. She looked about twelve years old.

"Yes, outside if you have it," Corinne said, "but inside is ok if you don't." Corinne looked at Jane. "That ok with you?"

"Sure, outside's fine." They followed the hostess to one of several small outdoor tables under a large awning. "So how is your son? Kindergarten going ok? Do you have a nanny or is he in after school care?"

Jane had so many other questions she would rather ask Corinne. What do you do if you've seen your lover -- that's it, that's the right word, lover. No financial implications on either side. Neither one in it for the other person's money, just thrills or physical attraction or some emotional need or pathology or may-be even love, but then he would be called a lover, that's it. So what do you do if you've seen your lover and later that same day your husband wants sex? Do you plead headache or have sex twice in the same day, with two different men? Does it mean lots of extra showers? Jane felt she could use one right then. Do you get mixed up about who you already told the funny story you heard from the clerk in the mail room? Or worse yet, do you tell your husband the joke you heard from your lover?

Jane knew Corinne's husband was a high school teacher. Did Corinne buy food for her family with his pay, eat some of it and then still go see what's-his-name? Or could Corinne make a convincing argument that since she made more money than her husband, her own pay was enough for all her food? Did that matter? Jane thought again about the story of Judah sending around a goat from his herd for Tamar in the Bible. Did Corinne take gifts from both men? And was there always passion or did Corinne sometimes wish her lover or her husband or both would lay off? And Corinne's little boy in kindergarten, what about him? If Jeff had agreed to start a family right away after they got married, Jane might have a kindergartner of her own about now. How she wanted that. And maybe another little one or two. And Corinne had everything and was risking everything. Was there a question about the father? No, Corinne hadn't been seeing the big shot lawyer that long. Jane didn't think so anyway. But if Corinne's husband found out about the affair would he wonder if there had been someone else in the picture too, earlier on, when their little boy was conceived?

The litany of childhood activities Corinne was describing, (play dates, T-ball, art lessons, music lessons, troubles with babysitters,) was winding down. Jane was going to have to say something.

"Art lessons and music lessons," Jane said. "Both? Really? Must be good for the left brain, or is it the right brain? He sounds like a really creative little guy."

Corinne had barely touched her lunch. Skinless grilled chicken on a bed of iceberg lettuce, dressing on the side. Probably not good to put on too many pounds. Not with two men to string along. Ok, that's enough already. More than enough. Jane resolved not to think even one more caustic thought. Not one more.

"So what about you?" Corinne said. "What are you up to these days?"

"Well besides work, of course," Jane said, "and there's a lot of that, I just finished up a few weeks ago with some volunteer work I was doing with an adult literacy program. I'm using the extra time to get some things done around the house. I'm thinking of building out an upper deck overlooking my back yard and I had a contractor look at it this past weekend. If I get it finished and get a railing up, maybe you and your son could come by sometime."

Why had Jane just said that? She couldn't believe she just said that. Did it mean she had to actually have Corinne over to her house? What if she brought her lover instead of her husband? Would Jane be condoning the situation by letting them in her house? On her deck? Not one more mean thought. Not one more. Focus, I've got to focus. But she'd never bring Frederick, that's his name, Corinne's lover's name is Frederick Harrigan, with her son. Her son would be too likely to say something about it later in front of his dad. Wait. Not one more mean thought. Not one.

"Oh sure, anytime," Corinne said. "We'd love to. We better

get the check and get back to the office."

That night after her dinner Jane called Sherri. No answer, just the voicemail on Sherri's cell. Asking her to leave a message.

"Hey Sherri," Jane said after she heard the beep on Sherri's voicemail. "It's Jane. Just wondering if you want to get dinner sometime this week? I'm free any night other than Friday. Let me know if you want to go for a walk even. What's up with you lately that your phone is off all the time? You ok? Call me, sweetie."

Friday evening Jane's meetings were finished by about 5:30 p.m. and she gave Roy a call. Then she ran into the ladies room and changed out of her power suit and into a dress and heels. Her trench coat was rumpled and not very sexy, but it was still cool in the evenings, and it could rain. She dug into her enormous handbag and pulled out her wallet, keys, cell phone and a lipstick, and she took a tissue from the box on her desk. Jane kept a supply of tissue boxes in her office closet and always remembered to grab a box to take into conference rooms for client meetings. A wills and estates practice often involved teary clients. Jane transferred the items she'd pulled out of her large purse into a smaller, (not exactly small, but smaller compared to Jane's usual handbag,) evening bag. She jammed her usual heavyweight, enormous hobo bag, with the rest of the assorted items she always carried, into the desk drawer where she kept her sensible shoes. Not taking the hobo bag would mean leaving behind her hairbrush, business card holder, coffee mug, water bottle, granola bars, eye liner, compact, flashlight, hand lotion, memo pad, hand sanitizer, phone charger, bottle of pain reliever, cough drops, extra packets of sugar substitute, and even her travel sized umbrella and pepper spray. She wanted to stuff those last two items, the umbrella and the pepper spray, into her evening handbag, but they couldn't possibly fit. Maybe just the hand sanitizer? No, she didn't want to have a lumpy bag ruining the lines of her dress. She took a few business cards out of the holder and put them in her wallet in the evening bag. They wouldn't take up any room and she might run into someone who asked for a card and could send some business her way. You never knew.

The night guard at the front desk buzzed her office phone

just as she hung her suit and blouse on a hook behind her office door.

"Jane Sidley."

"This is Jake," the night guard said, "from down here, on the front desk. There's some guy down here, standing here, at the front desk. He says he's here because he's supposed to see you. But I don't see his name on the appointment book. Not for tonight. I told him it's after hours and he's supposed to be in the book, if he's here to see somebody. For me to even ring upstairs, he supposed to be in the night appointment book. He says he knows you. I wouldn't even bother you, I mean I would have gotten rid of this guy, without him being in the book, but he said he has your cell number. And he was going to call you. So I figured I might as well call you, to let you know. That this guy is standing here and was going to call you. And he isn't in the book."

The night guard, Jake, was supposed to make the building safe at night after hours but Jane would have felt safer without him. Last Christmas he left a shot glass and a small bottle of whiskey on her desk as a gift. It was extra inappropriate because he didn't leave a gift for anyone else, just Jane. And he was always checking her car in the parking garage, with a kind of proprietary air, and then telling her he thought he'd noticed something wrong. A low tire or something with the way the exhaust pipe was positioned. As if he was a personal friend or someone with some kind of rights with regard to her car maintenance or her maintenance in general. Jane felt disgusted just thinking about it. How creepy was it that he figured out which car was hers and was spending time examining it?

And now Jake was making up some rule about the after hours night appointment book just to give her a hard time about going out on what was pretty obviously a Friday night date. Sure, you were supposed to put after hours appointments in the book, but that was just a courtesy for conference room scheduling. So people could reserve conference rooms for after hours meetings and not overbook. And that way the night guard could send people up to the right floor and the right conference room. There was no need to list someone if they were there just to meet someone and then leave the building with that person, instead of staying there, in the building, for a meeting. It wasn't like some kind of guest list for a private party at an exclusive club or something, it was the after hours conference room scheduling book. And there was certainly no rule about not calling upstairs if someone who wasn't listed in the book stopped at the desk and asked to see someone at the firm. How ridiculous would that be? Jake just didn't like it that Jane was going out with a man. That was more than a little disturbing. Maybe she should keep an extra pepper spray in her desk drawer.

"Ok fine," Jane said. "I'll be right down."

Roy was standing by the main reception desk. Both Roy and Jake turned their heads to look at Jane as she got off the elevator. Roy was wearing a turtle neck sweater under a worn leather bomber jacket. He had on men's dress pants, not jeans, with a good pressed crease. Jane didn't like turtle necks on men. It seemed a little too tame or Nu Age or something. A tattoo or piercings or a bare chest with gold chains might have been even worse in the opposite direction of too tame, and she didn't spot any of those on him, at least not so far. On balance, he looked ok. And no heavy men's cologne. So he smelled ok, which was even more important.

"Hi Jane," Roy said. "You look really nice."

Jane smiled. "Thanks."

"I know this place not far from the Shore Theater where we can get a quick dinner in time to get to the play by 8. It has the world's best sweet potato fries. And if we park in the municipal garage across the street, I won't have to move my truck if you don't mind walking three blocks to the theater after dinner."

"Sweet potato fries sound great," Jane said. "Sign me up."

Roy put his arm around Jane and they headed out the door that connected the parking garage to the reception area. Roy had cleaned his truck cab since their last date. And the restaurant he chose was good. Jane had a side house salad with vinaigrette dressing and then made a choice from the tapas menu to have as her entree. It was small pieces of duck in a mango sauce with some interesting vegetables. The restaurant decor was arty. Roy talked a lot and was even funny sometimes. They shared a carafe of house wine.

There was just one set for all the scenes in the play. It was the inside of two levels of a big house at the beach on Cape Cod. The audience had a view of a first floor living room and the kitchen, with a balcony upstairs that ran in front of a row of doors leading to imagined bedrooms. The characters were a group of couples and their children, some of them old friends and some of them friends of old friends. They had all rented the house together for a few weeks one summer in the sixties. There was a minister and his wife who had a troubled son who was approaching the end of his college deferment. The Vietnam war was going on, of course, as it was set in the sixties. So the son needed to decide whether to enlist or wait to be drafted. Or he could run to Canada or be a conscientious objector.

Several of the couples had troubled marriages. Sometimes the bedroom doors would open and close very quietly at night and the audience could see people sneaking around. Jane wished there was a chart in the program as to who was supposed to be in which bedroom, because once or twice she got confused about who was sneaking around with whom, even with the scenes of stolen kisses and talk of assignations in the kitchen. Maybe the element of confusion was part of the theme of the play. Jane wasn't sure.

A few times the doors to the bedrooms were slammed during arguments, with shouting, on the balcony. Some of the arguments were even heard as muffled sounds behind closed doors while other people were standing and talking about life, or their hopes or ambitions or problems, on the balcony. One of the women was trying to find meaning in her life now that her children were leaving the nest. One of the men was trying to find meaning in his life after recently surviving a heart attack. Sixties music and the inevitable sixties' experimentation with drugs and free love kept the play moving.

Jane forgot herself completely as the scenes progressed. When it was over and they were clapping for Arthur and the other cast members, Jane came back to consciousness. It was as if no time had passed. Maybe they should put something about that on the posters advertising the play. So absorbing that even Jane Sidley, an attorney who never misses anything, and I mean never, got caught up in it and forgot to worry about her clients or her mom or her cats or her bank balance or her future for almost the entire two hours. That would sell some tickets.

They stood up to go and Jane looked back at the balcony railing on the set. With all the shouting, drinking and drugs, there were several times during the play when she'd held her breath as a character leaned out over the railing. No one fell, but the play did involve the aftereffects of a drowning, maybe an accident, maybe a suicide, in the ocean.

After the play they found Arthur backstage. He was beaming. "My friend, my dear, dear friend, tell me you loved it. Tell me this little play of ours changed your life." He grabbed Roy and Jane in a big bear hug. He smelled like gin, maybe rum.

"You were magnificent, Arthur," Roy said. "I laughed, I cried. It did change my life."

Arthur released them from his hug and turned toward Jane. "And you, young lady? Was it life changing for you as well?"

"This is Jane, Arthur," Roy said. "We met at the birthday party you and Mindy threw for me."

"Yes, yes, of course, Jane," Arthur said. "Well, did the play move you to new heights, dear?"

"Actually, I loved it," Jane said. "I forgot I existed it was so absorbing. Great job, Arthur, really."

"You hang on to this one, Roy, my boy," Arthur said. "She's a keeper. Listen, lovebirds, this band of humble thespians is headed to Hailey's Pub for libation and song. Comest thou with us, wilt thou?"

Roy begged off and they slipped out a side door onto the sidewalk. Jane saw a Hi-Grade Window Cleaning van just ahead, parked under a street lamp. Were they everywhere these days or was it that same van she'd seen at the Community Center and then at Church? One of the back doors was open and she smelled chemicals and body odor as they walked toward it. There was a sleeping bag in the van. Was someone living in there? Jane tried to read the array of bumper stickers on the open door of the van as they walked past. One said something about Texas, another was about Alaska and then one was in a foreign language or maybe something in symbols? She was trying to decipher it when Roy interrupted her thoughts.

"So how about a drink, just the two of us?" Roy said. "I know a nice place near here."

"Ok," Jane said. "But just a quick drink, it's getting kind of late."

"You turn into a pumpkin at midnight?"

"No, I don't. It's just been a busy week, that's all. And I usually go in to the office on Saturdays, at least for part of the day, so I don't like to stay out too late on Friday nights."

"Or Saturday nights, what with Church on Sunday mornings." Roy was smiling. "Just giving you a hard time. C'mon, here's the place I meant." He took hold of her upper arm with his right hand, the way he had when she was on the ladder at her house, and then put his left arm around her, steering her toward some tables lined up on the sidewalk outside a bar with lots of hanging plants. His grip felt reassuring and he was warm and close in the night air. "I think it's a warm enough spring night that we can sit outside if you keep your coat on." The waitress came by their table. "I'll have a draft beer. What about you, Jane?"

"A glass of Chardonnay."

"How about that Arthur?" Roy said. "Not bad for an old guy, hunh?" Arthur was Roy's age.

"I thought he did a great job as the father of that girl who drowned," Jane said. "His grief seemed so real."

"Did you think it was an accident or suicide?"

"Whichever it was, they could have kept a better eye on her."

"She was a teenager. They can slip out at night. You can't watch a teen 24/7 like a toddler."

"I thought that was part of the point of the play," Jane said. "That with Vietnam our whole country was so focused on controlling things that were not our business, like the government of a country half way round the world, that we couldn't pay attention to things that were our business right here. We couldn't take proper care of what was given into our own hands to manage."

"Speaking of taking care of things that are ours to manage," Roy said, "have you thought about a build out for a deck over your bonus room? I've got some extra lumber so I could get it done for you for just about nothing. I've been picturing it in my mind and I'd really like to get started on it."

If she let Roy get started on the deck as a favor, would Jane then owe Roy favors? Favors like sexual favors? Jane was not about to have sex on a second date. Even one that was going as well as this one. She'd liked the play and there was a lot she liked about Roy. He'd asked for this date in advance, planned ahead, picked her up and paid for everything. Other than taking her hand a few times and putting his arm around her while they were walking to the bar from the theater, he was being an absolute gentleman. No groping, no crass remarks. And other than the turtle neck, he looked good. And besides liking how he smelled, she'd liked the work smell, kind of a wood and tools smell, riding in his truck. His truck also meant he was employed. These days, especially given Jane's previous experience during her marriage, that was a real positive, not to be overlooked. But it was still the second date. A goodnight kiss, maybe a few kisses was all she was doing tonight. Accepting his offer to work on her deck would make that line a lot more difficult to hold.

"I've been thinking about it too," Jane said. "I'm still not sure what I want to do. Can I have some more time to think it over?"

"Sure, no hurry. But if you're going to do a project like that, spring or summer at the latest is a good time to start. If you start in the fall, and you run into any kind of delay, or get a rainy fall, it can stretch into winter and that's a problem for an outdoor project."

"I see," Jane said. "I'll try to make a decision as soon as I can." The waitress arrived with their drinks. Jane took a sip and looked at Roy. "What do you like to do besides your work? Do you do carpentry in your spare time too or do you have other hobbies?"

"I have these friends who like to play a little touch football sometimes. And I ride mountain bikes on the trails around here. My favorites are the trails at Scattered Rock State Park. Do you have a bike? Maybe we could ride on one of the trails sometime together."

"I actually do have a mountain bike," Jane said. "I haven't been on it in a while. Work doesn't leave me a lot of time. But I've had it since college and I still have my helmet."

"Great. The trails are beautiful. The other thing I like to do, as kind of a hobby I guess, is play bridge with my family. Usually it's my parents and Anita and me, but I've got cousins who play and sometimes one of them will come over if Anita is busy with her kids."

"I played a little in college so I know the basic rules," Jane said. "I never did learn much in the way of bidding conventions and all the unwritten rules and strategies. I guess it can get pretty complicated for some people."

"My family is pretty laid back," Roy said, "so we do some of that but not a lot. The funny thing is, even though I went through a phase where I was learning a lot of the inside stuff, the bidding strategies and codes that signal things to a bridge partner, and I even memorized a whole lot of that stuff and read books on it, I never really thought any of it made much difference. I always thought, even while reading all the books, that as bridge players we're all just fooling ourselves. Making it complicated so we can feel like we're making a difference in the outcome. When so much depends on the luck of getting dealt good cards. I mean there are so many rules to the game, and so many unwritten practices and conventions on top of that, the players feel like they have some control, but really that's so little, such a small part, compared with getting dealt cards with a lot of points or not. How well you play the cards you're dealt makes a little difference, but getting dealt a good or bad hand makes a big difference. And all the complexity of the rules and conventions is just an attempt to hide that and not make it seem like everything is pretty much decided once the cards are dealt, even before play starts."

"I don't know," Jane said, "I've messed up some hands with lots of points in them."

"Well, I suppose I'm exaggerating some," Roy said. "Knowing more about the rules and at least paying enough attention to know what cards have been played does make some difference. But the dirty little secret is that for all that people get absorbed in the intricacies of the rules and conventions, a lot of winning or losing has to do with chance, just as much as a game of Go Fish. But I still like to play. Maybe sometime you could meet my parents, although you might already know them if you were in Anita's class at school. Maybe we can play a few hands of bridge with them sometime. Just be sure you don't mention my theory about it being mostly a game of luck, not skill, especially not to my dad. That would be serious heresy in his book."

He's suggesting that I play bridge with his parents? This soon? Is he sincere or feeding me one of his standard lines? "Got it. If your dad asks, I say 'it's not the hand you're dealt, it's how you play the cards.' No problem. And I think I did see your mom now and then at school events. I even remember a party at your house when Anita and I were in junior high. But I don't remember seeing you."

"No, if Anita was having a party, even if I was still home in high school and not yet at college, I made myself scarce. Didn't know what a good thing I was missing by not meeting you."

"Thanks," Jane said. "But I'm just as glad you didn't first meet me in junior high."

"Can you leave your car in the garage at work overnight?" Roy put his hand over hers and leaned in for a kiss. Then he stayed close, speaking softly and directly, looking at her with clear, honest eyes. "I'd like to go to your house, or take you to my apartment, and then I can take you to your car in the morning."

He's good. The dinner, the play, the conversation, the kiss, all good. And those eyes. But second date, no way, no exceptions. "I'd like to take it slow. It's not anything about you. I'm having a nice time with you tonight. I'm just not ready to invite you in."

"Ok," Roy said. "I can wait, but I want you to know I'm waiting. I'm interested in you, Jane. I like being with you."

Jane smiled. She was glad he was interested. Glad he was waiting. She felt she was waiting too. But for the first time in a long time she wasn't waiting for Jeff. Not waiting for Jeff to move to her city after law school. Not waiting for Jeff to propose. Not waiting for Jeff to find a job. Not waiting for Jeff to say yes to starting a family. Not waiting for Jeff to decide if he was leaving her for Cassie. Not waiting for Jeff to sign the final divorce papers. Not waiting for Jeff to marry Cassie so she could stop paying alimony. Not waiting for memories of Jeff to fade. No, she was waiting for herself this time. Taking her time with her own feelings. Waiting until she decided she was ready for something, for someone. And that felt very good.

A couple came out of the door to the bar. The woman was laughing. Jane looked up. Was that Sherri? Who was she with? Oh no, not John Hauser. Jane could hardly believe it, but there was Sherri with Hauser.

"Hey," Roy said. "For a minute there with that smile I thought you were going to change your mind about tonight. Now you look like you just bit into a lemon. I'm hoping it's not the thought of me naked."

"What?" Jane said. "No, sorry, I just thought I saw someone I knew. I mean someone I thought I knew. But no, nothing about you. For a lawyer, I guess I'm not much of a poker face."

"Not even a little. But I like that about you. A lot." Roy put a twenty on the table under his empty glass. "Let's get out of here. I'll drive you to your car and then follow you home. Not trying to pressure you, I promise. I just want to follow you to see that you get home safe."

As soon as Jane got home she started calling Sherri's cell. By Sunday afternoon she'd left eight or nine messages, maybe more, on Sherri's voicemail. "Sherri, it's me again, Jane. I know why you're not picking up. We're friends. You can tell me anything. I'm not your mother. Call me. Or don't. But I am your friend. I care about you." Sherri picked up.

"What do you mean you know why I'm not picking up," Sherri said. "I've just been busy, that's all."

"It's none of my business," Jane said, "and you don't have to say a word about it if you don't want to, but I went out with Roy Adams and we were at Fernanza's for drinks late Friday night and I saw you with John Hauser."

"Ok, busted. But it's not like you think. He's practically separated. He and his wife are hardly speaking to each other. He's practically moving out."

"Do you hear what you're saying? Are you even listening to the words coming out of your mouth? What is practically separated or practically moving out? It's practically bullshit is what it is."

"That's exactly why I've been avoiding you. I knew you'd never understand and you'd just get up on your high horse and be all judgmental about it without even knowing the particular facts of this situation."

"He has kids," Jane said. "This isn't just about you and Hauser. It's also about his wife and those kids."

"I'm hanging up now."

"Ok, ok, I'm sorry. You're right. I have no right to tell you what to do. Let's talk about something else."

"No, I'm sorry," Sherri said. "I understand you went through an awful betrayal with Jeff, so everything looks like that to you. But this is different. I think it's true love with us, really. We can't help ourselves. We just have to see each other. We have to be together as much as we can. He calls me every minute he can."

Jane remembered all those questions she wished she could ask Corinne about her affair. Now that she could ask Sherri anything she wanted, Jane didn't want any answers to any questions. She just felt sick.

"You do remember," Jane said, "that he hit on me, right?"

"I know you think he did, but what did he say, really? He ran into you at the Justice Center one night, right? And he said he wanted to get coffee and ask you some questions. So what? That's not exactly propositioning you, now is it? And then what, he called to ask you to lunch? He's in the investment business. He does have clients who need wills. You draft wills. I know you like to think he was attracted to you, but let's face it, you do get business referrals from stockbrokers over lunch, right? Hard to argue with that, isn't it?"

"Ok, whatever," Jane said. "I just don't want you to get hurt."

"I'm a big girl."

But his children aren't. They're not big girls. They're little girls.

CHAPTER FIVE

Work was busy. By Tuesday, Jane was already exhausted. She had a difficult family situation with some very wealthy clients. The matriarch, who held the family purse strings, finally decided to sign her will and trust but wanted to make a speech to her children at the signing. And she wanted it videotaped. Except now it was CDs or DVDs or digital, not video tape, and the production crew, handpicked by the family matriarch herself, was headed up by the matriarch's nephew, an aspiring filmmaker whose credits so far included taking pictures at several weddings and posting short pieces on the internet. He brought along some of his friends who seemed to know at least a little about cameras and recording equipment.

Even with that level of distraction, Jane noticed that she hadn't heard from Roy. He didn't ask for another date when he dropped her off at her car after their second date. He did follow her home in his truck, but then waved and drove off without a word. How long ago was that, maybe about six weeks now? What was all that talk at Fernanza's, about him wanting her to know that he was interested in her. That he wanted her to know he was waiting. What a phony. Maybe we never leave junior high. Just like standing in the gym, waiting for some greasy boy to ask for a dance.

Ted Willingham was in her doorway.

"Jane, I've had people from our accounting department in my office, two days in a row, complaining about those production people of yours. I don't like having accounting people in my office. I like to get e-mails from them once in a while, letting me know that we're making lots of money. Other than that, I don't want to see or hear from them. And they've been in my office two days in a row. The accounting people said the I.T. people said your production crew crashed our whole computer system, twice in two days. Do you know how much revenue that costs us? Our firm bean counters do. They know. And now I know. They brought me estimates and projections on it. Let's just start with yesterday, how about that? Yesterday we were down, even the branch offices, thanks to those film people of yours tapping into our computers with whatever they're doing with their equipment, a full hour. A full hour. Do you know how much revenue we lose when the computers are down an hour? It's not just the combined billing rate of seventy-five attorneys, which is plenty. It's even worse than that. After fifteen minutes of no computers, half the associates went out for coffee, or went home or went out shopping for new suits. I don't want half the associates going home or out shopping. I want them sitting at their desks, billing time. That's what keeps the lights on."

Jane's phone rang. It was her mother. She pushed a button diverting her mother's call directly to voicemail.

"I'm really sorry," Jane said. "I know it's been crazy but they should finish up with the recording this afternoon and then they'll be out of here, I promise. And I wouldn't do this for just any client. Max Bowden's estate just made a partial distribution and now Adelaide is the major stockholder in Integrated, and she's who we're taping. A lot of the work those associates are doing is asbestos and other product liability defense work for Integrated. So keeping Adelaide Bowden happy is keeping the lights on." Her phone rang again. Roy's cell number appeared on the caller id screen. No way to get rid of Ted fast enough to take the call, so she pushed the button to divert Roy's call to voicemail too.

"I appreciate that," Ted said, "I know you know we value our relationship with Integrated, but even if those associates who went to the Mall were working on Integrated files, they weren't working on those files while getting lattes or burritos at the food court at 10:00 in the morning. What good is it to nurture our valued relationship with the Bowden family if that doesn't translate into associate productivity? And when it doesn't, that's when I have accounting people in my office, and I don't want that. When our accounting people aren't happy, I'm not happy. Because I know if our accounting people aren't happy then when bonus time comes around no one will be happy. Am I making myself clear?"

"They'll be gone by close of business today," Jane said. "You can count on it."

"Good, good," Ted said. "Glad we understand each other. You ever think about getting some art up on the walls in here?"

Ted was gone and Jane put her head down on her desk. Was this what she'd hoped for in law school? Running herself ragged for cranky rich clients and imperious managing partners? Ted was right about her having nothing but her framed diplomas on her office walls. She could at least get some art on the walls if she was going to be practically living in her office.

Jane called her mother first.

"Hi Mom. Everything ok?"

"Yes, I just hadn't heard from you since Sunday. I was a little worried about you."

"That's sweet of you, Mom, but I'm fine. Things are a little crazy at work just now, so I can't really talk. Could I stop by after work? I'll pick up one of those big falafel sandwiches at the Mediterranean place and we can split it for dinner. How about that?"

Next she rang Roy's cell.

"Roy, it's Jane. Sidley. You called me?"

"Oh, hi," Roy said. "I'm glad you called. I've been thinking about you. I know it's been a while since we've seen each other, but I wanted to ask if you could come to a reception at this building I've been working on. The thing is, it's a reception for investors. In this building I bought. Three of us contractors pooled our money and we got this apartment building to renovate and then sell the units as condos. But we didn't have enough money to put up, just the three of us, to buy the building and do all the renovations too. So we got financing from a lot of people. They're called angel investors, but believe me, they're no angels. So we finished the renovations and we're having this reception for the investors and some real estate people." Roy paused. Jane didn't say anything.

"So, you know, it's kind of a way to show off the building for the investors, and to drum up some interest, a little buzz, so we can start getting these units sold and finally make some money on this thing. And I'll tell you, I could sure use a little celebration. This project has been just crazy busy. I haven't had a spare minute. So I finished up with the building yesterday, which is good because we were a month past our original deadline, well, maybe more than that, but at least a month, and some of the investors were threatening to pull out. And the reception is Thursday, starting at 5, at the building. I'll need to pick you up at about 4. I mean, if you could you do that. I'd really like you to be there."

Six weeks of dead silence and he calls and says he's been thinking about me? Where, down a well or something? Sure, he's been busy, but how long does it take to dial a phone? And what was it that slimeball Hauser said? 'You gotta eat.' He could have met me for coffee or a sandwich at least sometime in the last six weeks. And now he says he'd really like me to be at his reception for his investors? If I'm so important to him, why hasn't he called before this?

"This Thursday?" Jane said. "I've got a meeting with a client scheduled for 3:30 that day. Best I can do is try to meet you there. I'll try to get there by 5:30 or 6. But no promises. I might not be able to make it at all."

"Yeah, my fault for the short notice I guess," Roy said.

And for not calling for six weeks. How about an apology for that?

"I am sorry about the short notice," Roy said. "I'm good at the build out, but not so much with this investor party stuff, or remembering to call ahead."

Or remembering to call at all.

"It's 3712 West Lambert, near Liberty Park. It would mean a lot to me if you came. I miss you, Jane."

I miss you, Jane? That's what he says? I haven't been on another continent. I've been right here. If he missed me, why didn't he call me sometime in the past six weeks?

"I know where that is," Jane said. "I'll try to come by if I can. Bye."

Jane wore a sleeveless dress to work on Thursday. It was lined and had a little jacket that was appropriate for the office, but she could leave the jacket in her car for the reception at Roy's building. She also changed out her sensible pearls and sensible shoes for some flashier accessories and higher heels before driving over to West Lambert. She thought about not going, but Roy had said he was really busy with this project. And if he was overextended financially and behind schedule with it, she could understand if he decided to put his social life on hold, to get the building renovations done. That was a good thing, right? It showed responsibility and was probably nothing personal. It didn't mean he wasn't interested enough to call, it just meant he was really busy and maybe a little overwhelmed with such a big project. Maybe. Maybe not. But worth wasting an hour at his reception to try to find out. Who knows, maybe some of her clients would be there. A lot of them liked to invest in real estate projects.

She tossed her purse into the trunk of her car and tucked her car key into her bra. The building had a brick front with cute shutters on the windows and colonial lanterns by the steps leading up to the front double doors. The lobby of the building was spacious with a marble floor and antique looking mailboxes set into a glass brick wall. The other walls were painted in neutral colors, with some exposed brick even on the interior. The built in station for the doorman looked like Roy's work. The wood was partially covered by a cloth as the caterers were using the doorman's counter as a bar, but from what Jane could see of it, it was a cherry finish, and obviously custom built for the space. Jane looked around for Roy and instead ran into Gordon Wendell.

"Jane, how are you? Gordon. Gordon Wendell. Remember, we spoke on the phone about insurance trusts?" He held out his hand.

"Sure, I remember. I'm fine. How about you?"

"Good. Still hoping we can do some business together sometime."

"I appreciate that." Jane looked around for Roy, but still didn't see him.

"You know a Jeff Rogers?" Gordon said. "He said he knows you. That you'd vouch for him. He wants to work with me on a new product some insurers are coming out with. It's this deal with selling shares and these derivatives, which are like shares in the shares, in SOLI policies. You know what SOLI is, Stranger Owned Life Insurance policies? You familiar with SOLI products?"

"Jeff Rogers is my ex-husband. And yes, I know what SOLI is. Just never heard of selling shares or derivatives in that kind of thing." SOLI, wouldn't you just know that would be something Jeff would want to get into. Companies, who were actually the strangers, in Stranger Owned Life Insurance, would buy up insurance policies from insured people at a deep discount, sometimes paying twenty-five percent or less of the full policy death benefit amount. It gave the insured people some quick cash for medical bills or other expenses, even if it meant their family members or other beneficiaries lost out on the death benefit from the life insurance policy when the insured person died. Sometimes people sold out to the SOLI companies because they could no longer pay the premiums on an old policy and were going to let the policy lapse, so at least with the SOLI payment, they got a little something out of the policy. What the SOLI companies got was a chance at a nice profit. They could collect the full insurance proceeds when the insured person died, even though they bought the policy at the discount price. Jane had heard there were hefty commissions involved for people who could steer people with policies to the SOLI companies. But she'd never heard of a scheme to sell shares or derivatives in the policies the SOLI companies bought up. Selling a piece of the SOLI action to ordinary investors, was that what Jeff wanted to get into? Was that even legal? Typical Jeff.

"Your ex? Then you probably don't want to vouch for him. Just as well. Derivatives in SOLI policies sounds a little too complicated even for me. I told Rogers if you'd vouch for him or if it gave me a shot at getting you to steer some of your clients who need big insurance trusts my way, then maybe, but if he's your ex, I guess working with him won't get me the time of day with you, will it?" Gordon laughed.

"He is my ex, and he was a lousy husband, but you can't say he's not a good salesman." A good talker, that's for sure. "He has a background in insurance and he's a bright guy, energetic anyway. Our marriage didn't work out. It ended pretty badly, in fact, but enough time has passed that I wish him well and I guess I'd still vouch for him. As a salesman, just not as a husband." As bitter as the divorce had been, Jane didn't want to stand in the way of Jeff earning a living. SOLI derivatives sounded like a really bad idea, but there might be something in it for Jeff. Jeff as a functional and self supporting person would mean he'd be less likely to show up in Jane's life, hit on her and ask for a loan. Sounded like a better deal in terms of Jane being free to get on with her life without interruptions from an impoverished and needy ex-husband.

"Well, honey, that's a first," Wendell said. "A woman wishing her ex-husband well. Don't hear that too often."

"Excuse me," Jane said. "I need to find Roy Adams, one of the contractors."

She found Roy by the elevators.

"Was that Gordon Wendell you were talking to over there?" Roy said. "He put together the insurance for this project. Not my favorite guy to work with, but he got us the best rates. How do you know Wendell?"

"I know a lot of insurance agents," Jane said. "Their clients need wills, my clients need insurance."

"Would you like a drink? I'm having tonic water. I want to stay on my toes in front of the investors."

"Tonic water, sure, that's fine."

They headed to the bar.

"So that's what Wendell was talking to you about all that time?" Roy said. "Sending clients? That's what you were talking to him about for that long?"

"I was only talking to the man for two minutes," Jane said.

"It was more than that. And it seemed pretty intense. And now you're avoiding telling me what you were talking about."

"I'm not avoiding anything. What are you talking about? Are you jealous of my chatting up Gordon Wendell?" First he doesn't call for six weeks, then he gets upset because I spend five minutes talking to an insurance agent who must be pushing sixty? Where is all this coming from? Has he been thinking about me? Thinking about me for the past six weeks without picking up the phone and calling? Is that possible? He couldn't take two minutes sometime in the last six weeks to call and say he's sorry he couldn't go out with me, he's working 24/7, but he's been thinking about me? Nobody's too busy for that. So if he hadn't called for six weeks because he isn't interested or doesn't care, what is with this possessive, jealous vibe tonight?

What's with this guy?

"No," Roy said. "I'm not jealous. It just seemed like you were talking about something personal, more than a casual business conversation, over there between the two of you."

"I guess. Wendell was approached by Jeff Rogers, my ex, about a new line of business and he wanted to know if I'd vouch for Jeff or if maybe I'd be interested in doing some other business if Gordon helped Jeff out. Something like that."

"Your ex? Wendell wanted you to vouch for your ex? Who vouches for an ex?"

"He didn't know he was my ex. Jeff didn't tell him. And actually I did vouch for him. He was a rat personally, but this is business."

Roy had an odd look on his face.

"Roy," Jane said. "You've got a bit too tight of a grip there on my arm. How about letting go of me and getting me that tonic water. Ok?"

"I thought he cheated on you and left you when he got his girlfriend pregnant. You vouched for him?"

I know I didn't tell him any of that. On our two dates it was casual conversation all the way. Hobbies, the play we saw, family, maybe religion a little, but nothing about Jeff having an affair or Cassie getting pregnant. Nothing that personal. Ok, I said I was divorced but no way did I give him any of the gory details. It just didn't work out. That's all I said about why I'm divorced and not a word more. Maybe later, maybe if he can manage to call more often than once every six weeks, and we're in a real relationship, maybe then I would blab about Jeff's affair and Cassie's pregnancy and the alimony and all of it, but no way does any guy get the dirt on my love life on the first or second date. No way. Chances of sex on dates one and two are near zero. Chances I'll run my mouth about my divorce, even less.

So if Roy knows about Jeff's affair, has he been asking people about me? Trying to find out things about me? Maybe he's more interested than the average guy who can't manage to call for six weeks, after all. Maybe so. His sister Anita. If I had to bet, he got the scoop on my mess of a marriage from Anita.

"I'm not still in love with him or anything," Jane said. "But if he can make a living and get on with his new life, he's that much more likely to stay out of mine. So yeah, I'll vouch for him if it could help him with a business deal. But that's all it is. Helping him get on with his life so he'll stay out of mine. That's all."

Roy was quiet for a moment. He still had a tight grip on her arm and he was frowning, looking down at the floor. Jane waited. She wanted to tell him again to let go of her arm, but she didn't say anything. What was up with this guy? Talk about running hot and cold. Nothing from him for weeks and then he's upset that I vouched for Jeff. If he didn't care enough to call all this time, why would he care if I put in a good word for Jeff on a business deal?

"I want to fix that deck for you," Roy said. "I want to do that for you."

If he does, it might cause problems down the road in our relationship, but I'm not risking much, given that we don't exactly have a relationship, at least not now. And his voice. There's something in his voice.

"Ok," Jane said. "I have been thinking about it and ok, yes, I guess I would like you to finish the deck. But I want to pay for the materials."

He let go of Jane's arm. "We can fight about that some other time. I have to spend at least a few more hours here. I'll come by later and take some measurements of the roof."

"It'll be dark in a few hours. How about over the weekend?"

"No. I have portable lights. I'll be there in a few hours."

"There's no railing. I don't want you up there in the dark."

"I have lights. It won't be dark. It's just measurements. It'll take 20 minutes. See you later."

It was still light when Jane got home. She went out to the back yard to fill the bird feeder. She'd read that some people stop feeding in the spring, but then the birds were nesting, and the new crop of seeds was not available yet, so spring was the worst time to stop filling the feeder. Jane didn't stop feeding the birds in the spring. She didn't stop in the summer either. She filled her backyard feeder year round. That way the songbirds and robins had their best chance of avoiding starvation in the winter and raising baby birds through the spring and summer. Jane topped off the feeder and saw a hawk circling. She nearly stepped on a bird one of her cats had left on the back stoop as she headed back inside the house.

Jane was at her desk in the corner of the bonus room, catching up on a few things from the office, when she heard Roy's ladder against the side of the house. Then footsteps on the roof. She could see the backyard lit up from above. He did have lights. She went upstairs and out onto the roof through the French doors in the bedroom. The lights were very bright. She could barely make out Roy standing by his lights. Roy saw her and switched off the lights. There was some light from the other houses and the street lamps, but with her eyes accustomed to Roy's lights, Jane was plunged into darkness as he switched them off. Roy walked across the roof and pulled her close. Then he was kissing her.

"I want to stay here with you tonight," Roy said. "I want you to let me stay here." His voice was hoarse. Jane knew it was probably a mistake, but she liked his kisses, and, more than that, just like her decision about the deck, the urgency in his voice made her decide to kiss him back. Then she reached for his belt buckle and pulled him even closer. Roy kept Jane close and started walking her backwards toward the French doors. She could see well enough now to make out the lines of the roof and the overhanging trees. They were in the middle of the roof, away from the edge. She felt the doors at her back and he reached around, pulling them open. Then they were in the bedroom, in the dark, on her bed.

The same bed? Is that ok? Roy pulled a condom from his pants pocket. Can I have another man here after it was my bed, my marriage bed, I mean, with my husband? Would it be better if I had a new bed in here? At least a new mattress? Roy took off her dress. When did I buy these sheets? They weren't a shower gift, were they?

CHAPTER SIX

*W*eeks went by. Jane left for work these days a little later in the morning, especially when Roy stayed over, which was more and more often. This morning when she left, he was up on the roof of the bonus room. He hadn't done much so far, other than getting the materials and putting them up there. But it sounded like this morning he might actually be putting a few boards in place before he left to work on some custom upgrades for a new house in the swanky Fox Haven subdivision. Jane headed out the door just before 10 a.m. Before Roy, even when Jeff still lived there, she was always out before 8.

Look at this traffic. So much lighter. What a difference. Hardly anybody out here this late in the morning. After all, I am a partner. Let the new associates get there at dawn. Plenty of the old farts don't come in until 10 a.m., I know they don't. Then they read the paper, (in paper, not even on the computer,) and take a two hour lunch. And then it's off to the club or the driving range. Practicing their putts. At least I work once I get to the office. That's something, right?

Her phone was ringing as soon as she got to her desk. The caller id showed Roy's cell phone number. She had just left him a half hour ago.

"Hi Roy. What's up? You ok?"

"Yeah. I meant to ask you about something last night and just forgot. Arthur and Mindy Ogden got this idea, from that play Arthur was in, to rent a big beach house with friends. So they rented this house at the beach in North Carolina, on the Outer Banks, for the month of July and invited a bunch of their friends. Anita and her kids are out there already and Mom says they're having a great time. Anita's husband is just going for a couple weekends I guess because he can't get that much time off from work. Arthur called me yesterday and said one of the couples has to leave in the middle of the month, so they'll have a bedroom open if we want to come out. I have this job on a big house in Fox Haven that's driving me crazy just now, but it should be done in two weeks. What do you say we go out there the last week in July? Can you take time off from work?"

Jane hadn't been on a real vacation in years. A few long weekends with Jeff at some bed and breakfast a few hours drive in one direction or another in some little town or other while they were still married. Then, when they weren't, she'd taken a few weekend trips with Sherri to a bigger city to see a show and do some shopping. That was about all Jane had managed in terms of vacations. The lack of vacations was good for her career. That was some consolation. Never taking a real vacation was just great for her in terms of racking up billable hours at her firm, and may have been a factor in her already being a junior non-equity partner at thirty-one. But even Jane had to admit it was a little unbalanced. Even those idiot consultants the firm had hired, even they said so.

Could she get her calendar cleared for a whole week at the end of July? She clicked on her calendar on her computer screen. Nothing unusual. Just some client meetings and a few firm group meetings, department meetings and section meetings.

"I can get my assistant to reschedule the clients I have on my calendar for the last week in July," Jane said. "And I have some firm meetings, but people miss those all the time. This sounds like fun. I've never been to the Outer Banks, but I hear it's really beautiful."

"Great. I'll tell Arthur we're coming."

"Um, Roy," Jane said, "do you need a check from me for part of the rent for the beach house or anything?"

"What is wrong with you, honey? I'm inviting you to spend a fabulous week with me. With your toes in the sand. I'll settle up with Arthur. You bring the tiniest bikini you have. Ok?"

"Got it. You bet."

"Ok, bye."

Jane's assistant Helene leaned in the doorway.

"Oliver Bowden is here."

"Oliver Bowden? Oliver Bowden is here to see me? Does he have an appointment?"

Oliver Bowden was the CEO of Integrated Products, and in

her mind's eye, Jane could imagine the rows of associates in their offices all around the firm, churning out the hours on Integrated files. But those files were litigation files, so why would Oliver want to see her? Jane had managed to win the war with the lunatic film crew that Oliver Bowden's mother, the family matriarch and largest company stockholder, hired to record her epic scolding of her children while she signed her estate planning papers, so that was over and done with. Sure the filming was a huge fiasco, and upset just about everyone at the firm, but the point was that the documents got signed. And if you actually watched what the film crew managed to record, it showed a woman who was difficult to deal with, but clearly of sound mind. And the documents she signed got the job done, let's not forget that. Besides her will, she signed an assortment of trust documents and limited liability company papers that should make those very same children, who got a such a thorough dressing down on the recording, including Oliver, into incredibly wealthy people in the event of their beloved matriarch's passing, while minimizing the tax bill to boot. If Oliver wanted to go over that, his mother had authorized Jane to talk to him, but during all the time Jane spent working with Adelaide on her estate plan, Oliver never contacted her. Why speak up now after everything was finally signed, not to mention digitally recorded? Maybe he was here to ask about his father's estate? Max Bowden's estate was still open, but it just made a substantial distribution. Surely Oliver could wait at least a little while before complaining that he wasn't getting his inheritance fast enough. And in any case he was going to have to wait for his mother to die to get most of it, and even then it would be tied up in limited liability companies or in trust.

The other possibility was that Oliver was here to talk about his own estate plan. That wouldn't be any problem, but Oliver had asked another firm to prepare wills and trust documents for him and his wife Monica. Jane had been told what was in the documents in general, but she wasn't Oliver's estate planner. So why was he here now?

"No, he's not on your calendar," Helene said. "But I thought you'd want to see him anyway so I put him in conference room Q."

"Right. Good thinking. Can you send in a tray with coffee and a pitcher of water?"

"Already did."

"Of course you did. I should've known. Thanks Helene."

Jane walked into conference room Q. "Oliver, sorry to keep you waiting."

"No problem. Thanks for seeing me this morning. I need to talk to you about my mother."

"Your mother? I don't mean to interrupt, but please understand that while this firm represents you mother and also represents Integrated, and while we have signed conflict waivers on file from your mother and on behalf of Integrated, and while you are the CEO of Integrated, you are also an individual and your mother's son. I don't have written conflict waivers between your mother and you individually. She has verbally authorized me to talk to you and to your sister about the contents of her documents, so we can talk this morning, but please keep in mind that as your mother's representative, I can't keep secrets from her. Especially not any secrets that could cause her a problem in any way. If you're here to tell me about to tell me something that you wouldn't say in front of her, then please understand and keep in mind that I am duty bound to disclose it to her. As it is, I'm going to have to tell her that you came to see me today and wanted to talk about her."

"I appreciate that, but the situation with Mother is getting out of hand. You know how she is. You just went through all that nonsense with her will. With Mother insisting that you hire my cousin, the aspiring film director, to film the signing." Oliver sipped his coffee.

"Her affairs are in good order."

"I know, I know. And I do appreciate that, certainly. I'm not here to complain about the planning you did for either of my parents. Bang up job, Jane, under tough circumstances, we all realize that. But with Mother, even with a good estate plan, the difficulty is keeping it that way. When Father was alive, no one could get past him. The leeches and hangers on would make a run at him now and then, but they'd get just exactly nowhere. Were you here when some Ivy League snot nosed kid from Wall Street they'd hired at Kensington Investors tried to convince father to put half the Company's profit sharing plan funds in commodities? Father got him transferred so fast, it was just stunning. Where did that kid end up? If Kensington had a Siberian office, Father would've had him sent there I'm sure."

"I think that was before my time. But I seem to remember Jack Dempsey talking about it."

"Good man, Jack. Sorry he passed so soon after his retirement. Reminder to us all I guess. Carpe diem and all that."

"You're right about that. And it was such a loss for the firm. We were all expecting that Jack would be 'of counsel' to the firm for years after he retired. Having him around would have been so good for the new attorneys. He taught me so much when I was first here with the firm and fresh out of law school. There are still so many days when I wish I could ask him about files I'm working on. But you were saying there's a problem with keeping your Mother's estate plan in place?"

"Right, right. Yes, that's right. Now that Father is gone, Mother is more vulnerable. Especially as she's getting up in years."

"Is someone bothering her?"

"It's complicated," Oliver said. "Do you know Gordon Wendell?"

Gordon Wendell. Turning up under every rock. "Not well, but I've run across him several times."

"Then you might know he's an agent for Regents Mark. And you worked on Mother's trusts. Her insurance trusts have most of their policies through Novalife, but some are with Regents Mark. The thing is, Novalife is a division of Novaline and we have just about all of our business and property/casualty insurance for Integrated with Novaline. But since Wendell is the agent for the Regents Mark policies in Mother's trusts, he's been telling her she can get the trustee to do some kind of 10-something exchange to put all her trust coverage with Regents Mark, and drop what we have for her trusts with Novalife." Oliver pulled a fountain pen out of his inside jacket pocket and tapped it on a legal pad on the conference room table. "It's not too terrible an idea in terms of how the premium costs compare, but it's also not necessary. Just churns some big commissions for this Wendell character."

Jane poured herself some coffee and refilled Oliver's coffee mug. "I'm with you so far. Integrated has coverage with Novaline, and Wendell wants Adelaide's trusts to do a 1035 exchange, swapping its Novaline policies for Regents Mark."

"Yeah, 1035, I think that's what it said on some papers Wendell left with Mother. But if Mother does this policy swap or exchange or whatever you call it, then long story short, all of the trust policies will be with Regents Mark, not Novalife."

"It's called a '1035 exchange' because 1035 is the section of the Internal Revenue Code that applies if one insurance policy is replaced with a substitute policy."

"A little too much information there, Jane. But I guess that's why we pay you the tall dollars. The point here is that getting rid of the Novalife policies and putting Regents Mark policies in Mother's trusts instead is not such a bad idea financially, but it's a big headache for me because Novalife is a division of Novaline, which covers Integrated. The people at Novalife aren't happy that Mother is thinking of dropping their policies. They're talking to the Novaline people and we don't need to rock the boat there just now."

"Can a few policies make that much difference?"

"These days, if there's a nickel on the floor, everyone dives for it. And what makes the situation worse is, as you may know, we've got all kinds of litigation exposure right now at Integrated and we don't need any wrinkles, if you catch my drift, with our coverage with Novaline." Oliver shifted in his chair. "Can I tell you something in confidence?"

"Not from your mother, I can't keep secrets between the two of you. But otherwise you can."

"I'm on the Board of the bank that's trustee of Mother's trusts," Oliver said, "so when I called the trust officer and said that if they go along with this Wendell guy I'll make them regret it, they listened and said no to Wendell. I know the trust officer is supposed to do what's best for the trust, but I got her to see it my way. At least we agreed that it's a gray area or a judgment call or who knows what, but bottom line she agreed the trust's policies could stay with Novalife."

"So problem solved?" Jane said.

"Not quite. Now Mother is threatening to fire the bank as

trustee unless they go along with Wendell and the bank is reconsidering. It's just ridiculous. And it's not just the trust insurance policies I'm worried about. I mean this Wendell guy shows up at Mother's house way too much. I'm starting to worry he's angling to get her to give him power of attorney over her money or put him on her bank accounts or something like that."

"Your mother is a very independent person," Jane said. "I'll call her and see if she wants to meet with me to discuss any of this." Jane knew charlatans could move in quickly, especially where the wealthy and elderly were concerned, but often the worst fleecing was done by members of one's own family, so she wanted to move slowly and carefully here. "But let's keep in mind that I represent your mother. If moving more of the trust insurance coverage to Regents Mark is a good idea, I won't tell her not to do it just because it isn't good for Integrated." Jane had a brief mental picture of the look Ted Willingham would have on his face if Oliver ever complained to Ted about what she'd just said. Probably result in Jane having to listen to another cliché filled lecture from Ted on keeping bean counters happy, keeping lights on and keeping one's ethics intact without having to walk over hot coals or beat yourself up, you know what I'm saying, can we play ball here, Jane, for heaven's sake? "Frankly, I prefer Novalife to Regents Mark because Novalife and Novaline are more conservative companies and I think 're a better bet for weathering the ups and downs in the global insurance markets. They're more likely to still be in business when these policies mature, as we say. But if Wendell has something significantly better with Regents Mark, I'm not going to turn a blind eye to it. I just can't do that, Oliver." Not much of a line in the sand, but something.

"Understood, of course, goes without saying," Oliver said. "But if it's close to even money, I hope you'll encourage her to leave well enough alone. Never hurts to keep the big picture in mind, Jane."

Jane put down her coffee mug. "And I'm going to have to run all this past our conflicts attorney here at the firm. If he thinks I have a conflict here, we may need more written waivers."

"I'll sign whatever you need. But what about Wendell visiting my mother so much? Can we stop him if he's trying to get Mother to give him power of attorney or access to her personal accounts?"

"It wouldn't be the first time I've seen that happen to an older client. Wendell is fairly reputable, I mean he's known for pushing the envelope sometimes to get a good price, but he's not the worst by far, and even a sterling reputation is no guarantee he won't overreach in your mother's case. I'll talk to your mother about him. If Wendell's been telling her to name him as her attorney-in-fact, I think that's a really bad idea and I'll say that to your mother. If she feels she needs more help with her finances, my recommendation is to put more assets in her living trust at the bank."

"But if Wendell worms his way in to the point where she insists on giving him power of attorney or adding him to her accounts, can we stop her?" Oliver said. "Better yet, can we get a restraining order to prevent him from going to the house and just cut him off now?"

"She's an adult with legal capacity. She can see who she wants to see. And if she wants to give someone power of attorney or add someone as signatory to her bank accounts, she can." Jane stole a glance at her watch. "But let's not get ahead of ourselves. Let me talk to her and see what's going on. In any case, I don't know anything about restraining orders. Our criminal defense attorneys might know more, but before we go into any of that, let me talk to your mother."

"Ok, but don't take too long, he's over there every few days." Oliver got up from his chair at the conference room table. "She does listen to you. At least sometimes. I'll tell her you'll be calling to arrange a time to drop by and see her."

Jane walked Oliver to the elevators. How different he looked than Jeff had looked standing by that same bank of elevators. The last time she saw Jeff, back in January, his pea coat fit tight on his lean frame and in his jeans and boots he could pass for a teenager, at least from a distance. Oliver was not much older than Jeff, but he was solid, expansive in his well-tailored dark suit, crisp white shirt and bow tie. When she married Jeff was she thinking he would somehow morph into someone like Oliver? No, she'd liked Jeff just the way he was, wiry and on edge.

She wouldn't trade a minute with Jeff for someone steady like Oliver, well, generally steady anyway. Oliver did have a few indiscretions in his past, one of them pretty serious, a real mess actually, but even with all of Oliver's money and ease in the business world, his type was not what Jane wanted.

But when she'd moved back here after law school and then Jeff, after several months when Jane wasn't sure if she'd ever see him again, suddenly showed up and asked her to marry him, Jane had expected him to find a job. They were both in their mid -twenties and able bodied, after all. Why couldn't they both work for a while and then start a family? Everything seemed so simple back then.

After the wedding they'd decided to build a house and at first Jane could see the advantage of Jeff not working right away, so he was available to make decisions about the house on the spot if the builders had questions. The construction crew would quit for the day if no one was available to choose the color of the counter tops or even the tile grout. So having Jeff around kept the house construction on schedule, well mostly anyway.

But once the house was finished, Jeff should have gotten serious about finding a job then. Really, he should have, right? So they could start a family. That way, if he was working too, she could cut back at work once they had a baby. With no more commotion from the house construction and expenses down, wasn't that a good time for Jeff to look for work and the two of them to start trying to have a baby?

But it didn't work out that way. He didn't spend much time looking for work. And he said it was her fault he didn't find anything. Because of her, he'd moved to a city where he didn't know anyone. Contacts are everything in sales. That's what he said. Absolutely everything, especially in insurance. Personal contacts, babe. Personal. And he didn't want to start a family. He still wanted to wait. Just until he found a good job in the insurance industry. Jane would have to wait until he could make some contacts. Personal contacts.

Two years, no, it was closer to three, went by like that. Looking back, Jane couldn't believe she'd spent all those years with Jeff unemployed and not seriously looking for a job. All those years wasted arguing with him about money and wanting to start a family.

Finally, Jeff looked through the online classifieds for the local newspaper and answered an ad for a position in sales at an industrial parts manufacturing company. Sounded good to Jane. Jeff wasn't sure, but he got the job and was finally going to work in the morning. That was what mattered, right? Now they could start a family. The job paid commission on sales, with no salary or benefits, but there was a lot of potential upside. Jeff said so. Only he didn't do that well. And he met Cassie who was working in the shipping department. And he got Cassie pregnant. And he left. Jane had to pay him half their equity in the house and give him half her 401(k) retirement account in the divorce settlement. Worse than that, his income was so low she had to pay alimony until almost a year after that when he finally got around to marrying Cassie. And Jeff, who didn't want a baby, at least not one with Jane, now had a beautiful baby boy.

The elevator doors closed and Jane headed for Helene's desk to give her the notes from the meeting with Oliver.

"These need to be scanned into the file for Adelaide. And please put a reminder on my calendar that I need to call her in a few days."

"Got it," Helene said. "Also, speaking of the Bowdens, I meant to tell you that the litigation file on Oliver's sexual harassment case is on the central filing list of old matters to be closed next week. If you want any of the records in that file copied to any of the Bowden estate planning files let me know and I'll get that done before the harassment file is closed."

What a mess that case had been. Who could imagine that Oliver would try to step out on his wife? Oliver? I guess you just never know. At least Jeff showed his true colors before we had children. That's got to be better than if he cheated and left after we had kids. Right?

"No, but thanks for the head's up," Jane said, "I don't need anything copied from the harassment case file."

When Jane got home that evening there was no sign of Roy. No note or message on her cell or the voicemail for the landline at her house. Not that he needed to leave a note or a message, exactly. He was still living in his apartment and just staying with

Jane sometimes. And they hadn't really talked about what the rules were for how often that was or wasn't. She'd given him a key, but just because it made it easier for him to work on the deck. Not because they had reached the stage of their relationship where keys were exchanged. So even though he had a key to her house, Roy hadn't given her a key to his apartment. But that was understandable. After all, having a key to her house was in his capacity as carpenter, not in his capacity as, well, what, maybe boyfriend, or maybe even partner, or at least significant other, but in any case, since it was just because of the deck, and not because they'd reached some milestone in their relationship, a key for Jane to his apartment was not required. Jane could imagine what her mother would have to say if she tried to explain any of that to her. Not something Jane wanted to hear, that's for sure.

Two days later she had a text message from Roy.

"All ok w Arthur for week @ bch. Wrkng hard to finish job Fx Hvn nxt 2 wks. Ok to stay @ your place fri. night 7/21 leave for bch 4 am sat 7/22?"

Was he saying she wouldn't see him for the next two weeks? And then was he scheduling sex for Friday June 21, followed by a week at the beach? Was Jane OK with that? Who was this guy? Mr. Hot and Cold himself? One day he's kissing her and saying he can't stand to wait too long for her, then he disappears for six weeks. Then he's all jealous of her talking to anyone, even Gordon Wendell, especially if the talk is about Jeff, and they have this hot sex. Then he's practically living in her house and calling to invite her on a vacation. Then he wants to disappear again for several weeks.

On the other hand, with the Bowdens and all her other pending matters, it was looking like she would also be working hard to finish jobs next 2 weeks too. So OK, maybe Mr. Hot and Cold does really need to focus on his work now so he can take a week to go out of town on vacation. And maybe she needed to put her social life on hold too and focus on work for the next two weeks for the same reason. Anyway, a hard working guy is a good thing, right? At least he texted this time instead of just disappearing without a word.

"Ok see u 7/21"

"Great. Luv u"

"Luv u?" Really? Mr. Hot and Cold saying "luv u" even as he says he'll be ignoring her for two weeks? Go figure. All the same, Jane was sure she was not going to text back "luv u 2." Mr. Hot and Cold could just wait for that.

Jane called Adelaide Bowden, the Bowden family matriarch, and agreed to drive out to meet with her at her home Thursday morning.

The drive out to the Adelaide Bowden's home was less than an hour. The day was bright and already very hot, even though it was just before ten in the morning. The humidity felt about 100%. Even Jane's board straight, shoulder-length brown locks were showing signs of frizz. She had the windows closed and the A/C cranked up in her Sierratti. The Bowden mansion was on six or so incredibly valuable acres at the back of the Fox Haven subdivision. Jane wondered if she would see Roy's truck parked at one of the other mansions.

Jane entered a long, circular driveway, parked, walked up the palatial front steps and across a wide front porch, carrying a briefcase full of copies of the various Bowden estate planning papers. On her shoulder was her usual enormous handbag. The latest essentials added to her bag were summer items such as two pairs of 100% UV protection sunglasses, bronzer, sunscreen, band-aids and a sun hat. Jane knocked at a door she thought was more suited to the entrance of a museum than a home.

The housekeeper, not in uniform, unless bright green stretch pants and a wrinkled pink T-shirt could be considered a uniform, answered the door.

"Hello Drema, it's Jane Sidley. I'm here to see Adelaide."

"Oh sure Jane honey," Drema said. "Come right in. She's in the front parlor. She's been waiting all morning for your visit."

Adelaide Bowden was seated on a plush velvet loveseat. It had elaborately carved legs.

"Adelaide," Jane said, "I'm so glad we could get together this morning. Your son Oliver has been worried about you."

"Jane, sit down," Adelaide said. It was more like an order than an invitation. "I know Oliver is unhappy with me. That boy always has his own ideas. Didn't listen when he was little. Still doesn't. That's for certain. That boy has never listened to anyone, not a day in his life."

Jane took a straight backed chair from beside a table that was loaded with silver candlesticks, a tea service and some other silver items she couldn't readily identify. Jane carried the chair over to the edge of Adelaide's loveseat.

"Oliver tells me you've been meeting with an insurance agent, Gordon Wendell," Jane said.

"Yes, he never would listen. I can still see him in his short pants running away from me every chance he could." She picked up a bell. "I'll have Drema bring in some unsweet iced tea."

"Thank you," Jane said. "Tea would be nice. And I'm sure Oliver was a handful as a boy. Did he tell you he came to see me last week?"

Adelaide picked up a photo album from underneath a nearby coffee table. "Look, here he is all dressed for the first day of kindergarten and trying to squirm away from me. Always moving, always busy, that one. Not like my Nora."

Two hours later, Jane wasn't sure what she'd accomplished. She thought she had extracted a promise from Adelaide not to sign any papers, especially not anything from Wendell, without letting Jane see them first. But even that much was not entirely clear. She also wondered if Adelaide was having short term memory problems. More and more she tended to talk about events from the distant past and to be less clear about recent events. Would she even remember this meeting? So many of Jane's clients had some sort of short term memory loss. Most of them could still manage on their own, more or less, without needing a child or someone else to step in as guardian, but it was often bad enough to make them vulnerable to the Gordon Wendells of the world.

Jane remembered how sharp Adelaide had been when Jane's mentor, Jack Dempsey, had first brought Jane to a meeting at the Bowden house. Jack spoke mostly to Max Bowden but Jane could tell from the few questions Adelaide asked that she understood everything Jack said. And it was complicated. They were talking about techniques for gifts of minority stock interests, with lowball valuations, to minimize taxes and still someday pass control of Integrated to one or both of their children, Oliver and Nora. Which one would get control now that Adelaide had outlived Max, well, Jane knew the answer to that even if Oliver hadn't yet figured it out. But the point was that it wasn't very long ago that Jane was a new attorney meeting the Bowdens for the first time and now Jack Dempsey and Max Bowden were gone and Adelaide was remembering twenty years ago better than twenty minutes ago. Carpe diem indeed.

That Sunday, during the sermon, the preacher asked the question, 'What holds you back?' Jane knew she meant greed, or fear or pride or selfishness, holding a person back from being more charitable or from becoming a better Christian. But Jane thought that what she wanted was a baby and what was holding her back was an ex-husband who had walked out of her life before he would agree to have one with her. Not to mention Mr. Hot and Cold, Roy Adams, who was either absent or reaching for the condom drawer. That was what was holding her back.

After Church, Jane and her mother went out to lunch at a restaurant that was brightly lit and had reasonably good sandwiches and salads. And air conditioning, which Jane's mother thought they turned up too high.

"How's that deck of yours coming along?"

This was code. The unspoken translation, which Jane comprehended instantly, goes something like this: By letting Roy work on your deck, you gave him access to your house, and presumably to you, without Roy having to continue to take you on dates or, better yet, propose marriage. I, your mother, think this is a grave error, but I'm not going to say so, at least not out loud, or other than by the use of broad hints. I also suspect that he's not even getting the work done on the deck so you've shut yourself out of proper dates that might have led to a proper proposal and you're not even getting a deck out of the deal. Your mistakes are costing us valuable time that you could be using to give me grandchildren.

"Oh, Roy's gotten a good start on some of the flooring, I think." Jane looked around for the waitress. "Anyway, he has a big job in Fox Haven, so my deck is kind of on the back burner right now."

"I see. You two lovebirds go out to eat or see any new plays lately?"

"Not exactly, but funny you should mention plays. I've been wanting to tell you that Arthur Ogden, he's this friend of Roy's and he was in the play that Roy and I went to see in May, anyway Arthur and his wife Mindy have rented a big house for the month of July at the beach in the Outer Banks, on Hatteras Island, North Carolina. Cape Hatteras. I've heard the beaches are really beautiful. It's supposed to be quiet and not too overbuilt out there. So Roy asked me to go with him to stay in this big beach house with the Ogdens and some other friends for the last week in July. If you need to talk to me that week, be sure to call me on my cell. And could you look in on my cats while I'm gone? It's only a week, so I'll leave a big dish with dry food, and a couple of big bowls of water, but if you wouldn't mind just driving over once or twice that week to check on them, I'd really appreciate it."

"I'll check on them Jane. And you think about hiring someone to get that deck finished and a railing on there before someone falls and breaks their neck."

"Right, Mom."

Almost two weeks later, when Jane got home on Friday night, July 21, Roy's truck was parked, as promised in his text message, in her driveway. She pulled in behind him, figuring they would take her Sierratti to the beach. Roy was dressed in a T-shirt, cargo shorts, white athletic socks and sandals. No, he can't be wearing socks with sandals. Black socks with sandals would be worse, but white socks with sandals was bad. Worse than the turtleneck on their second date. What if he left them on at the beach, or, oh no, during sex?

Roy put his arms around her and gave her a slow, deep kiss. Still holding her close, he spoke softly in that clear, direct way that he had.

"All packed I hope. I've missed you so much. You feel so good to hold. And you smell so nice."

Jane was packed. Work had been crazy, as usual, but she had packed. She had one small suitcase with sandals, flip-flops, pool shoes and running shoes. Another large suitcase had T-shirts, shorts, a summer skirt, two summer dresses, a few pairs of capris, fourteen pairs of underwear, six pairs of socks for her running shoes, gym shorts, three nightgowns and two sets of summer pjs, two bikinis, four beach towels, a large beach tote bag, a set of queen sized bed sheets, matching pillowcases, two jackets, four sweaters and three beach hats. She jammed a few paperbacks into the outside pocket of her suitcase, but figured if there was any time for reading it would be some of the files she was bringing in her briefcase. She also had a makeup case, a toiletry case loaded with sunscreen and hair products and a first aid kit. Jane had a defibrillator in her car which she had bought recently because she made visits to so many elderly clients. She thought she'd leave it in her car for the trip to the beach, just in case. And she had a beach umbrella, two beach chairs and a cooler with soft drinks, a six pack of beer, three bottles of wine and some water bottles. Metal, not plastic.

"I've been meaning to ask," Jane said. "Does this beach house have wi-fi?"

"Wi-fi? We're supposed to be getting away from civilization. Taking time for walking on the beach, swimming in the ocean. Why even bring a computer?"

"I need to check e-mails from work. And if there's a problem I might need to work on some documents. I can't go a whole week without my laptop."

"Why not?"

"Never mind, I have a wireless card I can bring. It's just slow sometimes."

They left at 4 a.m. because Roy said they could beat the traffic that way. The drive was uneventful. Once they reached the ocean and headed through the tunnel and over the long bridges onto Hatteras Island, the view out the car window was beautiful, just spectacular. Jane looked out at the expanse of blue water. She could smell the salt air and felt herself relaxing. Roy may have been right. She might not spend very much time on her computer after all.

They called Mindy's cell when they passed the town of Frisco, headed south along the National Seashore. Arthur and Mindy were waiting to greet them, drinks in hand, when they arrived at the enormous three story beachfront house. It was on stilts and they parked in a space on a concrete pad under the house. Painted turquoise with lacy white trim, the house was wrapped round at every level with porches. There was even a widow's walk surrounded by a railing at the very top.

Mindy and Arthur hugged Roy and Jane. Then Anita and her children, Brooklynn, Patrick and Katy came up from the beach and there were more hugs. Ansel, the drummer Jane had met at Roy's birthday party, emerged from one of the porches and, smelling faintly of rum, he gave Jane a big hug and a sloppy kiss. Two of his bandmates were also there, but still sleeping even though it was already afternoon. Jane thought Arthur was about three sheets to the wind already as well. Apparently Mindy's sister and her family were also staying at the house, but they had gone a little further down the island to some T-shirt and souvenir shops and weren't back yet.

"How fine to see Jane Sidley once again, kindergarten friend of Sherri Winger," Ansel said. "But no longer a kindergartener, that much is certain. It's been a long time since I've set eyes on you, Lady Jane. Much too long." The weeks in the sun had deepened the tone of Ansel's olive skin. His curly hair was a little unkempt when Jane first saw him at Roy's birthday party, but now it was just wild. His light brown eyes were striking with his darker olive skin tone and wild mop of very wavy, very dark brown hair. Jane couldn't help smiling. She had been a little anxious about fitting in with a group of people who all knew each other better than they knew her. But Ansel, with his big kiss and beach bum demeanor, made her feel very welcome.

"Hi Ansel," Jane said. "Good to see you again too."

"Fresh grilled mahi mahi tonight, campers," Arthur said. "Nothing finer." Jane wasn't sure how good an idea it was for someone in Arthur's present state of inebriation to play with fire, but fresh grilled fish sounded very appetizing.

Mindy showed Roy and Jane their room on the oceanside of the first floor just past the living room. Anita and her kids helped haul their luggage up the steps from the carport underneath the house. Jane and Roy's room had sliding doors leading to a porch looking out over the ocean.

"Just like your house, Jane," Roy said, "only with quite a view."

"No kidding," Jane said. "This is absolutely stunning. I'd like to get changed and get down to the ocean for the late afternoon sun. Would you put sunscreen on my back?"

"Count me in."

That night Roy and Jane sat for a long time on the porch outside their bedroom listening to the sound of the waves and feeling the ocean breezes. A bright moon rose over the ocean, casting an eerie light on the water. The clouds were patchy, drifting out over the waves. Then they made love in their bed, still a little sandy even though they'd showered before dinner after coming in from a quick swim in the breakers and a walk along the beach. Jane felt her worries about her law practice, her half finished deck, her aging mother and her uncertain future ebbing away with the sounds of the lapping waves.

Later that night, in their slightly sandy bed, Jane was still awake as Roy held her in his arms. After their lovemaking had finished he drifted off to sleep, but Jane lay awake for some time, feeling relaxed, but still awake. Roy felt so peaceful and strong. Jeff was like holding a live electric wire. Jane couldn't help remembering. Jeff was a bundle of energy even when he was spent. She'd liked that energy. His small, sinewy body was always in motion. In bed and out of it. He was always after the angle, the edge. And to hold onto him, to have his energy inside of her, there was nothing else like it. But then she remembered how all that energy meant Jeff could carry on with Cassie while still stringing Jane along and how it had all blown up in her face. Best to feel the peace here with Roy. Roy, heavy and warm. Snoring softly.

CHAPTER SEVEN

*T*he next day was even better. Slathered in sunscreen, Jane spent the morning on a beach chair under her umbrella reading paperbacks and ignoring the files in her briefcase. If she got too hot, she went out in the waves. Then she'd lay in the sun long enough to dry, more or less, and then back under the umbrella for more trashy novels. Heaven. The whole morning was just heaven.

Then lunch was the best barbecue pork Jane had ever tasted. Anita made a take-out run and Jane could not stop raving about how good it was. Jane did the unthinkable in the afternoon. She took a nap. Then grilled fish and good wine for dinner. Another long walk along the ocean. Jane couldn't remember the last time she felt this relaxed and happy.

The following morning at ten o'clock her cell phone rang. It was the number for Helene.

"Helene?" Jane said, "It's Jane. What's up?"

"I'm so sorry to bother you at the beach. Oliver Bowden has been calling. He sounds frantic. He says he wants to send his private plane to get you today, to talk to his mother. Can you call him right away?"

"He wants to send his private plane? Couldn't I just talk to his mother on the telephone?"

"I don't know, but I think you need to call him. And Ted Willingham has been circling. Pacing past my cubicle. He wanted your cell number. I think he's going to call you too."

"Terrific. That's all I need. An upset Ted Willingham. Thanks for the warning. Call me back if anything else breaks. Bye."

Jane called Oliver Bowden's direct dial office number. Gautier, his assistant, picked up on the first ring.

"Integrated Products. Oliver Bowden's office."

"Gautier," Jane said, "it's Jane Sidley from Hantler Vintberg. Is Oliver available?"

"Hold please."

Jane saw the call from Ted come through on her cell phone's call waiting. She let it go to voicemail. That would make things worse, but she couldn't have Oliver pick up and get her voicemail.

"Jane, is this Jane?"

"Yes, Oliver, it's Jane. What's going on?"

"Your secretary tells me you're where? North Carolina? Mother is completely unreasonable. Drema says Gordon Wendell was there first thing this morning with some lawyer and they're coming back tomorrow morning. They asked Drema if she can be a witness tomorrow if they sign documents. Documents, Jane! They're going to bring documents to sign. Why would they need Drema to be a witness unless they're trying to get mother to sign a new will? You're the only one she'll listen to. You've got to be at the house tomorrow morning when Wendell gets there with this lawyer of his."

"Look, I am in North Carolina. So how about if I just call your mother today and talk to her about this?"

"You know as well as I do that won't help. She'll forget you called the minute she hangs up. The only thing that's going to stop Wendell is if you are standing between him and my mother tomorrow morning, and you know it."

Jane looked out at the waves. She was going to have to leave all this to go do damage control tomorrow with Adelaide Bowden. Really rotten luck. Not likely to go over well with Roy either.

"Oliver," Jane said, now using the calm, deliberate voice of the seasoned attorney she was, "if your mother wants to sign a new will, she can. But I'll try to get a look at whatever papers Wendell puts in front of her tomorrow morning, and if I think signing the papers is not good for her, or her estate plan, I'll tell her."

"That's not the A answer. Not even close. And there's quite a lot at stake here. But I suppose that's why Mother listens to you."

"You know, Oliver, I'm not saying you should give in to this kind of shenanigans, and it's kind of like feeding stray dogs, because once you start you can never get rid of them, but it might be easier to get Wendell to back off if you throw some business his way. I didn't draft your personal documents, but my understanding is that you and your wife have big insurance trusts of your own. And most of your top executives at Integrated have split dollar agreements backed by some very sizeable insurance policies that Integrated owns. If I'm remembering right, I don't think any of that coverage is currently with Regents Mark. So could I promise Wendell tomorrow that Monica and you will sit down with him to at least discuss the possibility of moving some of your personal trust policies to Regents Mark? And if I could hint that you're thinking about tossing him some of the Integrated split dollar insurance policies, Wendell won't be able to talk to your mother into anything foolish, because he'll be drooling too much. Bottom line, he might let go of your mother if we let him think you might toss some opportunities like that in his direction."

"It's not going to make our agents at Novalife and Novaline very happy," Oliver said. "But I agree, it might get Wendell to loosen his grip. Dammit, Jane, this is just ridiculous. He's preying on my mother. Can't I just have him arrested?"

"Tell your pilot I'll be at the airstrip near Frisco, North Carolina at two this afternoon," Jane said, all business now. "You need to fly me back here tomorrow after I meet with your mother. Are we good?"

How was she going to explain this to Roy? Her phone rang again.

"Jane, Jane!" Ted was shouting on the phone. "Are you there Jane!?"

"Yes, Ted."

"Oliver Bowden is upset. He's upset. So I'm upset. I don't think I need to remind you of how many of our very capable new litigation associates are cutting their teeth on some very thick Integrated files. And how much we have to pay our very capable new litigation associates these days for sitting around while teething."

"I know, I just spoke to Oliver—"

"And I might mention that your review is coming up which I believe involves an up or down vote on your potential to advance to senior non-equity partner or even junior equity partner. Junior equity is not out of the question, at this point for you, Jane. You know I always thought you had a bright future here at Hantler Vintberg. But we are still an up or out shop. Are you hearing me?"

"Ted, I get it, ok? And don't worry, I told Oliver to send his private plane. I'm getting on it at two o'clock today and then I'm going to throw myself between Gordon Wendell and Adelaide Bowden tomorrow morning. And you know what? You might try having a little confidence in me. I've been with the firm for seven years now. And I've held clients' hands and wiped their noses with the best of them."

"I believe we understand each other. I like that about you. Just don't disappoint me tomorrow. And good for you for going to the beach. A little R and R once in a while is a very good idea. Hope you get a few days of it at the end of the week."

But that still left the matter of telling Roy she was leaving Hatteras at two that afternoon, flying out of the airstrip at Frisco, and would not be back until tomorrow.

"I can't believe this," Roy said. "You're leaving in the middle of our vacation together?"

"I'll be back by tomorrow night. Just pretend I went shopping overnight up in Nags Head or Kitty Hawk or something."

"For two days in the middle of a one week vacation? Can't somebody else cover this for you? Aren't"

Hadn't the consultants the firm hired said something about that? About Jane not delegating enough? "This isn't something a new associate could handle. It's a delicate situation and I'm the one who's had the most contact with this particular client. She trusts me and I have to go. That's all there is to it."

"Can't it wait until next week?"

"No, I'm sorry. It can't."

"I feel like you don't care. That your work is all you care about and other people's feelings, especially my feelings, just aren't important to you."

"Roy, it's like this," Jane said, once again in her calm, no-nonsense, seasoned attorney voice. "I make my living working at a law firm. And law firm clients don't have problems on a schedule. Things just happen sometimes at inconvenient times.

It's not perfect. And I'm single. I'm on my own. I have to look out for myself. I like you and I like being here on vacation with you. But I can't take a sledgehammer to my career for this relationship when I have no idea where it's going."

"What are you saying? Are you saying you wouldn't leave to go to this meeting if I asked you to marry me or something?"

"No." Jane let go of the tote bag she was holding and squared her shoulders. "You did not hear the 'm' word come out of my mouth. I'm not ready to marry anybody. All I'm saying is that it's too soon for either of us to be able to tell if this relationship has a future or not. I don't know and you don't know. That's where we are. And I can't take a bullet in terms of my career for this relationship, not at this stage. And who are you to tell me not to get on that plane, when you disappear for weeks at a time for your work?"

"Is that what this is about? I don't recall disappearing, as you call it, for my work, in the middle of a vacation with you. I quote disappeared unquote, before we came here on vacation, so that I could get work out of the way to be here with you."

"I'm sorry, but I can't do this now. I need to go get packed so I can get on a plane at two. I'll be back tomorrow and I hope you can forgive me, but that's how it is with me right now."

The view on the flight from Frisco in Oliver's six seater private plane was breathtaking. Jane hadn't felt a sense of patriotism in a long time but seeing a piece of America from the air like that, at a low enough altitude to really see it, without the press of humanity she normally had to deal with in coach on an airplane, but just floating up there with the gentle noise of the engines, Jane realized how much she loved her country. How vast it was and how lovely. And its crazy, inefficient, often sclerotic legal system, it was the best in the world and the best ever in history. And Jane appreciated that she could make a living here in this vast, beautiful country, even after being abandoned by a faithless husband. How many women in other places in the world would starve if their husbands left them to start another family with some other woman? And here she was, making her way. In this spectacular land. Roy could just wait for her. She would be back tomorrow.

The following morning, Helene drove Jane to the Bowden

mansion. Two hours later Jane once again left the Bowden mansion without much of a sense of what, if anything, she had accomplished. No papers were signed, which was key to getting Oliver and Ted off her case. She convinced Adelaide to let her look at the new will prepared by the attorney that Wendell had dragged along. Being Jane, if the new will was any good, she was going to let Adelaide sign it, even if it meant kissing off any chance Jane might have at making junior equity partner.

Fortunately or unfortunately, the new will wasn't any good. At least not for Adelaide and her heirs. If she signed the new will, it would be a bonanza for the IRS. It was like a smart bomb that would target and explode all the tax planning of Adelaide's other documents. So Jane not only told Wendell she needed more time to think about it before she could advise Adelaide whether or not to sign, she also mentioned that she'd heard Oliver was thinking about making some changes in his own estate plan. Not only that, but she'd heard he might be considering some changes in insurance policies they had at Integrated for a few of the other top executives. Jane could maybe, just maybe, give Wendell the direct dial number of Gautier, Oliver Bowden's assistant. So Gautier could set up a meeting for everyone to get together and discuss possible changes in coverage for Oliver and Monica Bowden's own insurance trusts and maybe some other changes in Integrated's executive split dollar life insurance policies too. If Wendell was interested, that is, well, it just might be arranged. But that would probably mean a delay in any changes in any documents for Adelaide, to give everyone time to look at the big picture. Surely Wendell could understand that. Apparently he did. He beat a pretty hasty retreat after Jane gave him Gautier's number. We live to fight another day.

Back on Hatteras Island, Jane drove from the Frisco airstrip to a supermarket in the town of Avon she'd heard Anita mention. She thought it might be better to return with a car full of groceries, rather than empty handed. Anita came out to help her unload the groceries when Jane returned to the beachfront house.

"Roy's still pretty upset," Anita said. "He wouldn't say a word to anyone at breakfast this morning. Then he took my kids parasailing on the dunes. They should be back by dinnertime but there's no telling what kind of mood he'll be in. I know you two have your differences, but Roy really is a good person. He's great with my kids. He'd be a great dad someday if you were thinking about a family."

"If he's such a terrific family man, how did he get to forty without ever marrying anybody?"

Anita and Jane started up the steps from the concrete pad where the cars were parked.

"I guess he was late getting started," Anita said. "Our parents had their basement built out for him. Besides a bedroom, there's a full bath down there and a finished rec room. He needed it to save money while he got his business started. And then he liked to spend time watching sports down there with his friends and my dad. Mom cooked and did his laundry, so he just stayed there through his twenties and most of his thirties. He's only had his own place for about the past year and a half. But he still brings his bags of dirty laundry to my mom, and she still brings him leftovers. He's dated around, but I think with being an uncle to my kids and having my mom take care of him, he really didn't see any need to start a family of his own. Now with my parents slowing down, and Roy just turning forty, I think he's ready. And he likes you, Jane. He really does. We all do. And we'd all like to see him more settled. From where I sit, the two of you have a good thing going. Could be even better."

"Thanks. Your brother is a good guy, no argument there. And I hope you're right about the two of us having a chance at a future together, but so far, I just don't know. I mean sometimes it seems like everything is going great, but then it's like we just stumble. I'm glad to hear you're rooting for us, but this week hasn't exactly been smooth sailing."

Roy came back with Anita's children just before dinner. He didn't say anything to Jane, not even a sullen hello.

At dinner, Anita sat between them. "Jane bought the shrimp and made the salad."

Roy pushed aside his shrimp cocktail and salad bowl.

"Mom, the parasailing was awesome," Patrick said. "You could see everything. For miles. Can we go again tomorrow, Uncle Roy?"

"We'll see," Roy said. "It really was amazing up there. Not like being in a private plane, or anything like that, but still way up there."

Anita brought a platter of fried fish to the table. "This is compliments of Jane too. She went shopping in Avon."

Roy left the table. Jane looked at the napkin in her lap.

"So how was your flight back to civilization, our fair Lady Jane?" Ansel said. He handed her the glass of beer he'd just poured and reached over to a nearby cooler for another bottle.

"Like Patrick said about the parasailing, it was awesome. My client's son sent a six seater plane and I could see the coastline and then every green hill between here and home. We were below the clouds the whole way. We take for granted what a beautiful country this is, but it was just awesome."

"Amen to that. And he'll get over it. If he has any sense, that is."

After dinner, Roy told Anita he was going out to hit the local bars with Ansel and the guys from Ansel's band. After Roy left, Jane decided to leave Hatteras. She would drive back home, that night. But when she asked Arthur and Mindy if they had room in their car to take Roy home at the end of the week if she left now, they convinced her to at least stay until the morning. That made sense. It had been a long day. She agreed she would stay until the morning.

Mindy and her sister packed up supplies for s'mores and juice boxes for the children. Arthur packed a cooler of beer and wine for the grown ups. They all headed down to the beach with the children. Jane thought the children would be exhausted and sleepy from a day of parasailing, but they were revved up and way past tired. Arthur built a fire on the beach. Jane watched the flames dance and listened to the ocean.

"Jane, what's the meaning of our sorry existence?" Arthur said. He put his arm around her as they sat on the sand by the fire. He'd been knocking back glasses of wine since dinner and he was expansive as he spoke. Arthur had a natural stage presence that carried over into his real life, especially if a little wine was added, which was often.

"Little kindnesses, Arthur," Jane said. "That's all there is. Little kindnesses."

"Like what, dear?"

Like putting one's arm around someone who has spent half a

beach vacation fighting with her boyfriend.

"Like feeding a bit of bread to a seagull. Or letting someone into traffic."

He gave her shoulders a squeeze.

"I think the meaning of life is to have fun," Arthur said. "To dance, to sing, to embrace while we can, before we wither and blow away like dry leaves."

"Did you really get the idea to rent this house from being in that play?" Jane said.

"Yes, sweetheart, I did. I was hoping we'd have more fun than they did in the play, of course, and less door slamming, less drama, and no drowning of course. Except for your little lover's quarrel with Roy, which will blow over, I hope you know that, we've had all sun and fun and none of the strum and drang."

"And no musical bedrooms," Mindy said. "Could you believe how they snuck around at night in that play?"

"They sure did," Jane said. "But the after effect of the drowning, that was what was so striking. Your grief was so real, Arthur."

"Thank you, my dear. The Ogden Method of acting. I imagine getting nothing but bad reviews and the sheer terror spurs me on to dizzying heights of thespian greatness."

The conversation continued on one of the porches after Anita and Mindy's sister put their children to bed. By about 2 a.m. Jane decided she better get some sleep if she was leaving in the morning.

Jane was sound asleep when a tapping on the sliding glass doors in her room woke her. Roy's side of the bed was still empty. She pulled a robe over her summer pajamas and went to the glass doors that led to the porch outside her room. In the moonlight she was able to see Ansel standing on the porch, looking unsteady on his feet. Jane slid the doors open just enough to talk to him, but not wide enough to let him into the room.

"Ansel," Jane said, trying to keep her voice to a whisper, but still loud enough to be heard over the surf. "What are you doing out there in the middle of the night?"

"If that idiot's gonna sleep on the couch," Ansel said. "If he's too stupid to come up here and sleep with a beautiful woman like you, you're so beautiful Jane, Lady Jane, then he doesn't deserve you. But I do, Janey Jane. Let me into your broken heart. I will rush in, yes rush in, I will do that, my angel Jane, where that fool feared to tread."

"That's sweet, I guess, in a sick way, but no way. You're not coming in here. You need to go to your own bed. How did you get up here?"

"Climbed up, oh my darlin'."

"Climbed up from where?" There were no stairs from the porch. "Look, you have to leave, ok? Now."

"My heart breaks, but if that is your wish, I can only obey. If you don't want me, you don't want me. Just let it be that way, if that's the way it is. I'll be on my way." He lurched to the side of the porch and began climbing onto the railing.

"Wait, no," Jane said, "you'll fall. You can come in but just to get to the hallway, no stopping, ok?" The porch was on the first floor of the house, but it was still one story above the ground, as the house was set on stilts to avoid damage from flooding during hurricane season. Ansel could get badly hurt if he fell. He kept trying to climb onto the railing. Jane went out on the porch to stop him. He turned to wave her away, lost his balance and tipped over the porch railing. He landed on the sand one floor below, narrowly missing the edge of the driveway and the concrete pad for the cars.

"Ansel!" Jane ran inside and then started down the outside stairs from the kitchen. Lights came on and Roy was on the stairs behind Jane. By the time Jane reached the bottom of the steps, Arthur, Mindy and Anita were at the kitchen door, asking what was going on and flipping on the outside lights. They saw Jane and Roy reach Ansel. He was lying on the sand, looking up at the stars. Soon they were all standing over him.

"Wow," Ansel said. "What great friends. You guys are the best. Best friends ever. You all ran down here. Wow."

"Are you all right?" Mindy said, kneeling down on the sand next to him. "Do we need to call the paramedics?"

"He is a paramedic," Anita said.

"Ansel is a paramedic?" Mindy said.

"Yeah, he says he likes to help people," Anita said. "He also says picking up a few shifts here and there pays the bills, whenever it's lean times for his band, which I gather is most of the time."

"I'm fit as a fiddle," Ansel said. "Right as rain."

"Can you get up?" Roy said. He reached out a hand and helped Ansel to his feet. "Wait, did you fall from the porch up there? Outside Jane and my bedroom?"

"I'm sorry, man," Ansel said. "But you weren't there. I needed to console our Lady Jane."

"Nothing happened," Jane said. "Ansel showed up on the porch up there by our room. He woke me up by tapping on the glass and I told him to go. That's all. He's drunk. He's not thinking clearly. He probably won't remember any of this tomorrow morning."

"I'll beat your lights out." Roy shoved Ansel back onto the sand.

"Boys, boys, break it up," Arthur said. He stepped between Roy   and   Ansel.
        "Roy," Jane said, "Ansel didn't mean anything. I mean even if I said yes, which I didn't, and I wouldn't, and I think he knew that, he's too drunk to do anything. In a way he was trying to be your wing man."

Roy looked at Jane. "My wing man? By climbing onto that porch up there and making a pass at you, he was being my wing man?"

"I get it," Mindy said. "I agree with Jane. He was making a stupid, obviously ineffectual pass at Jane in a very public way, designed to wake us all up, to get you to realize how much you care about her."

"That's it. Mindy's right," Anita said. "That's exactly it. Ansel wanted to make you jealous. As a way of getting you back with Jane."

"Possibly," Arthur said. "I mean I'm just throwing this out there. For your consideration. But possibly, Ansel was provoking the latent homosexual feelings we men all have for each other by making this play for Jane, in hopes that Roy's latent feelings for Ansel himself would propel Roy back into Jane's arms."

"I'm not sure I get that part," Jane said. "It's a little too complicated for me to wrap my brain around this late at night. I think we should stick with the 'making Roy jealous' theory."

"Wait a minute." Roy said. "For me to buy any of this, I

have to believe that Ansel planned to fall off the porch. Otherwise how would I know about this? And if I didn't know about it, how would I be jealous?"

"Are you?" Jane looked directly at Roy.

He looked back at Jane, but hesitated.

"Ok, people," Arthur said. "The fall off the porch may have been an ad lib on Ansel's part. Plausibly so. In any case, I'm putting Ansel to bed. If you still want to beat his brains out in the morning, Roy, you can. But until then, I suggest you make up with Jane, so we don't have you sleeping on the couch and the boys in the band trying to play musical bedrooms. Life imitates art."

Ansel was asleep or passed out on the sand and they heard him start snoring. Roy was still looking at Jane. Sure, he had dropped the ball when she asked him about jealousy. Still, she couldn't help smiling, thinking of him ready to fight Ansel, to defend her honor. Roy looked back at Ansel and then again at Jane.

"Truce?" Roy said.

"Truce," Jane said. "Let's go to bed."

When they pulled into the driveway on Sunday after the long drive back from the beach, Jane wondered if Roy was about to disappear again. He put his duffel bag into his truck.

"Except for the rough start to the week there," Roy said, "I had a great time. I'll call you, ok?"

"See you."

Roy gave Jane a careful kiss goodbye.

CHAPTER EIGHT

*B*ack at her desk at work, Jane's voicemail was full and she had hundreds of unopened e-mails in her inbox. The extra trouble she had coming back to the office after a vacation made it almost not worth it. Almost. Her phone rang and she couldn't believe the name on the caller id. Jeff Rogers. And he had a phone in his own name. Cassie must have gone back to work after all.

"Jane Sidley."

"Janey baby," Jeff said. His restless, edgy voice was so familiar. "I need to ask you something." For something, no doubt. For money most likely. That was way too familiar too. "It'll only take a minute. Can you meet me at that coffee shop we used to like, you know the one, in an hour?"

"I just got back from out of town and work is really piled up. Can it wait or can you just tell me over the phone?"

"No, meet me baby, you owe me this much. At least. Just meet me. I mean I came to this town because of you and I can't catch a break. If I stayed where I was I'd be a millionaire by now. But I'm here because I couldn't live without you back then baby, so come on, meet me in an hour."

"I do not owe you anything. If I ever did, I've paid. And paid and paid. And I'm paid up." And fed up.

"One hour, Janey. I know you'll be there. See you babe."

One hour later Jane was in the coffee shop and Jeff, if he was even coming, was late. At least the coffee was good. And Jane liked the thick white ceramic coffee cups they had in the coffee shop. It was a bright, sunny day and light was streaming in from the big front windows. She looked up and saw a man in coveralls outside the windows, just standing there staring as cleaning fluid dripped down the outside of one of the window panels. When she caught his eye, he went back to his work, wiping the window with a squeegee.

Jane remembered having some good talks in the coffee shop with Jeff, back when things were good between them. About Jeff's big plans. His big ideas. And about the house they were building together. Jane sighed. What a stupid dream it was. A delusion, lasting what, four years? Seven, if you count the two years she'd known him while she was still in law school, then the eight months before he moved here and four months after that when they were engaged. She could have a kindergartner and maybe even a second grader by now if she'd never met him.

And then there he was, coming through the door at the front of the coffee shop, heading straight for Jane's table. Edgy and lean, with that head of shiny straight thick black hair and those bright blue eyes that were animated, moving, taking everything in. Taking her in. She put her ceramic cup back on its saucer. She was lucky she only wasted seven years.

"Jane, baby," Jeff said. "You look great. What ever happened to us? You figure we just grew apart or something?"

"No, I don't. I don't figure we just grew apart. But let's not go there, ok? I'm kind of in a hurry so is there something you wanted to talk about? Some reason you wanted to meet me here?"

"Hey, I'm glad to see you too. And here's the thing." He turned to signal the waitress. "Coffee here darlin'." He flashed a perfect smile. "So I've got these brochures. I didn't want to talk on the phone because you need to see them. It's a sure thing, if I can just get my foot in the door."

The brochures were from a SOLI company called Life's End. They described how people could sell their life insurance policies to Life's End at a discount. A big discount. Jane estimated that compared to the amount of the policy proceeds, and without doing the math on life expectancy or interest rates, a rough ballpark for Life's End's payments was less than twenty-five cents on the dollar. But Life's End would pay cash, while the insured people were still alive. Their loved ones wouldn't get anything when they died, but the insured people could get money now, right away. They could use the cash to pay bills or for whatever they wanted. The brochures suggested that they use the cash to buy new policies from Life's End. Maybe better ones.

There was another brochure that told about the commissions

that insurance agents or even attorneys could get if they could find people who wanted to sell their policies to Life's End. For the agents, they could even get two commissions. One for getting someone to sell a policy for cash to Life's End, and then another commission if the person used some of that cash to buy a new policy. And the commissions were top dollar. The brochure promised.

Then there was a separate, very large and glossy brochure about the derivatives or shares that ordinary investors could buy in the SOLI policies that Life's End already owned. It was like a mutual fund. The investors put in money and depending on when people died, and whether Life's End collected on its SOLI policies sooner or later than expected, the shares would be worth more or less. Shares could go up or down in value too, based on trading in the shares. There were some complicated charts on life expectancies, numbers of deaths per thousand people in different age groups, and likely, but not guaranteed, rates of return. Were they hoping for a plague, so that people would die a lot faster and the shares would really go up?

"So let me get this straight," Jane said. "You make a commission if you get somebody to sell a policy to Life's End. And you get another commission if you get that same person to then buy a new policy from Life's End. And you get even another commission if you sell some shares to investors in the SOLI policies Life's End already owns?"

"You got it, baby. Every step of the way, there's a piece of the action for me."

Jane remembered her conversation with Gordon Wendell about Jeff and the SOLI products. Wendell didn't want to work with Jeff unless Jane vouched for Jeff's business skills, and unless it got Wendell a chance to pitch some insurance policies to her clients. And Wendell wanted to give her a percentage of his commissions on those policies, to make sure Jane would keep her clients from shopping elsewhere for insurance. No way was she going to take money like that. Not ever. Not going to happen.

"And let me guess," Jane said. "You want to do all this through the Wendell Agency and you want me to put in a good word for you with Gordon Wendell, right?"

"Personal contacts. I've told you that. And you're my personal connection to this opportunity, doll." He started jabbing his finger at one of the brochures. "Look, it says right here that Life's End has got actuarial certification. These people are sure to die and Life's End, they know when. It's statistics." The waitress brought Jeff a cup of coffee and set the pot on the table. "Not only that," Jeff paused to look at the waitress' backside as she walked away, "but Life's End, they give these poor dying people a chance to live before they kick off, with whatever time they have left, by buying their insurance policies. They get cold cash when they can still use it. Pay for medicines or treatments if they want. Fat lot of good insurance money does people when they're already dead and lying in some grave somewhere. Then we let lots of people in on the action, people like you and me Jane, just ordinary people, for no risk. You see, Life's End sells these derivatives, which are like shares or a stake, in the pool of these policies they bought. If people die faster, the investors make a fortune. Everybody wins."

"So why exactly do you need me?"

"I can be an agent for Life's End, but they'll only let me if I can hook up with an established agency, one that has, you know, a good reputation, like what you mentioned just there, Gordon Wendell's agency. You can get that for me, Jane. You can get my foot in the door with Wendell. He wants to do some kind of business with your law clients so you scratch his back and he'll scratch mine. And if you do that, then I get a piece of the action, like you said, for every policy I get signed over to Life's End. And I get even more if the suckers use the cash to buy more polices from Life's End. And then, if I line up investors to buy into these shares in the policies, then I get even more. I can't lose."

"I didn't think insurance agents could sell derivatives."

"Oh yeah, right. That's another thing. Besides Wendell, I might need somebody with a broker's license to help me out with the part about selling the shares to the investors. I'm trying to get a meeting with this broker, his name's John Hauser, who I think can help me with that. Do you know, is he banging that friend of yours, Sherri Weiner or Wanger or something?"

"Sherri Winger. And I'm not going to discuss Sherri's personal life with you."

"That's Janey-speak for yes, ain't it babe?"

"Look, Jeff, I did happen to run into Wendell not too long ago and he mentioned some of this and asked me if I'd vouch for you business-wise. I said I would vouch for your skill as a sales-man, even if you were a rat as a husband, which you were. So if that's all you want, I already did it and I think we're done here." How many times had she heard Jeff's wheeler-dealer, get-rich-quick song and dance? Not about SOLI, that was new, but the 'I can't lose' and the 'everybody wins,' she'd sure heard all that from Jeff before. Too many times. Probably even in this very coffee shop. Maybe in this exact booth even. And it always came to nothing. Or worse. As devastating as his affair and the divorce had been, maybe she should send Cassie a big thank you note for taking him off her hands.

"Calm down, hold the phone," Jeff said. "I'm getting to that. Wendell said you talked to him, but he's still not sure if he's ready to let me work through his agency. Sure, I could try to get Life's End to let me work as an agent on my own, but so far they're saying no dice, and anyways I get real credibility, real credibility, Jane, if I work through Wendell's outfit. It would be like I'm selling magazines or encyclopedias out of the trunk of my car if I don't have an agency. But with Wendell, he's got a reputation and the personal contacts. Clover, Jane, this would put me in tall clover." Jeff was shifting in his seat, fingers tap-ping on the table. "But like I said, Wendell's still not sure he wants to work with me on this. He says he's never heard of Life's End before now and he's never heard of selling people shares in pools of SOLI policies. That he thinks it sounds too complicated, but it's not, Janey, it's real simple. You saw the brochures. They've got these color charts with numbers and eve-rything. But here's the thing. Wendell still wants this shot with you and your clients. Every time I think he's not even going to talk to me anymore, not even going to think about this as a pos-sible even, then I mention you, and he's still listening. We al-ways were a good team, Janey. You know that. So I said to him, how about this, we all of us meet, just one time, at his office, and we go over all of this, and some other things he wants you to see. He gets a chance to pitch whatever to you, and I get one last chance to pitch the SOLI thing to him with you sitting there saying I'm ok. I know it'll work, baby, he won't say no to me with you sitting there and him thinking you'll finally play ball with him on selling his policies to your clients. You'll do that for me, won't you babe?"

"You need to understand something," Jane said. She was trying to catch Jeff's eye, but he kept glancing around the coffee shop. "Wendell has asked me to get involved in some things involving commission splitting that I've refused to do for a long time. If he still wants that, the answer is still no. I can vouch for you again, sure, but if that's not all he wants, then this is not going to work and we should just forget about any meeting, because it'll just be a big waste of time."

"I'm not saying you have to actually promise Wendell anything. I just think if we meet, in person, and he hears my pitch with you there in person, making the personal connection, I'll be in. He'll let me in his agency. That's it Janey. That's all you have to do. One meeting. Can I set it up?"

"I don't know. I'm not sure I want to get mixed up in this."

"Janey, baby, Cassie is screaming at me about money all the time. That baby we had, needs something every damn day. All you have to do is sit there and nod when Wendell asks if I'm ok. That's it, then you're out. One meeting. Do this for me, Jane."

"Ok, ok," Jane said. "Set it up. Call my assistant Helene and get it on my calendar. But only on one condition. That this is the last favor. You never ask me for anything ever again. After this meeting with Wendell, you're out of my life forever. Forever. You understand that, forever? We're strangers then, Jeff, get it? Like we never met. You don't call, you don't show up at my office, you forget my address. Forever."

"So I hear you're seeing some old guy."

"He's forty, not old. And I am absolutely not going to discuss my personal life with you. Period. Off limits."

"Hey, I'm not asking the particulars. You want to see some old goat, that's your business."

"Damn straight it is."

"Take care of yourself, Janey baby."

"I always do, Jeff."

By Friday, Jane had worked her way through the backlog of e-mails and cleared out her voicemail. She'd even managed to see a few clients in person. With no word from Roy, and Sherri busy with Hauser, the weekend ahead was looking a little bleak. It crossed her mind, just for a minute, kind of like a joke, that maybe she should find out if Ansel's band was playing somewhere. He probably had a gig somewhere. She could go be a groupie. She wouldn't exactly be stepping out on Roy, if she just went to hear a band. And if Roy kept disappearing out of her life with no word on when she might see him next, then she wasn't expected just to sit home, was she? But she could use some extra billable hours after her vacation. If she worked late Friday night instead of going out, and then came back to the office Saturday morning, it would help her productivity numbers. And she could still make it to the gym this weekend and the grocery store. And Sunday she could go to Church and visit her mom.

When Jane got home Friday evening, Roy's truck was parked in her driveway.

"Hey there," Roy said. He'd opened the front door and was standing in the foyer looking out at her when she got out of her car. "I brought Indian take out. Chicken tikka, chana masala and goat curry. I hope you like Indian food."

Goat curry? Jane couldn't believe she actually had a man standing in her doorway offering her goat meat in exchange for sex. Like the Bible story she remembered from her course at college on women in the Bible. Judah offered a goat to Tamar in Genesis if she would have sex with him. And Tamar got healthy twin baby boys out of the deal. Jane would sure be happy with that. But fat chance Jane could tuck into that carton of goat curry Roy was offering and end up pregnant. No way could she convince Mr. Hot and Cold, not yet anyway, to stop using condoms. On the other hand, Tamar had long odds against her, and she had to wait a long time and risk her life to be a mom, but things still worked out in the end. What was it St. Paul said about hope? That hope did not disappoint?

Late at night, lying in bed, Jane looked past Roy's sleeping body, out the French doors, past the unfinished deck, at the night sky and the overhanging trees.

"Jane?" Roy was awake. She thought he had dropped off to sleep pretty much right after the lovemaking.

"I thought you were asleep," Jane said.

"I wanted to ask you about something. Anita said she saw you in a coffee shop with your ex."

"So?"

"So why would you be seeing him?" Roy turned on his side toward Jane. "It's not like you had kids with him that you need to discuss. Is something going on?"

No, she didn't have kids with Jeff. That is correct. First her mother, then Roy, skewering their way right to her sorest, most vulnerable places, in seconds only. How come the people in her life were so good at that? Did she have too many sore spots, too many vulnerable places? Was that the problem? Was there a way to get rid of some of the sore places in her heart? Some kind of brokenness reduction program? Like a weight loss program, only the heart and soul were unburdened, not the hips and thighs? And it was not lost on Jane that Roy waited until after the sex to pick a fight with her. Clever bastard didn't want to risk getting into an argument beforehand and losing the mood.

"Nothing is going on," Jane said. "Jeff is down on his luck and wants me to help him get into Gordon Wendell's agency. I think I mentioned this to you at your building reception."

"I still can't believe you're going to help this guy. He totally burned you. You should hate him."

"Thanks for pointing that out. I hadn't realized it quite yet in every fiber of my being. There were one or two fibers left unaware, but you've taken care of that now. I am officially, totally and completely aware that Jeff burned me. Rest assured."

"So why did you see him?"

"I feel sorry for the guy, ok? It's no big deal. He wants me to go to one meeting with Wendell and him. And I just have to vouch for him. That's all."

"Wendell too?" Roy sat up in bed. "You're seeing that slime ball? I don't like this Jane."

Jane wanted to pull the covers over her head. "It's one meeting. It's business, that's all. I'm not 'seeing' Wendell, I mean for heaven's sake, get real, and I'm not seeing Jeff either."

"I just don't like this. But you'll do whatever you want, won't you? Doesn't matter what I like or don't like."

"I do care about your opinions," Jane said. "But you're being unreasonable here. And jealous for no reason."

"I'm not jealous."

"Are too."

"Goodnight Jane."

Next morning Jane woke to the sound of Roy's truck pulling out of her driveway. She checked the fridge to see if he at least left her the rest of the curry.

On Sunday, the Gospel lesson was about the kingdom of heaven being like finding a treasure in a field and then hiding it and selling all you have to buy the field with the hidden treasure.

"Where is your treasure?" The preacher asked in her sermon. "What would you give up everything for?" What would Jane go all out for? Was there anything that would make her go all out? She thought she had thrown caution to the wind and given her all to marry Jeff. But that turned out so badly. So where did her treasure lie now? She knew the answer was supposed to be Jesus. Her treasure was supposed to be her spiritual life in Jesus. But Jane couldn't help thinking that her treasure, the one thing she would gladly sell all that she had to obtain, was a chance to have a baby. And with Roy dropping in and out of the picture, was she ever going to get that chance?

Jane and her mother stayed after the service to socialize at the coffee hour.

"Jane, are you bringing Roy as your date to cousin Annie's wedding or are you just going by yourself?"

"Mom," Jane said, "I don't even have an invitation yet. I don't even know when it is."

"It's the last Saturday in September, I forget the exact date, but it's the last Saturday. At noon at St. Luke's Episcopal. Then a pre-reception and later a formal dinner."

"As soon as I get the invitation, I'll be sure to RSVP."

"Annie's mother, cousin Beth, has been calling me. She wants to know if Roy and you are coming. She needs to know if you're coming as a couple, otherwise you're a single and she needs to know how many of those she needs to seat. You can understand."

"Mom, look, next time I see Roy, I'll try to remember to ask him."

"Can I tell Beth we'll be able to let her know this week?"

"I think so Mom, but I'm not sure exactly when I'll see

Roy." Oops. Couldn't she have just said ok? Even if she didn't see Roy this week, she could still call him and get an answer about the wedding that way. But no, she had to open her mouth and tell her mother she didn't know when she'd see Roy next. Her mother was sure to give Jane an earful about that. And it would be a lecture that Jane didn't need, not even a little. Because Jane's mother's opinion about her relationship with Roy already exactly matched Jane's own opinion about the situation. Not that Jane would ever admit it, at least not out loud, and not even entirely to herself.

"You don't know when you'll be seeing him? I tell you it was a lot simpler when I was young. Your father and I had what, two dates? He took me to a dance and then to meet his parents. Then he got called up for the Korean War and we got married before he had to go to basic training. Then a lifetime together. Simple. Now you date for three years and you get married and what happens, he's tomcatting around and then he's left you for some tramp. And now you're dating again, and this one has a key to your house even, but you still don't know when you can expect to see him."

Jane could have kicked herself. Why on earth had she let her mother know she gave Roy a key to her house? Her mother was not happy about Roy having a key for so many reasons. Jane had lost count. Not just because of her mother's unshakable belief that 'you'll never get a marriage proposal from a man who can get what he wants without it' but also on the grounds that Roy might lend it to a member of his work crew. Who might copy it or lend it to who knows who. And then some night some random stranger might walk right in Jane's front door or her back door or her side door. Any door. Any night. Just walk right in. A valid concern if you didn't trust Roy's judgment. Which her mother definitely did not, unless and until he had the title of son-in-law, and even then with certain reservations, given Jane's track record with husbands so far.

"Mom, I don't have time for lunch today," Jane said. "I really need to get to the gym."

Two weeks later Jane drove out to a nursing home to see a new client. It was one of the better nursing homes. No smell of urine. Bright plastic flowers in vases on tables in the lobby where one of the residents was playing a piano. It was accompaniment, more or less, for an aide leading a group in continuous rounds of 'If You're Happy and You Know It.' Clap your hands. Stamp your feet. Some did. Some didn't.

Jane signed in at the reception desk and walked down the hall past people in wheelchairs staring into space or looking into a corner. So much was needed even for that. Someone to help them out of bed and to the toilet. A little breakfast, spoonful by spoonful. Then clean up. Teeth brushing. Getting dressed for a day in the hallway. Was this the worst part of her job or was it going to so many client funerals? Hard to tell.

"Mrs. Mondrian," Jane said, entering the room and approaching the bed of her new client, "I'm Jane Sidley. The attorney from Hantler Vintberg. Your daughter called me. Then she gave you my office phone number and you and I spoke on the phone. Do you remember speaking with me?"

"Yes, yes," Mrs. Mondrian said. "My memory is fine. It's my pancreas that's not, like I told you on the phone. Cancer."

"I'm so sorry."

"I tell you, I've never been sick a day in my life and then three weeks ago I had this stomach pain. I wasn't even going to go to the doctor but it got so much worse. And now here I am and they say it's not even worth trying surgery. So I have to get things in order. That's what I have to do."

"Yes, of course. Do you feel well enough to talk now?"

"We'd better talk now, no matter how I'm feeling. The doctor says I might not have much time left at all. Maybe just a few weeks. And before then I may be out of my head, or so they tell me. Can you get me a will that fast?"

"When we spoke on the phone it seemed like this could be a very simple will, so I can do that quickly," Jane said.

"That's all I need. Something simple. But couldn't you just write the will from what we talked about on the phone?"

"I wanted to go over everything with you in person, just to make sure what I write is what you want." And to get a look at you, and ask a few questions to see if you're still of sound mind. Jane scribbled a few words about her impressions of Mrs. Mondrian's lucidity on a yellow legal pad. She would have Helene scan her notes into the computer file for the Mondrian estate plan when she got back to the office.

"Everything goes to my children, just like I told you on the phone," Mrs. Mondrian said. "I don't know if you need more than their names, but my daughter thought you might need addresses, phone numbers and social security numbers, so she wrote it out on a piece of paper for me to give you. It's here in the drawer." Mrs. Mondrian reached from the bed toward a small bedside table with a single drawer. She tried to pull it open, but it was stuck. "I told them this is broken. They need to fix this drawer." She kept pulling on it, trying to yank it open. "I told them several times but no one listens. It's broken and they need to fix it."

"Here, let me try." Jane tugged at the drawer and pulled it open.

"But I guess it doesn't matter, does it?" Mrs. Mondrian sighed and looked down at her hands, on top of the bed covers. "Why would it matter? It doesn't matter, does it?"

"I've got it. The list is right here," Jane said.

Mrs. Mondrian leaned back on her pillow. She closed her eyes.

"Are you alright Mrs. Mondrian? Would it better if I came back tomorrow?"

"No, no. I'm just a little tired all of a sudden, but I can talk a little longer."

"Everything is to be divided in equal shares between your son and your daughter. Is that right?"

"Jewelry. My daughter." Mrs. Mondrian's eyes were still closed and her voice was getting very quiet. Jane knew she needed to hurry.

"Your daughter gets your jewelry? Then everything in equal shares?"

"Yes, yes."

"Do you know what an Executor is? That's the person to handle the estate paperwork."

"My daughter."

"Ok, you're daughter is to named Executrix, with your son as alternate? Is that ok?"

"Yes. I am feeling very tired now. Are we almost finished?"

"Yes, we're just about done. I can get this ready and be back here in a few days." Jane hated to keep talking when Mrs. Mondrian obviously needed to rest, but it really was important. "Besides the will, I recommend that you let me prepare some other documents for you so your daughter or your son can make decisions for you. I could prepare papers letting either of them make medical decisions and financial decisions, if the time comes when you can't make decisions for yourself. But you need to understand that these are very powerful documents. They can be a great help, but they can also be misused. You should only sign if you completely trust each of your son and your daughter."

"I trust them. Go ahead." Mrs. Mondrian waved her hand as if to wave Jane away.

Jane knew she should leave. "Just one more question, I promise. Katherine, "K A T H E R I N E," Hanover Mondrian, is that how you want your name on the will?" Clients rarely did more than flip through the documents Jane sent them, but they sure noticed if she didn't get their names right. Misspelling Mrs. Mondrian's name, or using Katherine H. Mondrian in the will when she wanted Katherine Hanover Mondrian would not only upset Mrs. Mondrian, but it would mean showing up at the nursing home, with Helene and one other person from her office in tow, to serve as a witness and a notary, only to find out that she had brought useless documents and needed to schedule another trip to the nursing home. And she would have to write off the extra time and eat the costs. She'd have Helene call the daughter to make sure Mrs. Mondrian's nod to her spelling of Katherine with a K was accurate and not morphine induced.

Jane walked back through the lobby, past the vague singing and intermittent waving of hands or nodding of heads of the residents who were still paying attention, more or less, to the endless choruses of 'If You're Happy and You Know It.' She was relieved to get through the front doors and out into the parking lot where the mid August sun was hot and bright, baking the asphalt of the spacious lot. And there was Roy, rummaging in the back of his truck.

"Roy?" Jane said. She had neither seen nor heard from him since he brought the goat curry weeks ago.

"Jane," Roy said. "Hey. What are you doing here?"

"Seeing a client. What about you?"

"They're adding a deck out back. So the nursing home patients can get a little sun. I'm working on it."

"You're working on a deck. No kidding."

"Right, sorry about that. I need to get yours finished, I know."

The floor and the built in seating were finished, but still no railing. Jane wished she hadn't said anything about it. Wasn't really fair to bother him about it when she wasn't paying him, after all.

"I didn't mean to razz you about it. I mean you're doing it for me as a favor. I can hardly complain about that."

"Still, I should get it finished for you."

"Listen, Roy, my cousin Annie is getting married on the last Saturday in September and I need a date. Could you go to the wedding with me?"

"The end of September?" Roy pulled the ball cap he was wearing a little lower on his forehead. He pulled a tape measure out of his pocket and shifted it from one hand to the other. "This is not exactly the time or the place, I mean I didn't plan it like this. I had no idea you would be here and we would run into each other, but I've been meaning to talk to you."

This did not sound good. Not only did Jane think she was headed for the singles table at cousin Annie's wedding, but Mr. Hot and Cold seemed to be turning into Mr. Out of Her Life Completely.

Roy looked at the ground. "I've been thinking a lot lately about how I've only been out of my parent's house for a short time. In a way, I'm just starting out. Looking around in life a little. I've always been really busy with work and building up my business. And now I'm on my own for the first time."

Anita said he got his apartment a year and a half ago. And the man was forty years old. Jane really did not like where this was heading.

"I'm thinking we shouldn't see each other, at least not for a while. I mean we can still be friends."

Did he really say that? The 'let's be friends' line? Did anyone really say that anymore? And if he was thinking that they could be 'friends with benefits' he could forget that. And what did he mean, they shouldn't see each other at least for a while? They already only saw each other once in a while as it is.

"I'm sorry things didn't work out for us," Roy said. "I liked being with you. You're a terrific person. I just need to be by myself. I can't be in a relationship at this point in my life, that's all."

"I need my key back."

"Oh sure, here." He took it off his key ring and handed it back. At least her mother would be happy about that. But she would not be happy about Jane's prospects in the man department. No, not happy about that at all.

"I'll send some of my crew to finish up the railing on the deck. They won't need to get into the house. They can just stop by and have it done in an afternoon. You won't even have to see them."

"Never mind that," Jane said. "I'll hire someone. Don't send your crew. I don't want them or you at my house."

"I'm sorry Jane."

"Me too, Roy. Bye."

She was not going to cry. For heaven's sake, she had just been with a woman who was dying. She was not going to cry about losing some guy who couldn't make up his mind what he wanted. Great dates and even a week at the beach one minute, and booty calls with goat curry the next. She didn't need somebody she couldn't count on, that's for sure. She should be glad her life was now officially open for someone who would be crazy about her. Who would see her as a treasure worth giving everything for. Not as someone to toss aside. Not as someone to see when it was convenient.

In fact, she made it back to the office without shedding a tear. And then she went straight to a bathroom stall in the ladies room down the hall from her office and sobbed. How many times had she sat in that very same stall, sobbing her heart out, during her divorce? She couldn't believe she was back in there, crying again. Over another idiot.

When she calmed down a little, she had to admit, to be honest, if she was really honest with herself, that she wasn't exactly all that upset about losing Roy. Ok, she liked him some. There were things she liked about him anyway. She liked that he was able to think and talk about people other than himself. Not everyone could. And he could talk about ideas that didn't just concern his own desires or ambitions, like that conversation they had about Judas. And Roy liked that play, the one that Arthur was in, which was interesting to Jane too. And he could do things. Like carpentry. Jane respected that. The sex was good. Ok, it was better with Jeff, but Jeff was, well, something else. Like an alternate reality. Sex with Jeff was a delusion, like a drug. It was a lie. It wasn't real life. And it didn't last. But Roy was as elusive as Jeff, in his own way, wasn't he? Roy was deliberate and straightforward about things. But his honesty, even his dullness, was all the more confusing because it was followed up with his disappearing act. Hardly worth it to settle for someone with a more steady, deliberate personality, more boring than Jeff, if he wasn't really steady after all.

If Roy could commit, Jane thought it could have worked. For the long haul. Not like being married to, and then divorced from, the always agitated, never satisfied Jeff. But over the long haul. It could really have worked with Roy. But if not, then she was glad Roy was gone, and that she hadn't settled.

So why was she crying? She knew why. And she was embarrassed to admit it to herself. It seemed so crass and humiliating to admit it on the heels of being dumped by Roy. She was crying because she wanted a baby and she couldn't have one without sperm. And Roy, like Jeff, had sperm, and had walked away without making a baby with her. That was humiliating to admit, and seemed pretty cold and calculating on her part, but that was why she was crying. If she was being honest with herself about it. So now what? Maybe she should look into adoption agencies.

"Jane? Are you in there?" It was Helene.

"Yes, I'm in here."

"I'm sorry to bother you, but Mrs. Mondrian's daughter is on the phone. Things are not going well with her mother and she wants to know if we can get out there with the documents tomorrow morning so her mother can sign. You've got time at ten on your calendar tomorrow. Do you think we can get the documents ready that quickly? I can stay late if you need me to."

Ahh, work. Jane could anesthetize herself and forget Roy, at least for now, by working on Mrs. Mondrian's documents. A rush project was just what she needed to forget her troubles.

"Ask Mrs. Mondrian's daughter if her mother's name is Katherine with a K."

CHAPTER NINE

*I*nstead of the buffet Jane was expecting at her cousin Annie's wedding in late September, it was a sit down dinner with a mixed green salad and chicken kiev. The wedding cake was edible and not overly frosted but Jane left the frosting on the plate and had just a few bites of cake. She got to see a significant percentage of her cousins. Granted, she only had a few, but at least half of them were there. The faces from the photos that came every year with the Christmas letters.

Even better, the bride and groom had a lot of friends in their thirties. Jane danced with some of them. With enough champagne on board, she even joined the conga line. Best of all, the happy couple had hired Ansel's band. He spotted Jane right away and waved. She'd only seen him in T-shirts and beach shorts or jeans, even for his gig at Arthur and Mindy Ogden's party, but for the wedding the entire band was wearing tuxes with leather vests and bowties. A bit of a gimmick, but he looked sharp. When it was late enough that the bride and groom were gone and he didn't think anyone would notice or be sober enough to care, he got band to play a few songs they could manage without a drummer, so he could slip off the stage and dance with Jane.

Ansel was a good dancer. With his tall, lanky frame and Jane's thin, graceful figure, they made a handsome pair on the dance floor. "You are a beauty, Lady Jane. And you look especially pretty here tonight. Roy is a fool."

"Thanks Ansel," Jane said. "It just didn't work out for Roy and me. That's all."

"Why don't you come hear East End sometime at the Thin Dime?"

"Come hear your band? I guess I could. I mean I'd like to. You're sounding really good tonight."

"But that's covers. I want you to hear our own music. That's what matters. We've got a regular gig at the Dime on Friday and Saturday nights and we have to do the standard covers, oldies and eighties and stale indie and alternative, but the manager knocks off around midnight and it's the bartenders that close at two. They're cool with letting us do our own stuff once the manager leaves. Our real fans know to come late. And our music's good. If you came by some night late, you'd really hear something. And we'd be even better if you were there as inspiration."

Might be fun. Her social calendar was not exactly overbooked after all.

A few days later, Jane was sitting at a large conference table at a meeting of the Board of Trustees of a local arts council. She volunteered as a Board member. The arts council raised money and awareness for galleries, theater groups, dance, chamber music and so on. Back in the summer, the June quarterly meeting had been postponed to August because so many Board members had been on vacation in June and July. This meant the June meeting had been held just a few weeks before the scheduled date of the September meeting. So the Executive Director moved the September meeting to the beginning of October. Several Board members, including Lisa Wentworth, a longtime Board member and acting Secretary, were not happy about the schedule change. Jane was often a stickler for procedure, but today she was not one of the unhappy Board members. In fact, she was not even listening.

"I think we need to consider amending the bylaws to make Board attendance mandatory," Lisa said. "With enforcement provisions. Any member who misses more than two consecutive meetings, other than for reasons of serious illness or family emergency, should be automatically removed from the Board."

Lisa was the lone woman to make partner at the city's largest accounting firm. Relentless to the point of near brutality in questioning the executive director about any apparent inconsistency in the art council's financial statements, and a "take no prisoners" fundraiser, she usually left anything involving the charter or bylaws to whichever lawyer happened to be serving on the Board. Just now, that was Jane. Lisa shot glances at Jane, but when Jane didn't even look up, Lisa assumed her silence meant agreement, a strategy that had served Lisa well as she navigated the often murky waters of corporate accounting.

Jane was flipping through the Arts Council Calendar of Events in her Board packet. When she got to the cultural events listed for October, she saw that Arthur was the lead in another play. In a break up, friends went back to the side they'd been on before the couple got together. But Arthur and Mindy were Sherri's friends too. And even though Jane hadn't been able to get hold of Sherri in a while, Sherri was still her friend. So could she consider Arthur and Mindy still her friends too? She knew they'd sided with her in the disagreement, what did Arthur call it, he had some phrase he used, the tiff, the argument, no, wait, the lover's quarrel, that's what Arthur had called it, she'd had with Roy at the beach in July. But did they feel the same now that she was broken up with Roy? Probably they were still her friends, even if they were Roy's friends too.

Even if they weren't, it was a public play. She could go to a public event. She didn't have to have a friend in the cast, although that made plays more interesting if it happened. Which it did quite a lot in a city this size. Maybe her mom would like to go. It opened with Friday and Saturday performances next weekend and then continued for one more weekend after that.

"And we should amend to provide that we can hold meetings and vote without a quorum. That would prevent unnecessary postponement of meetings, as is the case today," Lisa said. That got Jane's attention. Power mad Boards members and busy executive directors were always trying to change the rules so they could vote without bothering to get enough people in the room or at least on the telephone, if the bylaws allowed telephone meetings, for a quorum. How many times had Jane recited her canned speech about no voting without a quorum? The State Code doesn't allow it. You can't have bylaws that don't comply with the State Code. No exceptions. None. She should get laminated cards printed with the relevant section of the Code and just pass them out at every meeting.

"So moved," one of the other Board members said.

Jane held up one hand. "No, no. Hold on. Don't second that. You have to have a quorum to take a vote."

"I know we do now, and that's why we need this vote today when we have one, so we won't need one next time," Lisa said.

"No, that's not how it works. It's not just our bylaws, it's the State Code. The State Code doesn't allow voting at a meeting without a quorum. You can't amend the bylaws to allow something the State Code won't allow."

"But we have telephone meetings," the Board member seated next to Jane spoke up.

"Yes, the State Code permits bylaws that allow participation in a meeting by telephone, and our current bylaws, with the amendments we passed last year, do allow that," Jane said. "But we still have to make sure we have a quorum before we take a vote, in person or by phone."

"What if we voted and then asked people who weren't there to just sign something later?" Lisa said.

"It would have to be a unanimous written consent," Jane said. "The vote at the meeting without the quorum would be invalid, but we can act by unanimous written consent anytime, even without a meeting."

"Unanimous?" The Board member next to Jane spoke up again. "I thought a quorum was a majority."

Jane looked at her watch. The agenda for the meeting had seven action items and this discussion wasn't even one of them.

Back at her desk several hours later, Jane checked the year-to-date statistics on her computer for billable hours and collections. Since the break up with Roy, she was over budget in every category. The firm's accounting people, and with any luck the Compensation Committee, although you never knew about them, should be pleased. Helene leaned in the doorway.

"Jeff Rogers called. He said you said it was ok to put him on your calendar for a meeting with Gordon Wendell. He seemed very sure about it so I put them on your calendar for next Friday. You don't have anything left open on your calendar for this week, but I could try to squeeze them in sometime earlier next week if you want. It didn't sound urgent, and maybe you might want a little time to think about canceling?" Helene had been there to see Jane get the divorce papers when the process server came to the firm. She had stood firm, giving not a crumb to the gossips who gathered around her cubicle, hungry for details about Cassie's pregnancy. Jane appreciated Helene's fierce, protective loyalty, but then again she would have gotten Helene fired or at least transferred to the word processing pool for any-thing less.

"Good point," Jane said. "But I don't expect to cancel, al-though heaven knows I probably should. I don't mind making them wait a week or so, the longer the better. Are they coming here or am I meeting them at Wendell's agency?"

"Their place. The Wendell Agency in the Shuley Building. Jeff said to plan on at least two hours. They want to feed you lunch and he said they have some sort of computer presentation to show you."

Helene's phone was ringing back at her desk. She leaned over, pushed several buttons, and took the call at Jane's desk. "Send them up to conference room R on nine." She put down the phone and turned to Jane. "Nora Bowden and Angela Monteri are here for your three o'clock. In conference room R."

Jane was always careful about confidentiality, but she thought she might need to take extra precautions in Nora Bowd-en's case. Nora was Oliver Bowden's older sister. And, Jane happened to know, she was in line to be the next family matri-arch. She knew this because she'd helped Nora and Oliver's mother, Adelaide, to set up a trust fund for each of Nora and Oli-ver, and the trusts were set up so that after Adelaide's death, the shares of stock in Nora's trust fund, together with some shares Nora would control through a limited liability company, would give Nora, not Oliver, controlling interest in Integrated Products, even though Oliver was currently the CEO.

Jane also knew exactly which family scandal involving Oli-ver had been the last straw for Adelaide and the reason why Oli-ver would eventually lose control of Integrated to his sister. It was one of the messier Bowden scandals. About six years ago, when Jane had been with the firm for only about a year, and about two years before Jack Dempsey, Jane's mentor had retired and then passed away, Jack and Jane had gone to an emergency meeting with Max and Adelaide Bowden. Adelaide was upset and wanted to change their estate plan.

There had been a sexual harassment complaint pending against Oliver. Oliver was accused of arranging the transfer of a young woman who worked in one of Integrated's facilities in another state, somewhere up north maybe, Jane couldn't remember exactly where, from the office up north to the main offices here, because she attracted his notice at some regional meeting up there and Oliver purportedly, allegedly and unfortunately wanted her close by so he could convince her to have an affair with him. Oliver continued, according to the complaint anyway, to bother the young woman, despite her clear refusal of his advances, for months after she started her work at Integrated's main offices.

Not only was Oliver accused of making a lot of inappropriate advances, but when the young woman was eventually transferred to an Integrated facility two hours from here, basically in the middle of nowhere, it was alleged to be retaliation for her refusal to have the affair, and because she'd filed a complaint, first with Integrated's HR department, then in court.

Adelaide would have stood by Oliver even though the young woman had witnesses and late night phone records of calls from Oliver's office, cell and even home phones, but then the poor girl's car went off the road and into a steep ravine while she was commuting from the remote facility, killing her instantly. Adelaide didn't think Oliver had done anything sinister like sabotaging the car, and she didn't even hold him responsible for the young woman having a wreck on her long commute, as people got transferred to that facility every day and managed to get to and from work without a problem, but just after the accident Oliver did something Adelaide was not willing to forgive or forget.

With the young woman's death, given that much of the sexual harassment complaint was based on her word against Oliver's, the court case was dropped. Oliver rented a private room at his country club and threw a drunken bash to celebrate, and he had quite a party, getting absolutely smashed, by all reports, along with some of the other Integrated executives and the attorneys from Hantler Vintberg who had defended him in the harassment complaint. At some point furniture was tossed out a window as part of a drinking game, and there was an incident with the police when a young woman on the waitstaff called 911 on her cell phone from where she was hiding in the coat closet. Adelaide didn't have all the details on why the young woman called the police, but she was bitterly angry and deeply disappointed that Oliver would celebrate so publicly and drunkenly when the

young woman he was allegedly harassing had died so tragically
in a car wreck. Adelaide thought it showed that Oliver lacked
something fundamental, in terms of respect for people. And she
thought it showed really poor judgment in terms of exposing
Integrated to bad publicity, for the son of Integrated's founder,
and the heir apparent, to engage in such a crass display of gloat-
ing over a young woman's death. Oliver said he was celebrating
the harassment complaint going away, not the young woman's
death, but Adelaide thought even having to say something like
that was just more evidence of bad judgment.

Back at that meeting six years ago, Adelaide wanted to
change the wills and trust documents she and Max had signed
several years previously. She wanted to take away eventual control of Integrated from Oliver and give it to their daughter Nora.
Max was upset at Oliver's behavior, but thought a good talking
to was in order for Oliver, that's all. He thought Adelaide was
overreacting to a youthful misjudgment on Oliver's part. Oliver
would mature over time. Max could bring him along and someday when Oliver took over control of Integrated he would be a
mature and seasoned leader. Max was sure of it.

Jack Dempsey, Jane's mentor at the firm at the time, agreed
with Max. Boys will be boys, that was Jack's attitude, and he
thought Oliver was the Bowdens' best choice for controlling
Integrated after Max and Adelaide someday passed away. Jack
had listened patiently to Adelaide's concerns at the meeting, but
it was clear that neither Jack nor Max had any inclination to
make a change in the Bowden estate plan.

Jack retired two years later and Jane began working more
closely with Adelaide. When Max died about a year ago, and
Oliver became CEO, Adelaide told Jane she still had concerns
about Oliver's judgment. She was convinced that she needed to
give Nora control of Integrated so that when Adelaide was gone,
Nora's majority ownership would balance Oliver's power as
CEO. Jane, unlike her mentor, didn't talk Adelaide out of it. She
helped Adelaide set up and fund the trusts and limited liability
companies that would, on Adelaide's death, put control of Integrated in Nora's hands, not Oliver's. The explanation of why
Adelaide made the change in her estate plan was part of the
scolding Adelaide recorded on the DVD of her will signing.

Given what Jane knew about Adelaide's estate plan, when Nora first called and told Jane she wanted to bring her partner, Angela Monteri, in to see Jane to discuss wills and some other planning, Jane immediately thought the highest level of security would be needed for the file. Jane didn't know whether or not Nora had told her mother that Angela was her partner and if not, whether or not her mother would approve if she found out. Jane didn't want to be the source of any leaks that might cause further changes in Adelaide Bowden's mind or her estate plan. Especially not if it cost Nora her chance at someday controlling the family empire.

But then Adelaide called to say she knew Nora and Angela were coming in to see Jane. Jane was relieved to find that the Bowden clan was well aware that Nora was a lesbian and welcomed Angela as part of the family. In fact, it turned out that Angela, not Nora, had serious concerns about confidentiality. Angela was a bank trust officer. Jane had just assumed that in this day and age Angela's sexual orientation wouldn't matter to anyone, but bank trust clients tend to be elderly and some of them apparently still had misconceptions and prejudices. So Angela wasn't out at her bank. She needed regular assurances from Jane that coming to see her, especially when Jane had clients who used the bank's trust services, wouldn't lead to knowledge of Angela's orientation leaking out. Jane knew she could trust Helene, and she set up the computer file for Nora and Angela with the tightest levels of security. Only Helene and Jane, and the I.T. people, who could see everything, no way around that, would have access. Jane felt sad that Angela had to be so careful. That things had to be so difficult for Angela, even today. What a shame that Angela couldn't be up front with her colleagues and clients without fear of discrimination. But Jane would do what she could to help Nora and Angela get their affairs in order, taking all the extra steps and jumping through all the extra hoops the law required in their case, given that Nora and Angela couldn't legally marry each other. And Jane would do everything she could to protect their confidentiality along the way.

Jane walked into Conference Room R and shut the door. "Hi Nora, Hi Angela. Good to see you both."

"Jane," Angela said, "I told Jonathan Crasner at the bank that I was coming here to talk to you about our new mutual fund products. If you see him and he mentions that, you might want to play along. They're actually pretty good products. I'll send you a link on them. There, we did talk about them. We won't be lying to Crasner."

"Don't worry," Jane said. "Anything we discuss here is absolutely confidential."

Nora and Angela were considering artificial insemination or adoption. The adoption might be international. They were looking at Honduras, Romania and China. If they went with insemination it might be through a sperm bank, but they were also thinking about working through a doctor's office with sperm from a selected donor. Someone they knew. They wanted help from Jane with wills, custody agreements and any waivers of parental rights that might be needed.

"I can help you with the wills," Jane said, "but I'm going to need to bring in another attorney on the custody and parental rights issues. We have some top flight family lawyers. One of them could help us here."

"Are they knowledgeable on LGBT issues?" Angela said. "And can they keep their mouths shut outside these rooms about my identity?"

"I have one in mind," Jane said. "Anthony Listerman. He's represented a number of gay and lesbian clients in custody matters. I trust him."

"Do you have a woman attorney we could use?" Nora was twirling a pen on a legal pad. "We're going to be discussing some very personal issues here. Some pretty personal biological issues. I don't know if I'm comfortable discussing insemination or surrogacy with a man."

Jane knew she lost out sometimes on business because a client wanted a male attorney. And probably her progress in the firm was slowed to some degree by bias against female partners, at least at the top levels of the firm. Ted's talk of junior equity partnership had somehow gotten lost in the shuffle once the danger was past with Adelaide over the summer. The appointment Ted's secretary sent a week ago to schedule Jane's annual review said 'Review and Consideration of Senior Non-Equity Status' with no mention at all of the possibility of junior equity. So she supposed she should be glad when the prejudice ran the other way. When men attorneys lost out on business to women attorneys, just because the men were men. But she wasn't glad. It offended her sense of fair play. An attorney should stand or fall on merit, not gender. That went both ways. For men and for women. Jeff would say that was nonsense. If she could hike her skirt and land a big client, he would say hike it, babe. Jane still hoped for the day when it would make no difference. When an attorney would be an attorney. Not a male attorney or a female one.

"Anthony is our best in terms of custody issues and surrogacy," Jane said. "He's who I'd pick for something like this, if I needed it myself." Would she? She was thinking about at least looking into adoption. She hadn't thought of artificial insemination or surrogacy. Maybe she should.

"I don't know," Angela said. "There's a lot at stake here."

"How about this?" Jane said. "I set up a meeting and you just meet Anthony. One time. Give him one chance. If it's not a good fit, it's not a good fit. I'll find you somebody else. After all, it's not his fault he's a man."

"Ok, I guess that's fair," Nora said. "If Angela agrees, that's ok with me. One chance, though, and either one of us has veto power."

"Ok," Angela said. "I suppose one chance is fair. Jane, I hope you're right about this."

Nora and Angela did like Anthony when they met the following Thursday. Angela was worried about making another excuse at her bank for seeing Jane during business hours, so the meeting was scheduled after hours. Anthony recommended that they have agreements drawn up to cover the custody issues if Nora became pregnant through insemination, or if either or both of them were approved for adoption in China, Honduras or Romania. Anthony explained that any of the options they were considering would take time, especially the international adoption route, which might take years. They would need to have patience, as there was a lot, and Anthony emphasized this, a lot of paperwork and red tape involved. They had a lot of ground to cover in the meeting, and when Jane and Anthony were finally showing Nora and Angela to the elevators, Jane looked at her watch and was surprised to see that it was almost 10 p.m. Jane had been so interested to hear about the adoption agencies and other possibilities for becoming a parent, she didn't notice that the meeting was running so late.

She should get home and get some rest because the meeting with Jeff at Wendell's insurance agency was scheduled for the following day. Jane drove home thinking she would have a quick bubble bath, then straight to bed. She wanted to be well rested and thinking clearly for the meeting the next day.

A car she didn't recognize was parked in her driveway. Jane pulled up but left her lights on, with the doors locked and the engine still running. She wanted to see who was there before opening her car door. Then Jeff appeared, rapping on the driver's side window. She rolled down her window part way.

"Janey baby," he said. "I thought maybe you weren't gonna come home at all. Maybe you were sleeping somewhere else, even though I heard you weren't seeing anybody. That the old goat was out of the picture."

Jane shut off the engine and got out of the car.

"He was only forty. Why are you here? Is the meeting off for tomorrow? And what happened to your car? I thought you were driving an Elixia."

"The meeting is still on, babe. It's on alright. It's right on. The wheels are Cassie's. I didn't want to pick up the option on the Elixia after end of the lease term." After the end of the alimony payments, no doubt. "You are looking good, babe, but what's with the late hours?"

"Work, remember that? I have a job. Sometimes it involves working late."

"That's what I told Cassie, that I had a late business meeting ahead of the big meeting tomorrow, but this is late for work meetings, babe. Seriously."

"No, it's not a lie. This is a business meeting. Strictly business. I need to tell you what to say to Wendell tomorrow."

"It's late," Jane said. "All I'm going to say tomorrow is that I vouch for you, whatever that means. And if Wendell wants me to take money on the side to send business his way, then the answer is still no. That's all."

"Janey, baby, it would really help me out if you would say you think you have some clients who are maybe dying and need money and want to sell their insurance policies. Or who aren't dying, but who might want to buy shares in the policies of other people who are dying. So Wendell will think this is a hot property. That it's got real potential as, you know, an emerging market. Won't kill you to say that kind of thing and it would really help me out."

"I'm tired and I don't have any dying clients who want to sell their insurance policies. If they can afford to hire me, they're not down to their last dime. They don't need this. My clients buy Treasuries and blue chips. They're even nervous about the blue chips right now. I can grit my teeth and say something nice about you, even if it kills me to do it. But if you're hoping I'll have anything nice to say about the SOLI thing, forget it. The best you can hope for, is that I don't say anything about it. Because if I do say anything about this Life's End scheme, you're not going to like it."

"Ok, ok, don't get excited. I know you won't let me down tomorrow, babe. I know you won't." Jeff jammed his hands in his pockets and shifted on the balls of his feet. "I got here before dark. Looks like you got some work going on, up on the roof of the back room. You finishing the deck?"

"Sort of. The work was going on, but it's kind of stopped just now. I need to hire a new contractor. It's all finished except the railing. There's a wood floor and some built in seating."

"Old goat couldn't get the job done?"

"Are we finished here? It really is late. I'm sure Cassie is wondering where you are."

"Hey, can I see what you've done on that roof? This was supposed to be our place."

"It was. But you wrecked all that, as I recall. Threw it away with both hands."

"But good hands, Janey baby. The best. C'mon, I'll keep them to myself, I promise. Let me come in the house and see what you've done with the deck."

"It's dark. You won't be able to see it. Maybe some other time."

"There's light from the inside. It'll be enough through those french doors if you pull back the drapes. C'mon, two minutes."

Jane knew there was a zero possibility that Jeff would just look at the deck and then leave if she let him in the house. Sure, he would actually look at the deck, and he probably was curious about it. But once he was in the house, no way would he leave without making a pass. And it wasn't anything personal, which was a big part of what had been so disappointing, so devastating even, in her marriage. If he made a pass, which he would, he was just being himself, an opportunist. And Jane noticed that he asked to see the deck when he couldn't get Jane to agree to everything he wanted her to say at the meeting tomorrow. At some level, he was thinking that a smooch or a hand under her shirt or up her skirt would be better, more powerful persuasion. Or maybe he just saw a chance at sex and couldn't pass it up without giving it his best shot. What a colossal jerk I was married to, she thought. What a jerk.

Then the words Honduras, Romania and China appeared in her mind. The three countries with the international adoption agencies Nora and Angela were considering. At the meeting with Anthony, Jane got some idea of the massive paperwork each of those agencies would require. And here was a man, with sperm, who was angling for a chance to make a pass at her. Granted it was her jerk of an ex-husband, but sex with him had to be better than filling out all that paperwork. With Roy out of the picture, this could be a chance for a baby that might not come her way again for who knows how long. Sure, she knew sex with Jeff was a drug, a cheat, an illusion, but what a drug it was. Potent. And this time, not like all the other times, she might get what she wanted out of it. Pregnant.

"Ok two minutes," Jane said. "Why do I listen to you?"

Jeff grinned and they were inside, headed up through the bedroom to the deck.

"Be careful," Jane said, "there's no railing yet."

"For an old guy, that goat of yours did some nice work. I like the benches he put in. Not bad, Janey. Not bad at all."

"Ok," Jane said. "You've seen it. Now you need to go. I need to get some sleep before tomorrow."

Jeff moved close to Jane.

"You don't need sleep, babe. I can tell. Sleep is the last thing you need." He kissed her. His hands were everywhere all at once. Jane always wondered how he did that. But it felt good. She kissed him back.

"Janey baby," Jeff whispered in her ear, "you're still on the Pill, right?"

"You know me."

But he didn't. And she wasn't.

CHAPTER TEN

*T*he next morning Jane woke up alone, with a feeling of dread. She remembered there was something she was just sick with anxiety about when she went to sleep last night, but what was it? Then she smelled Jeff's lingering scent in the sheets. Oh no. It had to be a bad dream, right? She couldn't have slept with Jeff last night. But yes, she had. She'd wanted to and she'd done it. And enjoyed it. Jane wished she could at least have been drunk so she could blame it on that, but no, she'd been absolutely sober. No excuse but her own poor judgment. A familiar theme in her life where Jeff was concerned. And now she had to go sit at a meeting and watch him smirk. Oh no. She would rather have an appointment for a tooth extraction, or a colonoscopy, or an IRS audit, anything but having to face Jeff at a meeting. He would be so pleased with himself. The high and mighty Jane brought low once again. What could be more humiliating? The guy breaks her heart, dumps her, gets alimony from her for heaven's sake, and she lets him get his rocks off one last time. In just about every position imaginable. Oh no. I'd better get a baby out of this, Jane thought. The paperwork for the international adoption agencies was looking better and better.

It was a beautiful October day. Still warm, but with a clear light and breezes that signaled the change of seasons. The summer humidity was gone. Jane thought she should be enjoying the walk over to Wendell's agency on such a spectacular fall day. She should appreciate even a few minutes outside, away from her desk and her phone. But she just felt sick. What had she been thinking? Letting that idiot into her bed again. What were the odds of getting a baby out of it anyway? Tamar, in the Bible, got twins from having sex just once with Judah. But with Jane's luck she was probably more like Rachel or Hannah in the Bible, and it would take years of trying before a baby came along, if one ever did at all. What could she possibly have been thinking? To win the lottery you have to buy a ticket. And Jeff was a lot like a lottery ticket. A very long shot, likely to come to nothing, even at his very best.

She pulled open the glass doors to the Shuley Building and rode the elevators up to the offices of the Wendell Agency on the third floor. Wendell and Jeff were waiting for her at the back of the reception area. "Jane, so glad you could come to this meeting," Wendell said. Did it seem like he knew about her and Jeff? Did it seem like he was appraising her like a piece of meat? Had Jeff told him? No way, she was just being paranoid.

"Janey," Jeff said, "long time no see."

"Hello, Jeff."

"We've got our presentation set up in the main conference room." Wendell led the way into a large room with a laminate topped conference table and high backed vinyl chairs on wheels. "Jeff has some computer slides to show you about sales of shares in SOLI policies by a company called Life's End. Then I have a few products to show you as well. I'm hoping we can put aside our past disagreements about how to structure our business dealings, if you hear what I'm saying, Jane."

It was downhill from there. Wendell wanted Jane to say that if he took Jeff in as an agent for the Wendell Agency, the Life's End product line Jeff would be selling would be a sure bet with Jane's clients. That would be an outright lie, so she wouldn't say it. Jane would on occasion stretch the truth, exaggerate, or sugar coat a painful fact or two, but this would be an outright lie, and even to help Jeff, she just wouldn't do it. The best she could manage was to say that she'd mention it to a few of her clients if an appropriate opportunity arose, but even that was mostly a lie. Then she could have salvaged the situation by hinting that she was willing to relent on taking a share of commissions from Wendell in exchange for steering her clients toward the Regents Mark and Livistar policies he was pushing. Again, the best Jane could muster was to say that when she recommended to her clients that they look at a variety of insurance products, she wouldn't exclude Wendell's. But she wouldn't agree to take any money from him on the side. Period.

Jeff followed her out the door from Wendell's agency, into the elevators and then out onto the sidewalk. "You bitch. You goddamn bitch. You screwed me. Last night and today. I thought we had an understanding, last night when you were on your knees anyway. But I should have known. You never change. You never could give me a break, could you? Would it just kill you to give me a break?"

"I'm sorry Jeff, I did the best I could for you in there."

"The best you could? You totally sank me in there. Totally threw me under the bus. And you owe me. I never did get a fair shake in our divorce. You got the house and now you're living like a queen and you can't even throw me a crumb. And I can't catch a break in this town and it's your fault I'm living in this one horse shithole in the first place. But this time you're going to pay. Cassie's brother-in-law is a lawyer and Cassie wants me to reopen our divorce settlement. Bet you didn't think of that. I've been holding off. I've been saying no, out of consideration, Jane, consideration. But not after today. No more Mr. Nice Guy."

No more Mr. Nice Guy? Did he really just say that? First Roy uses the 'let's be friends' line and now she's getting 'no more Mr. Nice Guy' from Jeff. Who writes their material?

Jeff got in the line for an idling bus at a bus stop.

"You're taking the bus?"

"Cassie needed the car today for work. We're working class people. Not royalty like you, you royal freakin' bitch."

"Do you need bus fare?"

"Save it. You'll need it when you hear from Cassie's brother -in-law." And he was on the bus. Jane watched the people pushing onto the bus with him, jockeying for seats. A picture from junior high health class of sperm, jockeying for position outside an egg, flashed through her mind. Let Jeff go ahead and hire Cassie's brother-in-law. Someone to accept service if someday Jane needed to go after Jeff for child support. It could happen.

The next night, Jane took her mother to see the Saturday performance of the new play Arthur was in. The action was set a small town in Indiana. A mail order bride had come to America from the Philippines in the 80's. She and her taciturn, depressive husband raise a daughter who, as the play opens, is about to leave for college in Chicago. The daughter has a fair dose of first -generation Catholic schoolgirl guilt about leaving her parents to embrace the freedom and temptations of life on a college campus in a big city. The mother is facing isolation and loneliness in a small town with a culture in which she never felt accepted. And then she finds she needs help from the townspeople, with their insincere smiles and puzzling customs, when she realizes she may be married to a man who murdered previous young brides, but who has left her alive, at least for now. Arthur had the part of the husband and father. He portrayed the man's reclusive depression and underlying sinister malice with an almost startling realism. Jane was amazed to see the affable, always friendly Arthur transformed into a secretive, morose and cruel man who may be a serial killer of gullible and vulnerable young women. Arthur could act, that was for sure.

At intermission, Jane's mother headed for the ladies room.

"I'll wait for you in the lobby, Mom."

Jane noticed a woman waving at her. It was Mindy. She was waving for Jane to come over to where Mindy was standing. With Roy and Ansel. Jane was going to just look away, but Mindy had already made eye contact and was waving pretty insistently. Jane walked over to them.

Ansel looked at Roy, winked at Jane and put his arms around her. He gave Jane a long, deep kiss and she felt his hand moving down her back to her behind.

"Ok, ok, Ansel, I get it, you're glad to see me." Jane couldn't help smiling, but still separated herself from Ansel.

"Jane," Ansel said. "Or should I say our beautiful Lady Jane. So good to set eyes and hands on you."

"You're one of a kind, Ansel," Jane said, still smiling at him in spite of herself.

"Roy," Ansel said, "are you not greeting our Lady Jane?"

"Not by putting my tongue down her throat and my hand on her ass, if that's what you mean." Roy was trying to make a joke, but Jane could hear the emotion in his voice. Had he missed her? Did she care? Roy turned to Jane.

"Hello Jane."

"Hello Roy," Jane said. "Hi Mindy." A bell sounded as a warning that intermission was almost over. "Nice to see all of you. I think Arthur is just great tonight. Tell him I said to break a leg. But please excuse me, I'm here with my mom and I need to see if she's ready to go back in."

Monday at work Jane's phone rang and the caller id showed Sherri's work number.

"Sherri," Jane said, "you're alive!"

"Funny, Jane, very funny," Sherri said. "I've got to see you. I have to talk to you. You're my best friend. Can you do lunch today?"

"What's going on? Are you ok?"

"I'm ok. I mean I'm not ok but I'm not dying or anything. It's this thing with John. I've got to talk to you."

"It'll have to be a late lunch," Jane said. "I've got clients coming in to sign every document you can think of. And there's sure to be a hundred last minute changes. Their appointment is in just a few minutes, at 11, and you wouldn't think signing documents would take very long, but I have a feeling this one is going to be a marathon. Second marriage, he's got kids, she doesn't."

"So what time can you do lunch?"

"How about if we shoot for 1:30 at Wiley's Grille," Jane said, "but keep your cell phone on and if I get in a bind I'll call no later than 1:15 to let you know I'm stuck, and we can go later or maybe just meet for a drink after work if it's looking hopeless. Do you mind something like that?"

"Ok," Sherri said. "Call my cell, otherwise I'll see you at 1:30 at Wiley's."

Helene leaned in the doorway. "Richard and Janet Bradley are in conference room Q. I'll get my notary stamp."

"Wait," Jane said. "Let me talk to them first. I'll call you when they're ready to sign."

Nearly two hours later, Jane was still gamely talking about the technicalities of retirement accounts to two people who had obviously managed to get married without ever having a serious talk about finances. Jane could relate to that. The conversation was going around in circles as neither Richard nor Janet wanted to speak plainly about how to divide what was enough, more or less, to live on now, into a piece for Janet and a piece for Richard's children in the event that Richard clutched his chest, fell to the floor and checked out. Which was seeming more and more likely, if the meeting didn't wrap up sometime soon.

"This is a consent form for Richard's 401(k)," Jane said. "Right now, even though your prenup says you can leave each other as much or as little as you want, federal law, called ERISA, overrides that. That means that you, Janet, as Richard's spouse, you are entitled to be the beneficiary of 100% of Richard's 401(k) account. If you sign this consent, that's no longer the case. Richard wants you to sign this consent so 1/2 of the 401(k) can go to your marital trust and 1/2 to his children. If you don't sign, all of it will go to you, Janet, outright, not in the marital trust. If you do sign, then as we've filled in here on this form, 1/2 will go to the marital trust, if you survive Richard, and 1/2 to Richard's children. One other thing you need to know, Janet, is that once you sign the consent, Richard can make other changes, without your consent. He could, just for an example, and I'm not saying he would do this, but he could, if you sign the consent today, go to his personnel office tomorrow, get a new beneficiary form and leave 100% of his 401(k) to his children and zero percent to you."

"What do you mean?" Janet said. "I thought you said Richard needed me to sign a consent to leave any part of his 401(k) to his children."

"Yes, he does now," Jane said. "But once you sign the consent form, Richard doesn't need it anymore. The next time he decides to change the beneficiaries on his 401(k), if he ever decides to make a change, he can do it without telling you and without your consent."

"Isn't he leaving me his IRA?" Janet said.

"Yes," Jane said. "The forms we are signing today name you as 100% beneficiary of Richard's IRA. But Richard can change that at any time. No spousal consent is needed for that."

"Wait," Richard said. "Which one is the IRA?"

"Can you excuse me for just a moment?"

Jane stepped outside the conference room and headed for her office. Helene was in her cubicle, eating a salad.

"I'm sorry Helene," Jane said. "I expected this would take a while, but never more than two hours. Thanks for standing by. They could be ready to sign at any moment, or we might need to reschedule for another day. I just can't tell how it will turn out at this point. If I ever get finished with this, you can leave a little early or come in late tomorrow to make up for missing your lunch hour today."

"That's ok," Helene said. "I left early one day last week and I need to make up some time. No problem staying through lunch today."

Jane called Sherri's cell. "Sherri, it's Jane. No way I'm going to make it to lunch. Quick drink at Janson's Cafe at 5:30 ok?"

"Sure," Sherri said. "See you then."

It was just past 5:00 when Jane finally put the Bradleys in the elevator, with the originals and a full set of copies of their documents. Janet finally agreed to sign the consent for Richard's 401(k), so his children could get half, but only after Jane revised their documents to give Janet her half of the 401(k) outright, instead of putting it in a marital trust for her. Janet said she would still leave something to Richard's children if she outlived Richard, but Jane knew that wasn't likely. It was not impossible, but if Richard died and as time passed his children didn't have much contact with Janet, then Janet would probably have a new will prepared that didn't include Richard's children and mostly likely whatever was left in Richard's 401(k) when Janet died would go to Janet's family. That was the most likely outcome. But that was something for another day. Right now Jane needed to get to Janson's to see Sherri. She grabbed her coat. She scanned her e-mails to see if there was anything that absolutely couldn't wait. She decided she didn't care. She hadn't seen Sherri in a while and really wanted to see her. Four of the e-mails were actually new voicemails, and Jane could have listened to them through her computer inbox, but why should they jump the line? They could wait, same as the e-mails that were actually e-mails, not e-mails of voicemails.

Jane thought about taking some files home, but the firm had been doing a fairly good job of switching to paperless files, so almost everything she might need, she could see by logging in from her home computer. When she thought enough time had passed that she could leave without running into her clients in the lobby, (too much risk of a zillion more questions or worse yet, requests for more changes in the documents if she did,) she headed for the elevators.

There was an odd smell by the ninth floor receptionist desk. Jane pressed the elevator button and heard the receptionist telling a disheveled man that he couldn't speak to the firm administrator. The receptionist explained that the management company for the building, not the firm, handled arrangements for all services and maintenance involving common areas or the exterior of the building. The man was very agitated. Jane slipped into the elevator. Just before the doors closed she heard the receptionist paging security.

When Jane reached the lobby she scanned it for any slow moving Bradleys, and at first she thought the coast was clear. It wasn't. There they were, with the oversized envelope holding all their documents pulled open, leaning against a post in the lobby. They seemed to be reading something in one of the shorter documents, holding it up and scanning through it together. Jane tried to get around in back of them, where she would have a straight shot to the revolving doors at the front of the lobby, but they spotted her.

"Jane, Jane!" Janet said. "We thought of one more question on the ride down in the elevator."

Sherri already had a table when Jane got to Janson's Cafe. Jane was out of breath from running the three blocks from her building to Janson's, after finally shaking loose from the Bradleys.

"Sherri," Jane said, "I'm so sorry to be late. I was still hung up with my 11:00 clients. Can you believe that?"

"No problem," Sherri said. "They have plenty of gin here."

"So what's going on? I've really missed you lately."

"I know, I know, I've been meaning to call you. Things have just been crazy. So crazy. But I just had to talk to you tonight. I'm going crazy."

"Are you ok?"

"Oh, yeah, I'm ok, I guess. Just going crazy. Or gone crazy maybe already. I can't believe my life."

"What's going on?"

"Ok, here's the story. So you know I've been seeing John Hauser."

Jane almost rolled her eyes at the mention of Hauser, but caught herself in time and managed to keep an expression of warm interest and concern on her face.

"And I know, I know, that you don't think I should date a married man. But I've told you, his marriage is a sham. He's just keeping up appearances. But ok, I get it, you still don't approve."

Jane thought about how she was not exactly in a position to judge Sherri's love life right then, given Jane's own lapse in the 'not sleeping with married men' department.

"Anyway," Sherri said, "long story short, two weeks ago, John and I are alone in my apartment, and he's used the old line about working late at his office a million times as his excuse for not being home." Jane thought of Jeff using that same excuse with Cassie so he could go to Jane's house the other night.

"I mean I know that's like such a cliché," Sherri said, "but it works, I mean every other time it worked, so that's what John tells his wife when he comes to see me. And then he sets his office phone to forward the calls to my phone, so he can pick up if his wife calls him at the office to check. Why the hell he didn't think to forward the calls to his cell, or just tell her to call his cell, I don't know, but the call forwarding thing worked, so what that's what he's been doing. So we're just hanging out at my apartment, but we're not, like, doing anything. I mean we might have been, but we weren't. We've been seeing each other since I don't know, for a while now anyway, so it's not like we rip each other's clothes off every time we see each other. Well, sometimes maybe, but not every time. We're not kids in high school. We're adults, right?"

The waitress stopped by their table.

"A ginger ale for me," Jane said.

"Another one of these for me," Sherri said. She looked over at Jane.

"A ginger ale? You're not pregnant or anything, are you?"

Actually, it was too soon to tell. It had been just a few days, even if it seemed like another lifetime ago, since Jane had sex with Jeff at her house this past Thursday. Jane was maybe about mid-cycle, and that was too early for a pregnancy test, right? Didn't it take a few weeks and didn't you have to be late for the test to work? Jane wasn't sure. But even if there was the slightest chance that Jane was pregnant, she wasn't about to take any chances by having a drink. Not Jane. She wanted this baby, if there was a baby, to be as healthy and to have as high an IQ as possible. No, if Jane was pregnant, this baby was going to hear Mozart and tapes of lectures on art history and architecture, even while still in utero. If she was pregnant and could figure out a way to start with flashcards before her baby was even born, she would. For now, until further notice, she was off alcohol, caffeine and tuna.

"I'm driving tonight," Jane said. "You know, driving home, after this. And I don't need a DUI right now, or ever for that matter. If you keep knocking those back, I'll be driving you home in my car too."

Jane wasn't sure Sherri would buy that explanation. Even if Jane was driving, she usually still got a glass of wine and then didn't drink much of it. But Sherri didn't ask any more questions, and Jane figured that whatever happened with Hauser must have been pretty serious for Sherri to miss any hints that Jane was hiding something.

"Oh sure," Sherri said. "Might come to that if I have a few more of these. Sure. Anyway, like I said, we're not messing around or anything. But the thing of it is, John never told me his wife had an after hours key card to his office. He said he gave her a card that works the gate to his parking lot so she can park and walk a block to the Mall and not have to pay for parking to shop, but he didn't say it was the same as a key card to get into his office after hours. Can you imagine, risking his marriage to save $3.50 in parking?"

The parking card put Hauser's marriage at risk? The parking card was not even close to the reason Hauser's marriage was at risk. Did people's brains just get soaked in some kind of delusional neurochemicals when they had affairs or was it the other way around? That people who had affairs were the delusional ones to begin with? At least she wasn't delusional about Jeff. He was a jerk. She wanted a baby. She expected nothing from him, or even less than nothing. It was not an affair. It was definitely a one shot deal. Baby or no baby. But who was she to criticize Sherri, having done what she had just done with Jeff? Ok, this was going to hurt, but Jane thought she could manage to say it.

"And then what happened?"

"Like I said, we weren't doing anything, thank goodness, just hanging around my apartment. But wouldn't you know Wendy Hauser actually does go shopping at the Mall, and instead of calling to check on John, as long as she's already in the parking lot, she uses her key card to go up to his office to check on him. And he's not there. And I'm thinking she's an idiot, I mean the way he describes her, but it turns out she's not. She goes into his office and figures out how to find out the number he's got his calls forwarded to. Sure, he has a passcode to get into the phone to check, but he uses the same password for everything, and she guesses it in no time flat. Then she's got my phone number. And she looks through the received calls directory on Hauser's desk phone and in no time flat she has my name and my phone number. Two seconds on the internet and she has my address. Ten minutes later and she's pounding on my door. Can you believe it? It's like a movie or a TV sitcom. What are the odds of her figuring out where I live?"

"Apparently pretty good."

"Don't get all snarky on me. Your track record with men is no better than mine." More than you know. "Anyway," Sherri said, "this is serious."

Ok. One more time. Jane just didn't know how many more of these she could muster for this sickening story. But here's one more at least.

"And then what happened?"

"Well, John lets her in and she screams at him for a while. And then, get this, she tells him not to come home. She says she'll pack a suitcase and drop it off and guess what, the next day she does. He's been in my apartment, Jane, for two weeks. And it gets worse. She keeps dropping off those brats of hers." Those brats of theirs, not just hers. "And guess what?" Sherri said. "They hate me."

"Imagine."

"What kind of mother does that?" Sherri said. "Isn't she afraid they'll be traumatized? They're what, five and seven or something? Shouldn't children be protected from this kind of thing?"

"You would think."

"And before he was a live in, I mostly saw John either in his business suits or naked."

"Sherri, honey, please, I passed up my chance with the guy, remember? Let's not overshare on the physical descriptions."

"Ok, ok. I mean, I know he could stand to lose some of that gut he has, but in a suit, he looks pretty sharp. But now I see him in these sweatpants he wears around the house. He looks like a homeless person. Which I guess he is, except that he's at my place. And these men's jeans, sized to fit Uncle Beerbelly down on the farm or something, I'm telling you, with that and those two brats screaming and sniveling and getting into everything, I'm losing my mind."

"Any chance he'll patch things up with Wendy?"

"I wish." Sherri drained her glass. "But he says he likes living in my apartment. He says he feels ten years younger or something. He says he likes being with a younger crowd, but it's just me in there unless Wendy has dropped off the brats again. And he keeps saying he's going to ask her for a divorce. What am I going to do? I'm going crazy. I can't stand to be in my own apartment."

"It sounds terrible. If you want to crash at my place for a while, I've got a spare bedroom. You know you're always welcome. But Hauser isn't, though, ok?"

"Thanks. I appreciate the offer, I really do. But I'm afraid if I leave, Wendy will drop those brats off again to be with their dad and the little darlings will trash my apartment. Besides, John wants me to watch them if Wendy drops them off so he can work late. Get that. Work late. Now he's telling me what he used to tell Wendy. He says he needs to work more, especially if he's going to have to pay for his and hers divorce lawyers. So I'm supposed to watch the brats. What kind of a mother leaves her own children with some homewrecker she's barely met?"

"You could break up with him."

"You think I should just pull the rip cord?" Sherri looked around for the waitress. " I guess it's more like cutting the umbilical cord with John. I could just dump his ass, couldn't I? But what about love? I thought I really loved this guy. That this was it. What if it is really love?"

"Love him, love his sweat pants and his kids, I guess," Jane said. "And his spending all his money on divorce lawyers."

"Great pep talk. That's so helpful."

Jane realized how tired she was, all of a sudden. Things had been crazy lately in her life too. "I am really sorry you're having all this trouble with Hauser. I shouldn't make jokes about it, when it's really serious. I know it is. It really sounds just awful. I do care about you and I can see how upset you are. If you need a place to hide out for a while, to get away from the situation, my door is open. But just now I'm exhausted and I need to get home. I'm sorry, but I haven't eaten anything since breakfast and I've barely had time even to pee today and I'm just dead on my feet. Let me get this. I'll run it up to the cashier. You call me if you need to talk or if things settle down enough that we can catch a movie or something."

"Thanks Jane. I'll call when I can or if I get crazy. Or crazier anyway."

Tuesday morning at work, her caller id showed the number for Roy's cell.

"Jane Sidley."

"Jane, it's Roy."

"Hello Roy."

"I was glad to see you at the play the other night. Really glad. You look great. Ansel was joking around and we didn't get a chance to talk, but if we had, I would have said I really miss you. Which I do. I miss you."

"I don't know about this conversation. I don't see the point of talking like this."

"Don't hang up. Just give me a minute. I want to see you."

"I don't think so."

"This weekend is the last one in October. Pretty soon November will be turning cold and all the leaves will be down. But it's still really pretty out on the bike trails, and the weather is supposed to be good this weekend. I know this great bike trail at Scattered Rock State Park that is awesome with the fall colors. Come with me. An afternoon of biking just to see the leaves, not so much to see me, how's that?"

"No thanks."

"C'mon, Jane. I know you're not seeing anybody."

Do they all say that? Hauser said that. Jeff said that. How do they know that? Is there an app for that? Some databank or website they can check? issheseeinganybody.com? Or is it a ploy? Are they just asking, whether they know for sure or not, just to see what the woman says? He says, "I know you're not seeing anybody' and then she says nothing, meaning he's right, or she's not telling and maybe willing to see him even if she is seeing someone else, or else she says 'as a matter of fact I am seeing someone." Either way, he loses nothing by saying that he knows she's not seeing anyone. Or Roy's been talking to Anita or even Sherri. Could be that.

"I haven't been biking in a long time. And I'm not interested in biking with you."

"A few hours," Roy said. "A nice drive. A beautiful bike ride. You'll have a nice time. I think we need to give this another shot. I miss you. We'll take it slow. Let me pick you up at 9 Saturday morning."

Jane didn't have plans for Saturday other than sitting here at her desk. Seeing Roy seemed like a bad idea, but maybe it wouldn't be so bad, just to go biking. But she sure didn't want Roy coming to her house. If he picked her up there, or worse yet, dropped her off there, he might get the wrong idea. And Jane might end up doing something really stupid, like she had with Jeff, just a few days ago.

"Ok, but I'm having an early breakfast with my mom on Saturday. Pick me up there. I'm sure she'll be delighted to see you." Let her mom give him the stink eye. Heaven knows he deserves it.

"Your mom's house? Really?"

"Maybe this just isn't going to work out."

"No, your mom's house is good. Saturday at 9. See you then."

Where had she put her bike helmet? The garage or maybe in a closet?

CHAPTER ELEVEN

*A*t 9 on Saturday Jane was finishing toast and coffee at her mother's house. They heard Roy pull into the driveway and park behind Jane's Sierratti. Roy honked his horn.

"Do you hear anything, Mom?"

"No, not a thing."

Roy honked again. Neither Jane nor her mother got up from the table. It was quiet for a few moments.

Jane's mother went to the window. "He's taking your bike out of the back of your car and putting it in the back of his truck." Roy saw Mrs. Sidley at the window and waved. Mrs. Sidley did not wave back.

Yeah," Jane said. "I left it unlocked so he could do that."

After a few moments, the doorbell rang.

Roy was right about the beauty of the bike trails at Scattered Rock State Park. The leaves were past their peak but there was still a lot of color. Reds, shades of orange and yellow. It was a clear, cool fall day. He was right too about having perfect weather for biking. They took one of the easier trails because Jane hadn't been biking in a while. She might have pushed herself and tried harder to ride one of the more challenging trails back when her relationship with Roy mattered so much to her. But now, when she was here only because she had nothing better to do that day, or at least that's what she told herself, she wasn't about to make much of an effort. No need to try to impress a guy who would probably just disappear again, not that she cared if he did or not, right?

The gently sloping trail took them over a bridge that spanned Scattered Rock Gorge. The view over the side of the bridge, down into the vast gorge, was truly spectacular. Roy and Jane got off their bikes on the bridge and took in the view over the side.

"How about that?" Roy said. "Isn't that something?" He

sounded like he owned the place. Because he'd been there before and suggested the outing, the park and the beautiful view
were somehow his. As if he was showing Jane the grounds of his
sizable estates. As if any minute now he would pull out his hunt-
ing horn and signal to his stable lackeys to release the hounds or
something. Ok, he was a little full of himself, but the view, that
was really something. And the fresh air and exercise did feel
good. Jane was having a good time. And if she was being honest, she would have to admit that she liked the familiar feeling of
being with Roy. More than she expected. Quite a bit more.

"Leave the bikes up here," Roy said. "Just for a minute. If
we go down along the base of bridge there's a place where the
edge of the gorge juts out a little and you can get a close up look
right down into the gorge." Roy pulled a small digital camera
out of his pocket. "The leaves are still really beautiful today. We
can get some great pictures from there."

"I don't know. I don't want to be that close to the edge of
the gorge. And the view is pretty great from up here. Can't we
just get a few pictures from up here?"

"C'mon, it's ok. And it's an incredible spot. You can see
right down into the gorge."

Roy walked over to the edge of the bridge and off the bike
trail, down along the base of the bridge, by the edge of the
gorge. Jane wasn't happy about it, but she followed him. The
spot he was trying to reach did jut out over the edge of the
gorge. He made small steps, inching toward it. If Jane had cared
about making a good impression on this sort-of date they were
having, she would have worried about getting dirt on the back of
her spandex bike pants. But she didn't care, she told herself. So
she sat down and scooted slowly, on her butt, toward the edge of
the gorge. Jane held on to small saplings as she edged toward
where Roy was, on a little natural platform of sorts where the
earth at the edge of the gorge extended out over the edge, just a
little.

"Wow, the view from here is amazing," Roy said.

Jane was looking mostly at the saplings as she scooted toward him. She did manage to glance out over the gorge for a
second or two here and there. When she was almost next to Roy,
she glanced up at him and realized he was losing his footing. He

was at the edge of the earth platform and it had crumbled away a little under his feet, leaving him off balance and over the edge, just a little too much. Time seemed to stand still and they both knew Roy was about to fall. That he was sliding too far, off balance and helpless, over the steep, rocky sides of the deep gorge. Jane, keeping hold of a sapling in one hand, shot up her other hand from where she was sitting and caught hold of the sleeve of Roy's bike shirt. She pulled on his sleeve and steadied him, just enough, so that his center of gravity moved back towards level ground, away from the emptiness of the gorge. It was enough, just enough, for Roy to regain a sure footing and his balance. If Jane hadn't reached up and steadied him, right then, he would have fallen down into the deep gorge. And they both knew it.

Roy looked wide eyed and pale. Then he got hold of himself and his face was expressionless. He didn't say anything. Didn't even thank Jane. Hardly even looked at her where she still sat on the ground. He headed back toward the bikes. Jane scooted back away from the edge for a foot or two and then got up and brushed off the back of her bike pants. She walked back up onto the bridge where Roy stood with the bikes. He still didn't say anything. Jane didn't either.

They rode for another hour in silence on the bike trail back to Roy's truck. The drive back to the city was pretty quiet too, although Roy eventually began to make some small talk, pointing out the little towns or historic sites along their route. But neither one mentioned what happened at the edge of the gorge. They stopped at a small town where Roy said they had good freshly pressed apple cider. Jane bought a gallon to take to her mother. Then they had a late lunch at a little diner in the town. They ate mostly in silence, not really even looking at each other. Jane looked out a window near their table as she ate. Roy concentrated on his plate, stabbing his salad and wolfing down his sandwich.

Roy dropped Jane off at her mother's house. He helped Jane unload her bike and put it in the back of her Sierratti. He mumbled goodbye and drove off.

Jane went in through the back door to her mother's house. "Hi Mom, I brought you some apple cider."

"Oh Jane honey, thank you. But a whole gallon? You'll have

to take some of that home with you. I'll never drink a whole gallon."

"Ok. I'll put some in a jar and take it home. But it should be really good. Roy and I stopped in this little town and they were making it right there. It's about as fresh as you can get."

"So you had a good time then?"

"I guess. The leaves are still so pretty, even though it's almost November and they're past their peak. It was really beautiful biking in Scattered Rock State Park. Our bike trail went across a bridge right over the gorge."

"The gorge? Is that safe?"

Was it?

"Mom, it's a bike trail. And the one we were on was not even one of the really challenging trails. No big slopes or anything."

"But I've heard of people getting into trouble going too close to the gorge. People have fallen. Sometimes they need helicopters to get the bodies out."

Jane remembered the panicked look on Roy's face in the moment when he realized he'd lost his footing. How time seemed to stop. Then, when she reached up to grab his sleeve, she must have grabbed for it pretty fast, but everything had seemed to go in slow motion. As if she was reaching from underwater. Everything had an almost cartoon clarity to it too. The big clear blue sky with only a few small, scattered puffs of sparse clouds. The bright yellows, reds and oranges of leaves on the trees lining the gorge. The sound of water running far below at the bottom of the gorge. Jane remembered how the small rocks sounded as they tumbled down the side of the gorge when the bits of ground were starting to break away under Roy's feet. Again, in her mind's eye, she saw Roy's face, as his expression shifted from concentration on getting a really good picture to the sickening realization the he was losing his foothold, just that much too far over the edge, off balance. Jane could see his face when he first knew he was too far over the edge. And then that silence between them, after he was safe. Jane was badly shaken and wanted to hug Roy and tell him how grateful she was that he was safe. That he didn't fall. But his silence had kept her from reaching for him or saying anything. He didn't like her seeing him unable to handle himself. Needing her help like that. And saying anything would just make things worse.

"Hey, Mom?" Jane said. "It's only 4. We've got another two hours or so of daylight. Want to take a ride over to the cemetery and visit Dad's grave? We could just go for a little while. Then I need to get home and get a shower, but I can drop you back here first. We can be there in ten minutes."

The cemetery was large. Mostly flat with grass around the tombstones. Well kept, with only a few trees. Jane and her mother hadn't been there for a while, but Jane's mother pulled the cemetery map out of her purse and they had no trouble finding her dad's headstone. Jane thought they had been there enough that they could have found it without the map, but she didn't say so. They stood in the late afternoon light looking at the headstone. 'William Arnold Sidley Beloved husband and father 1930 - 1995.' Never smoked, watched his weight, ran on a treadmill, went to his doctor for regular checkups. Never sick a day in his life. Then a heart attack, with no warning, at sixty-five. And he was gone.

Jane had been away at college when she got the news. Her parents were older than most of the parents of the other students. Jane had been a much longed-for, later-in-life miracle baby born to a mother and father who, at thirty-nine and forty-five, respectively, had given up hope of ever having a child. Jane missed her dad. She'd never dreamed when she went off to college her senior year that she'd lose forever the smiling, fit man who drove her to the airport and waved goodbye as she went headed to her gate. He was only sixty-five, after all.

No warning. No chest pain. Just a moment, standing on a stepladder, and then he collapsed and was gone. For a few seconds, Jane's mother thought he just lost his balance. That he'd reached for something on a high shelf, from the top step of the small stepladder, and taken a tumble. But he was gone. The paramedics couldn't bring him back.

And Jane remembered getting the news at college. One minute she was an ordinary senior, looking forward to the approaching day when her proud parents would watch as she got her diploma. Then hearing about her father was like the earth giving way under her feet, opening an abyss. How she missed his warmth, his jokes, his beaming admiration. Visits home from college had been so happy. Such a respite from classes and finals and crazy friends. But after that her visits home, to her lonely, grief stricken mother were like entering a deep cave. And school was the respite, a place to hide from the heartache of seeing her mother bearing up so bravely, so obviously not wanting to burden Jane. How she had wished she could have shown her father her college diploma and then her law degree. She wished he could have seen her office at work, the embossed notices the firm sent out saying that she made junior non-equity partner, and her wedding to Jeff. Well, at least he never saw her marriage go to pieces. That was something. But what if she was pregnant now? Oh, wouldn't he have been the best grandfather? The best.

"He would have been a great granddad," Jane said. "I mean if I ever have children."

"Oh yes. Your father loved children. All those years when we thought we couldn't have a child, he never said anything, but I knew it broke his heart. And then you came along. When we had lost hope. And there you were. A beautiful baby girl. He was the happiest man alive. He loved to sit and rock you in the evenings. And he went to everything. Every school play, every debate team meet. Do you remember that?"

"Yes, Mom, I do. I remember how knowing that he was there, in the audience, without fail, would chase away my stage fright and give me the edge I needed in the debates. Even if I couldn't find him in the audience because of stage lights or because there were so many people and so much to concentrate on, even if I didn't know which seat he was in, I knew he was there. He was always there for me, Mom, and for you." And then he was gone. Just a few steps up the stepladder and his heart stopped beating and he fell right out of their lives.

"C'mon, Mom, it's starting to get really cold. Let me run you home before dark."

Jane drove back to her mother's house and walked her mother to the door.

"Oh, Jane, wait, take some of the apple cider home with you."

"Sure, Mom. Do you have an empty jar?"

They poured some of the cider into an empty mayonnaise

jar. Jane would be glad to get home. She was still wearing her
sweaty spandex bike shirt and pants. She could get a quick
shower and then put something in the microwave for dinner.

Roy's truck was parked in her driveway. As she got out of
her car, she saw his ladder against the side of the bonus room
and heard hammering from the roof. Although the last light was
already gone, this time he wasn't using lights. The wind had
picked up and gusts of wind were making the leaves from the
trees in the backyard swirl around the driveway. It started to
rain. Not a driving rain, not all that heavy, but still cold, a har-
binger of the snow and sleet to come in winter. And with the
wind gusting, it was almost as if the rain was spitting in Jane's
face.

Jane couldn't believe Roy would even try a stunt like this,
especially when Jane had already seen his standard operating
procedure. Did he think she was that easy to manipulate? Jane
just couldn't believe it, what nerve for Roy to get back up on
that roof, working on her deck, as a way to get back into her
pants after one date. Oh no, we're not going down this same
road again. He's not getting up there on that roof after weeks
and weeks of 'let's be friends' and suddenly he's Mr. Hot-for-
me John Henry with his hammer in his hand. No way. If he's
thinking he'll sweep me off my feet again, and then he's back
into my bed, like the last time he pulled this stunt, he can just
forget it. Because guess what? I already know that tomorrow
he's Mr. Cold again, disappearing for weeks. Then round and
round we go, getting just exactly nowhere. No way. Not again.
Does he think I'm that gullible? That stupid?!

Jane wanted to shout at him that she was not stupid. That it
was not going to work this time. That he better get off her roof
and out of her driveway or she would call the cops. But with all
this wind, she didn't think he would hear. She sure wasn't going
to go into the house and end up shouting at him from the French
doors. To her bedroom. Dammit, the wind was picking up and
the weather was getting so bad right then that she was expecting
the Wicked Witch to fly past any minute, but she was still going
to have to go up that ladder if she wanted to yell at Roy. And she
did want to yell at him. All the excitement and then confusion
and humiliation of last weekend's encounter with Jeff and then

her grief at the cemetery with her mother formed a ball of emotion inside Jane and she wanted to yell at Roy more than anything. More than her fear of going up a wet ladder in a windstorm.

She didn't go all the way up the ladder. Just far enough so that only her head was above the roof line, with the rest of her still standing on the rungs of the ladder. "Roy!" Get off this roof! It's dark and raining and this wind is terrible. You'll break your neck. And let me tell you, the He-Man carpenter, show me you really care after a casual date thing, where you show up unexpectedly at my house, doing a little after hours work with tools, and then tell me how you really feel, and then as long as you've stopped by, and it's just the two of us at my house, then you think you're in, well, forget it, Roy. Just forget it. It's not going to work with me. Not this time. It's not going to get you anywhere with me. Been there, done that. Get off this roof and get your truck out of my driveway or I'm calling the cops!"

"You shouldn't be standing on the ladder like that in this wind. Let me help you." Roy came over to where Jane's head was just above roof level. He knelt down on the wet leaves that were blowing around the roof and gripped Jane's arm, intending to pull her up off the ladder onto the roof.

"Let go of my arm. Right now."

"Ok, ok. I'll hold the ladder and you come up here. What's that you're holding?"

"A mayonnaise jar of the apple cider. Mom said a gallon was too much." Roy reached for the jar, trying to take it from her and put it on the roof so she'd have both hands free to grip the ladder, but she pulled the jar close. "I'm not here to have a chat with you. I'm not here for anything with you at all, except to tell you to get out of here. Now I'm going down this ladder and into the house and if you're not gone by the time I get to the phone in my house, I'm calling the cops. And if you touch me again I'll call them from my cell even before that." Jane looked down, ready to start down the rungs of the ladder.

"Jane, wait, I want to give you this." The tone of his voice was pretty damn sincere. He was good at playing Mr. Hot, she'd give him points for that. Jane looked back at Roy where he knelt, holding the top of ladder with one hand to steady it for Jane.

Even in the dark and the rain there was enough light from the yard lights of the neighboring houses for Jane to see that he was holding out, in his other hand, a small velvet box.

"Roy?"

"That was so terrible today when I lost my footing. And you pulled me back. I don't want you to have to do that. I want to be there for you. I want to be the sure footing for you. That pulls you back from a fall, whenever you need me to. Not sometimes and then gone, like I was. And I'm so sorry about that. That's not how I want it to be for us. I want to be there every time. I want to be the one making you safe. Me for you. I want to be the solid ground under your feet. And I want to get the railing finished on this deck so you can lean on it and be secure. So you can lean on me, Jane. Every day, not just sometimes. And I want you to marry me. Please, Jane, please marry me and I'll be here for you, all in, every day. Please honey. I will never let you down. I was crazy not to be there for you. I was crazy to let you go. Please, give me another chance. A chance to be your rock. Your sure footing. I'm an idiot for the way I treated you, I know. But Jane please, marry this idiot."

Jane put the jar of cider on the roof. She looked at the box in his hand. Then she reached for it. And opened it. There was a large solitaire diamond ring inside.

"When did you have time to get this? This afternoon?"

"No. I got it a month or so ago, but I got cold feet. I broke up with you instead of proposing. I'm so sorry. I made a mistake. Let me put it right. Say you'll marry me."

If this was a ploy to get a one night stand, it was remarkably good. Roy was still kneeling on the roof. Were those tears on his face? It could just be the rain. Jane looked searchingly into his eyes. They were nice eyes. Clear, direct, big brown eyes. Did she love him? She'd been so angry with him. So hurt when they broke up. And if he dumped her once, would he do it again and she'd be back in divorce court, just that much older and not much wiser? But back when he said 'let's be friends,' even in all the hurt, she'd realized that a big part of the hurt was because she thought they had a real shot together. That this could work, long term. Over the long haul, that's what she'd thought. Is that love? Mrs. Roy Adams. Jane Adams. Jane Adams? Ok, Jane

Sidley Adams.

And what if she was pregnant? Jane startled, shifting suddenly on the ladder.

"Hey, honey," Roy said. "Let's get you off the ladder. I shouldn't have proposed to you out here in the wind and the rain. I tell you I'm going to keep you safe and then I pop the question while you're standing on a ladder in gusting wind and rain."

What were the odds? Jane never won contests or prizes. She never beat long odds. For anything to happen in Jane's life, it needed to be a pretty sure bet. Eighty percent at least. Things that happened to her tended to have about an eighty percent likelihood at least. Or better even. Maybe ninety percent. And getting pregnant from a one shot deal with Jeff, what are the odds on that? Ten percent tops, right? She'd have to check on the internet and see if there were statistics on the odds of getting pregnant from having unprotected sex just one time.

And, although Jane didn't like the thought, and felt guilty even for thinking it, there it was in her mind. It had just been a week since she had sex with Jeff. How would Roy even suspect that there was any, what, ten or so percent chance, that any baby she might have with Roy wasn't his, if she now had sex with Roy? If he reached for a condom, she'd make him put it back in the drawer by reciting his speech about being there for her, all in, every day. She could remind him of his promises, send them right back at him if she needed to.

That's cold. That is really cold. I can't believe this is me. I can't believe I'm thinking this way. But there it was.

"Yes," Jane said. "Yes, I will marry you and be your wife. Now let's both get down from here. Let's get out of this rain. Come in the house and we can get a good look at how this ring sparkles in the light."

Jane left Roy still sleeping in her bed, or should she say their bed now that they were engaged, and surely he'd give up his apartment and just move into her house after the wedding, that made sense, on Sunday morning. She wanted to go to Church to see her mom and tell her the good news. Jane almost called her mom last night but she didn't want to spoil the mood with Roy, and besides, she really wanted to tell her mom in person.

But she also wanted to go to Church because Jane had some praying to do. Her prayers would be mostly 'thank You,' but would also include some 'I'm sorry.' She wanted to talk to God about not telling Roy there was a chance she was already pregnant. A sort of confession, she thought, that's what it would be really, to apologize to God for not telling Roy right away, up front, that she had unprotected sex with Jeff a week ago. It wasn't cheating, not on Roy anyway. They were broken up. Did he expect her to be a nun at her age? Cassie would probably use the word cheating if she ever found out about it, but who was she to talk when Cassie took up with Jeff while he was married to Jane? But Roy was entitled to know Jane had sex just a week ago with Jeff, especially if Jane was now engaged to be married to Roy and having sex with him. He was entitled to know that Jane might turn out to be pregnant, without knowing which man is the father. Roy was surely entitled to a warning and some full disclosure on that. But Jane wasn't going to tell Roy, and she wanted to sit in the pews and discuss the matter with God this morning.

The leaflets in the pews asked people to sit quietly, in contemplation, before the service began. That didn't stop Jane's mother from exclaiming loudly with joy the minute she sat down next to Jane in the pew and saw the ring.

"Oh sweetheart, I'm so happy. I mean if you're happy. Are you happy?"

"Yes, Mom, I'm very happy."

"I want to hear every detail. Did he get down on his knees?"

"Mom, the service is starting. I'll give you the complete run down after the service."

The reading from the First Testament was about Rebecca getting her favorite son Jacob to fool his blind father Isaac into giving Jacob the blessing that should have gone to Esau. Then the Epistle from Romans, about how we're all deceitful, under sin. Then the Gospel, about being defiled by the deceit coming out of our mouths. Ok God, Jane thought, I get it. Please forgive me and please protect me, but I'm not telling Roy. However it turns out. Oh dear Jesus, please be with me, for I am a sinner.

For the first time in her life, after years of Church going and volunteering and giving to charity, Jane felt the real depth of her desperate need for God. She felt the power of deceit. The strength of its grip. Even though she could act like she always had, and people would think of her as a good person, she now knew she was clinging with all her strength to deceit. She was sorry about it, but felt helpless to stop. And after years and years of being vaguely annoyed in Church about all the endless talk of 'Jesus, Jesus, Jesus,' she now understood her only hope was in Him.

CHAPTER TWELVE

*M*onday morning at the office, a summons was served on her. Jeffrey Rogers v. Jane Rogers also known as Jane Sidley Rogers also known as Jane Sidley. A petition to reopen their divorce settlement. To award Jeff, due to his changed circumstances, more in cash. For the house, from her investments and retirement account, based on her earnings and based on his lack of earnings. It was ridiculous. At least she hoped it was.

Jane called her divorce lawyer, Harvey Whitman. She hadn't spoken to him in almost two years.

"This is Jane Sidley, I'm calling for Harvey Whitman. Is he available?"

"One moment."

"Yello," Harvey said.

"Harvey, it's Jane Sidley. My ex, Jeff Rogers, sent a summons. He's petitioning to reopen our divorce. Can he do that? He's remarried."

"Well, it doesn't set aside the divorce decree itself, Jane. It won't make him a bigamist, if that's what you're asking. He's just reopening the property division, or maybe separate maintenance payments, something like that, not the order dissolving the marriage."

"Right, I know that. But I thought this was over. That we had a final order and got on with our lives. He got married. I'm engaged now. We've moved on. And now I get this summons. Can that happen? Can a property settlement be opened after we're leading completely separate lives for this long?" Maybe not completely separate. But mostly.

"You're engaged? Congratulations. That's wonderful news. Who's the lucky SOB?"

Helene leaned in the doorway to Jane's office. "I'm sorry to interrupt. Ted is waiting on twelve in conference room X. You have your review."

Jane nodded to Helene.

"My fiance is Roy Adams," she said on the phone to Harvey. "He's a carpenter and a contractor. I went through school with his baby sister, Anita. So can you make this thing with Jeff go away? I can't deal with this right now."

"Send the papers over. I'll take a look. I think we will prevail in the end, but keep in mind these days the wheels of justice turn slowly. Any idiot can file a petition and it just takes time, even if there's no merit in it. It's the system. Keeps the rabble from rousing."

"I've got to run. I'll send the papers over. But I need you to take hold of the reins here and make the wheels of justice run over Jeff and get rid of this, ok?"

"I'll see what I can do."

Jane raced to the elevators, then decided it would be faster to run up the stairs. The first two floors she managed without any trouble, but the last two flights from eleven to twelve weren't so good. I have got to get to the gym. Top priority. Or maybe bike to work sometime. That's not going to happen. But the gym, for sure the gym.

"Sorry to keep you waiting," Jane said. "Got stuck on the phone."

"Have a seat." Ted said. "Now, today we're here to discuss your candidacy for senior non-equity partner. That's quite a move up for someone as young as you. I hope you realize that."

"Back in the summer, when we had that problem with Adelaide Bowden, you mentioned that I might be up for consideration for junior equity. What happened to that?"

"Junior equity? I'm not saying that it's a hard and fast rule. I'm sure there could be exceptions, in theory at least, but if I'm not mistaken, no one has moved from junior non-equity to junior equity without at least a year or two as senior non-equity partner. That's just not how we do things around here."

"What about Norm Harrison?" Jane said. "And Jim Canterbury? They went straight from junior non-equity to junior equity without having to park for a few years at senior non-equity."

"Norm and Jim are the exceptions that prove the rule. They're exceptional in terms of their community involvement. They bring in business by being community leaders. And they're well-liked by everyone here at the firm. They take time to be team players in the firm and in the community. Didn't our consultants say you could stand to spend some time just walking around the firm, talking to your partners, being a team player? If you want to just come in and do your work, we appreciate that, but the senior levels are more than that. You need to be a little more, I don't know, available. Maybe even a little nicer, maybe it's as simple as that. It's hard to describe. Maybe golf. Jim and Norm are out there, on the course, doing business. You're here working and that's great, but you're asking for upper level here. Now sure, you're not going to seal a deal with the boys in the locker room or the steam room, but you could still be out there at the ladies' tee. And these days, there are a lot of women who are in-house counsel, making decisions about who gets the company's legal work. You could golf with them or shop with them or something like that maybe. Do you see what I'm saying?"

There was a tap at the door.

"Come in," Ted said.

It was Helene.   "I'm so sorry to interrupt, but I just wanted to let Jane know that Harold Anderson is here early for his ten o'clock appointment. I put him and his nurse in conference room Q on nine. He says he doesn't feel well. Should I reschedule?"

"No," Ted said, "Jane and I just need another minute. We'll be done in five at the most."

Jane waited for Helene to leave and close the door. "I know I need to go take care of Harry Anderson, but I am involved in the community. I'm active in my Church and I'm on the Arts Council Board. And my collections are always well over budget. I'm handling complex matters by myself and sending work to other attorneys in the firm. I just sent a big matter to Anthony Listerman. And what I do keeps clients here, in the firm. It makes us full service. If the Bowdens had to go elsewhere for estate planning, we'd be at risk of losing Integrated too. You know that."

"Listerman, that's what I mean. He has that quality I'm talking about. He's going places here at the firm, you bet. It's the intangibles. Bottom line with you is, your numbers are great and you do great work. We appreciate that about you. The entire Executive Committee is very pleased with your work and your numbers. But senior non-equity is where you need to be right now. Junior equity is just not in the cards for you, at least not yet. Trust me on this. It's the right thing. And it's a good deal, for you, Jane. It's a step up. This is good news today for you, not bad news. Look, we're bumping up your pay quite a bit. Ahead of Corinne Eberly even."

"Ok Ted, ok," Jane said, knowing when to push, and when she needed to bide her time. "Thanks. You know I love the firm. I am grateful to make senior non-equity, especially in these tough times."

"That's my girl." If he patted her head, Jane would quit. No, she would sue and then quit. Jane ran back down the stairwell to nine.

"Harry, sorry to keep you waiting," Jane said. She turned to the nurse. "I'm Jane Sidley, Mr. Anderson's attorney."

"Savannah Hatfield. Pleased to make your acquaintance."

Harry's skin had a yellowish green hue. A hose snaked its way to an oxygen tank at his feet. "I need." Harry paused and breathed for a moment. Jane waited. "I need to make some changes, in my will."

"Do you mind if I ask Savannah to wait outside just for a minute, Harry? We have a sitting area by the elevators."

"No. She's who." The tank hummed. "I'm changing it for. I'm putting. Her. In my will. As my, you know." Savannah adjusted the hose. "My heir."

"That's all the more reason she needs to wait in the hall, just for a few minutes," Jane said. "If your children challenge this, it'll be better if I can say I heard you say what you wanted, without the new beneficiary being here in the room." Jane turned to Savannah. "I'm sorry, but you understand, don't you? If you're here in the room and Harry says he wants you in his will, it might look like you had some kind of influence. We call it emotional duress. I'm not saying you're pushing Harry into anything, I'm just saying if you step outside for just a moment, it's easier for me to defend whatever changes we make, should the need arise, down the road."

"I say. She stays," Harry said.

"If Harry wants me to stay," Savannah said, "I think I should stay. Anyway you can see how hard it is for him to talk. So short of breath and all. And I can tell you what he wants. He wants to leave everything to me. We've talked about it. It's all settled. Plain and simple."

Jane wondered if she should call Helene and tell her to order lunch to be brought in at noon. This was going to be a long meeting.

Late afternoon, her mother's name and number appeared on her caller id.

"Hi Mom, everything ok?"

"Everything's fine. I'm sorry to call you at work, but have you and Roy set a date yet? You really should let the preacher know as far in advance when you want the Church for a wedding. It's a large congregation. And to get a good reception hall, we'll need to plan ahead for that."

Jane had not asked Roy about setting a date. She should probably push for something soon, rather than a long engagement, if there was any chance she was expecting.

"We haven't set a date yet, but I'm thinking soonish. Not a long engagement this time." This time. The words struck Jane and brought back memories of last time. In the same Church. Did she want to walk down the same aisle as she had with Jeff just about seven years ago? And how big a deal should a second wedding be? It was Roy's first, of course. And did anyone still care about that sort of thing? First wedding versus second, like people used to care? No one cared about that anymore, did they? Did she care?

"You know, Mom, I do want our preacher to do the ceremony, but I'm thinking maybe not in Church. Roy was saying that he realized he wanted to stop just kind of being in a holding pattern in his life, and go ahead and get married, when we at Scattered Rock State Park that day last week. They have a beautiful lodge where people can stay overnight. It's like a bed and breakfast, but it has this big hall with huge stone fireplaces. You've heard of it maybe. The Eden Glade Inn. I think that might be where I want to get married. People could stay there overnight if they were worried about driving an hour or so to get home after the reception. I'll talk to Roy and see if we can set a date."

"What about bridesmaids? Just Sherri this time, or three like last time?"

There it was again. This time. Last time.

"I was thinking Sherri and Anita. You know, Anita is Roy's baby sister."

"Oh sure, she owes you."

"What, over the gym uniform still? I think the statute of limitations has expired on that one."

"What about flowers? All white again this time?"

"Mom, I gotta run. We'll have plenty of time to work out the color of the flowers. Honest."

Jane thought about her wedding to Jeff. It was a sudden, unexpected engagement, just like with Roy. After her law school graduation, Jane had accepted the offer she had from Hantler Vintberg. She was ready to move back home. But Jeff didn't follow her there right away. They'd been living together her third year of law school in her studio apartment. He said he didn't want to leave his job without having a new one lined up in her hometown. At the time, she thought that showed he was mature. That he wanted to be careful. Now she wondered if he was seeing someone else all along, and having trouble making up his mind which one to leave. He didn't seem exactly heartbroken when Jane packed up one of those move-it-yourself trucks and left.

Jane kept paying the rent on the studio apartment for several months after that, even though she was also paying to rent a small apartment in a large, prefabricated, sixties era building here in the city, not too far from Hantler Vintberg's offices. Jeff was short of cash, waiting for some new commissions to come in and Jane had a good salary. Money was tight for Jane because of her student loans and the two rents, but if she worked hard, she could look forward to bonuses and raises at her firm.

Jeff called now and then. They still talked about his ideas but then often got into arguments about money or whether or not Jeff was doing enough, or anything really, to look for a job where Jane was living. When Jeff sent her the papers to renew the lease on the studio apartment for another year, her mother asked Jane if it really made any sense for a young woman to pay rent on an apartment for a young man she hadn't seen in five or six months and who didn't even call all that often. Jane put the papers in a drawer in the desk she had in the living room of her apartment. She honestly wasn't sure if she would see Jeff ever again or not. While she didn't send in his lease renewal, and stopped sending rent to his landlord, she still didn't break things off with him.

Six weeks after the deadline for the lease renewal passed, Jeff showed up one morning at her law firm, without any warning. There he was, out of the blue, one fine morning, with his nervous energy, head of thick, shining hair and big grin, talking a mile a minute.

"I miss you baby. I can't live without you. Marry me, babe. Marry me. Say you will." He didn't have a ring, but he'd made a small payment on one and he was sure they could put together the rest in time for the wedding. No, he hadn't found a job yet but he'd decided he would never get anywhere with the search over a long distance. "Contacts are everything in sales," he'd said. "Personal contacts."

And the wedding was perfect. Just what Jane wanted at the time. Her beautiful white dress, the ceremony in the church she'd attended with her parents while growing up. Lots and lots of white flowers lining the pews and they matched the white flowers in her bouquet. Sherri was maid of honor. Two other good friends she'd known since high school were bridesmaids. Jane knew all brides thought so, and no bridesmaids ever agreed, but Jane really did think the light blue bridesmaids gowns she chose were absolutely lovely, and could be worn again to a fancy dinner or a cocktail party.

Jeff's dad, who was as wiry and energetic as Jeff, drove halfway across the country in a car that was on its last legs. Jeff's mom flew in from the West Coast with her husband. Since Jane's dad had passed away and Jane didn't have any other male relatives, no brothers as she was an only child and no uncles, not even any male cousins, she asked Jeff's dad if he would walk her down the aisle. She remembered how happy she felt. The pews were packed with people she loved. An assortment of female cousins and their families, friends from church, old friends from high school, a few friends from college and law school, her assistant and several of the attorneys from work, they all came to the wedding. And of course Jane's mother was there, looking tall and radiantly happy for Jane.

And that left so many questions. Did she want all the family and all the flowers again? The Glen Edge Inn was a good idea. The more she thought about it, the more certain she was she just couldn't walk down the aisle at her Church a second time. She might end up crying when a wedding was supposed to be happy. The happiest day of her life.

And there was a big question that Jane's mother had somehow managed to miss asking just now, by some miracle. Who would Jane get to walk her down the aisle when she married Roy? Obviously not Jeff's dad again, but who else was there? She could ask Roy's dad, but she hadn't spent much time at all with Roy's parents. She didn't feel that close to Roy's dad. She hadn't felt that close to Jeff's dad, come to think of it, but Jeff's dad was so charming, he seemed perfect to walk Jane down the aisle back then.

What about Arthur? Arthur could play the role of stand-in dad. He might be a really good choice. He could be expansive and avuncular. Why not Arthur? But Roy had said he was thinking of him for best man. Ansel. The wing man. At the play that night the weekend before last, Ansel's big kiss may have been the key to getting Roy to realize how much Roy loved Jane. Maybe she could go see Ansel if he still had his weekend gig at the Thin Dime. She could ask him if he would walk her down the aisle. She'd meant to go see his band. And if anyone was the right person to deliver her down the aisle, it was Ansel, right.

But first, she had to tell Sherri she was engaged. She dialed Sherri's cell.

"Sherri, it's Jane."

"Hey Jane," Sherri said. "What's up?"

"Can we meet for a drink after work? I have news."

"I wish I could. But I have to pick up the brats from ballet lessons after work. Then I'm supposed to take them to that place with really bad pizza and all those games and video machines. We're supposed to bond."

"That sounds horrible."

"You have no idea. Hey, why not meet me there? With two of us, we might actually be able to manage. I'll owe you for the rest of my life. We'll be there about six. It's on Dublanter

Road."

"I know where it is. And actually, I do have a favor to ask, so I suppose I'm in a position to owe you one."

"You're the best friend in the world. I love you. See you at six at Wacky Wheezies."

Jane was waiting just inside the door of Wacky Wheezies when Sherri showed up with two tired and sullen looking little girls in tow.

"Meredith and Lindsay," Sherri said, "this is my friend, Jane."

They stared at Jane. Jane crouched down to their level. She'd read in a book that speaking to children at their eye level instead of from a standing position, looking down at them, was better in some way.

"Hi there," Jane said. "I'm Jane. Good to meet you two. Did you have a good time at your ballet lessons?"

They stared more. Finally one of them nodded then pulled on Sherri's purse. "Can we have some tokens for the games?"

"Yeah, yeah," Sherri said. "Give me a minute to get us a table and get an order in for the pizza."

"Cheese," the girls both said at once.

"Just cheese," one of them said. "We only eat pizza with cheese."

They were shown to a table and Sherri waived away the menus, ordering two personal-sized cheese pizzas for the girls and a medium pizza with mushrooms and onions to share with Jane. Then they went up to the cashier to buy what Jane thought was a ridiculous number of tokens. The girls ran for the arcade area of the restaurant. Sherri and Jane followed.

"Used to be you could just leave kids with the games and maybe even enjoy a slice of horrible pizza in peace," Sherri said. "But now with so many pedophiles and serial killers out there, you have to stand watch right on top of the little darlings, every friggin' minute." Sherri was shouting over the sounds of gunfire, race cars, ringing bells, lazer guns and spaceships. Jane was wondering if it was the noise and the flashing lights that were making her nauseous, or something else.

Sherri leaned in close to Jane's ear. "On the phone you said you had news?"

"I do. I made senior non-equity partner." Jane couldn't believe what she just said. She'd meant to say she was engaged to Roy. That was the big news. That she was going to marry Roy.

"Wow. That's great. What does that mean? A bigger office? A bigger piece of the pie?"

"Same office. And not exactly a piece of the pie yet either. You have to be an equity partner to get a percentage of the profits. But I'll get a bigger salary." Bigger than Corinne Eberly. Big deal. But that wasn't the issue here. The big issue here was why, when she opened her mouth to tell Sherri about getting engaged to Roy, she told her about her promotion at the firm instead. Was it because Sherri had already been her maid of honor? Was Jane embarrassed that she was going to ask Sherri to do that again? For heaven's sake, Sherri had just asked Jane to help her babysit the disturbed children of the man whose home she was wrecking. Why should Jane be embarrassed to ask Sherri to repeat as a bridesmaid for Jane's do-over on the wedding front? Did Jane want to ask Anita to be her matron of honor? Was that it? She wasn't telling Sherri about the engagement because Jane wanted someone else as bridesmaid-in-chief? Or was it because Jane wasn't happy about the groom? Or the marriage itself? She saw the girls leave a machine that looked like a space ship and come running over.

"We need more tokens." The girls were standing and glaring at Sherri, with their hands out. Sherri pulled more tokens from the plastic Wheezies bag she was holding and filled their hands.

"You're just great with them," Jane said. "I think they're really warming up to you."

"Do you think so? I mean I'd hate me if I were them. And we've had some bed wetting from the little one. I know it's hard for them with their dad living in my apartment. Hard for me actually. There are days when I want to leave the country. But you think they're warming up to me?"

"Sherri," Jane said, "I did make senior non-equity partner, but I was kidding, I guess, in saying that was my big news tonight. Roy proposed. See, here's the ring."

"Oh my God, Jane!" Sherri said. "I'm so wrapped up in my own mess of a life I didn't even see the ring. Oh wow, you and Roy are getting married? I thought you two broke up. Wow, have I been out of the loop or what?"

"We did break up," Jane said. "Roy said we should just be friends. Can you believe that?"

"Cliché of the year award. But I guess that changed?"

"I saw him at one of Arthur Ogden's plays. Roy was there with Mindy and your friend Ansel. And Ansel gives me this big kiss and puts his hand on my ass."

"I thought you said you got engaged to Roy?"

"Not then. It's really hard to talk in here. Ansel just wanted to make Roy jealous. And I guess it worked. Roy called and we went out and then he proposed."

"No kidding. What a guy."

"Oh yeah, Roy's a great guy."

"I meant Ansel. Help me grab the girls. Our pizzas are ready. We need to bully them into leaving the games and sitting down to eat for two minutes."

Back at work, Jane saw Harvey's firm's name and Harvey's direct dial number on her caller id.

"Jane Sidley."

"Jane, it's Harvey. Look, I know you're not going to like this, but the court has sent this thing with Jeff Rogers to mediation."

"Mediation? What's there to mediate? He's not getting another dime. Period."

"I don't know why his lawyer would want it, but that's what they asked the judge to do, and she did it."

"So now what? Can't you get it dismissed?"

"So now we go to the mediation. I'm sorry but that's what we need to do. It's scheduled for a Monday in mid-December, at the mediator's law office. Jerris and Langer. It's a little storefront office on Mercer. I'll send you a copy of the notice. Put the date and time on your calendar and don't worry about it. We show up, argue for a couple hours and we're done."

Two weeks later Jane decided she couldn't wait any longer. Even with her erratic cycle, she was definitely late for her period. She stopped at a drugstore for one of those early pregnancy test kits. Turns out should could have taken the test even sooner. One kit advertised that it worked just nine days past ovulation. Given her variable cycle, ovulation could have been the end of the third week in October, when she saw Jeff, or the first or even second week in November, when she was having sex pretty often with Roy. It was past the nine days either way. Jeff or Roy. And maybe nobody. She was thirty-one after all. Almost thirty-two. Didn't fertility rates drop off for women in their thirties?

Roy was home. That's how she should think of it, that it was his home now too. He hadn't given up his apartment yet, but her house was on its way to becoming their house. Jane went into the bathroom and took the test. Positive. It was positive. Her dream was coming true. A baby. At last, what Jane really wanted.

"Roy, honey, Roy!"

"What? Are you ok?"

"Look," Jane said, "look at this. It's positive. We're going to be parents, Roy. You and me. We're going to have a baby!"

"That's just awesome," Roy said. "Wow. A baby. You'll be the best mom. Oh wow. I'll need to call my folks."

The next day at work, Jane called Sherri.

"Sherri, it's Jane. I have more news."

"You've decided we don't have to wear pale blue bridesmaid dresses this time?"

"Funny. Very funny." But there it was again, that phrase. This time. As if she would be having a wedding every few years. This time. Last time. The other time. The one time. "No, I'm not calling about the wedding plans. I'm calling to tell you I'm having a baby."

"You and Roy are having a baby? Oh that's so great. I'm so happy for you. Are you feeling ok?"

"Pretty much so far. It's still early. I get a little sick sometimes, but not much yet. Not too bad."

"So are you moving the wedding date up?"

"We haven't set it yet. But I guess now we really need to get going with that. I did have one kind of wedding question for you."

"Ok, shoot."

"You know my dad died back when I was in college. Jeff's dad walked me down the aisle." Jane almost said it. She almost said that Jeff's dad walked her down the aisle last time. But she managed to stop herself. "And I don't have any uncles or brothers. Or male cousins even. None that I know well enough to ask to walk me down the aisle. And I was thinking about Arthur Ogden, but I think Roy is going to ask him to be his best man."

"I'm sure John would do it," Sherri said.

"Hauser? Gosh, that's sweet of you to offer, but I just don't feel I know him all that well either. I was actually thinking maybe Ansel. I mean he helped get Roy and me back together. So it would somehow be appropriate if he finished the job by walking me down the aisle. What do you think?"

"Ansel? You want Ansel?"

"Why not?"

"I don't know. He got you and Roy back together by hitting on you at the beach. Then by kissing you on the mouth and putting his hand on your ass. And he has a nickname for you. Like a special sweet name, just between the two of you. Lady Jane, right?"

"So?"

"So it just strikes me funny. I can't really say why."

"Do you have a phone number where I can reach him? I'd like to ask him and see what he says, that's all."

"Roy knows him. Why don't you have Roy ask him?"

"I don't know. I guess because it's me he'd be walking down the aisle, not Roy. So I think I should ask."

"Ok, it is your life, I guess. He's got a gig at the Thin Dime this weekend. You could probably catch him there. Or wait, I do have the number for his cell in my cell. You could just call him and then you wouldn't need to see him."

Jane did call. Roy was working on a job two hours outside of town. There had been unexpected delays and he stood to lose all the profit on the job if he missed the deadline. The client had put penalties in the contract for missed deadlines. As the deadline approached, Roy was working longer and longer hours and had finally just rented a room in a motel to save the commute time. He would be gone at least through the weekend, if not longer. Saturday night, Jane put a frozen entree in the microwave and ate it while watching a sitcom and part of an old movie on television. Then she called Ansel's number.

"Hey," Ansel said.

"Ansel," Jane said. "It's Jane Sidley."

"My dear Lady Jane. So I guess congratulations are in order. I hear the Lady is engaged to her knight. And a little lordship or ladyship is on the way, too. Such glad tidings."

"Listen, I wanted to ask you something."

"Well, it's like this, love. You reached me just as I am about to embark on a sound check here at the Thin Dime. As we speak, I am in fact seated at my drumset." She could hear him do a few rim shots for effect. "So I can't grant an audience to my dear lady love. In fact, the manager is looking like his drawers are in an uproar watching me talk on this phone instead of doing his soundcheck. But come down and see me if you want. We're playing sets until 2, but I get breaks. Tell the ugly guy at the door you're here to see me if he gives you any problem. But I can't see him turning away such a beauty, Jane."

Well, why not? It's not like she had a big night planned. Maybe some more television. Or work from the office. Or laundry. Jane tried on seventeen outfits. And put sixteen back in the closet. Then she was out the door in a shiny shirt with a collar, unbuttoned quite a few buttons down, to show a frilly cami. She could still wear her usual jeans, but they were already just a little tighter than usual. With high heeled boots, instead of her sensible shoes, she thought she looked good. Then she wondered why that mattered. Roy was out of town. But looking good isn't about Roy. It's a matter of personal pride. Taking pride in her appearance, that's all.

Jane was grateful that Ansel's band took a break pretty soon after she arrived and took a seat at the bar. She ordered a glass of ginger ale and in just a few minutes no less than three men tried to buy her another drink or start a conversation.

"To what do I owe this honor?" Ansel sat down on the bar stool next to Jane.

"Ansel. Hey there." Jane smiled. She liked seeing Ansel. His hair was shorter than it had been at the beach, but still long enough to have an unkempt look that must be a good look for the drummer in a bar that was known not just for reliable covers, but for edgy, original music too. His light brown eyes brightened as he took in Jane's smile.

"Hey Jane." He leaned in for a kiss.

"I need to ask you something."

"How about if I refill that? They don't mind giving me and my dates a free drink or two if I'm working. As long as I keep it reasonable and don't drink up the night's profits for them and then pass out on stage. The manager frowns on that."

"I'm not here as a date, I just needed to ask you something."

"Of course. You have a previous engagement. But let me get that. One more of whatever this is for my lady, and a double of Shlivistaeger for me."

"The thing is, I don't have any male relatives. My dad died when I was in college and I don't have any brothers or uncles."

"A girl with daddy issues on a night in November at the bar at the Thin Dime," Ansel said. "Life is good." He drained the entire glass of Shlivistaeger.

"I was wondering if you would walk me down the aisle. At the wedding. You know, give me away."

"Give you away. Reveal your true, inner Jane. Give everything away."

"What? Was that a yes or a no?"

"I always say yes to you, Lady Jane. Just let me know when and where."

"Ok, thanks so much. I'll call you with details. That's so great. It means so much to me."

Ansel signaled the bartender to refill his glass. If Jane had even one Shlivistaeger, she'd be out cold. And he was downing doubles. "Tell me this. What kind of music do you like?"

"Let me think. I have a piano at my house. An upright. I don't have much time to play these days, but once in a while I play easy piano arrangements of some oldies or showtunes. I like those. And there are some female vocalists I like. Hannah Wright, Jenny Overton, that kind of thing. And I sing a little myself. I mean I used to. I wrote a few songs back in high school. They were kind of folky, acoustic kind of songs."

"You write?"

"I have. I mean I did. A long time ago."

"The garage at my house is rigged for recording. Why not come by and we can record your songs?"

"It's been a long time."

"Too long." He leaned in close and looked more serious than Jane had ever seen him. When he spoke there was no flowery, 'lady this and dear lady that,' and his voice took on a flat, maybe midwestern-sounding accent that Jane hadn't heard from him before and couldn't quite place. "Writers write. It's like you've been too long without breathing if you're a writer who doesn't write. Come by and we'll go over your songs. It's a great way to start writing again, to go back to your old stuff. In a new way. You'll see. Come by any day next week, except I'm working 4 p.m. to 2 a.m. paramedic shifts, Tuesday and Thursday nights, and then I've got the weekend gigs here at the Thin Dime. Otherwise come by anytime. But you need to write. Listen to me, Jane. Writer's write. If you stop writing, I mean it, it's like you're not breathing."

CHAPTER THIRTEEN

*T*uesday night, Roy was still out of town and Jane sat down at her upright piano. She worked through simple arrangements of songs from the eighties. Then she flipped through a book of songs from a Broadway show. What had Ansel said? How not writing was like not breathing. If she was a writer. Was she a writer back in high school? Was she still one now?

Nobody had taken her songs seriously back then. But Ansel sure seemed serious now about wanting to work on her songs. As if there was a creative part of her that was still alive and needed to breathe. Was there? Jane had been all work and no play for so long. Was anything left of Jane the songwriter? Ansel thought so. Jane remembered Ansel leaning in toward her, his light eyes getting just a little brighter, and his flat accent coming through, as if the real Ansel was trying to reach the real Jane. The Jane that wrote songs. Was she still there to reach? Jane started playing her own songs on her upright piano, surprised that the songs were still there, in her mind and her fingers. Ansel was right, something was still there that she shouldn't ignore. How had he seen that? Jane sang the brokenhearted lyrics of her teen years. Why had she stopped writing?

Wednesday afternoon Jane walked out the large double doors of a country club after attending an Estates and Trusts Institute lunch in the Magnolia Room. She sat in her car in the country club parking lot thinking she should get back to the office. Instead she pulled out her cell phone and dialed the number for Ansel's cell.

"Hey," Ansel picked up on the first ring.

"Ansel, it's Jane," Jane said. "Jane Sidley."

"I know who you are."

"I was wondering if I might come by. Were you serious about recording some of my old songs?"

"How soon can you be here?"

Jane drove out to the address Ansel gave her. She would have been surprised that a semi-employed musician had a house, but Sherri had mentioned to her sometime that the house was how Ansel landed in this city in the first place. He had a sister who died and left him her house, and enough life insurance to pay off the mortgage. It was a detached house with an attached garage in a suburb with decent schools. It looked like something built in the post WWII baby boom, so the returning soldiers could marry their sweethearts and have a place to raise families.

Jane and Ansel played her songs in his garage for hours. They added his drums to her keyboards. They mixed tracks. Ansel played enough guitar that he could strum a little and sing some of his own songs so Jane could hear them too. She was able to figure out a few chords and a little melody here and there on the piano to go with his songs. When Jane finally looked at her watch it was almost 8:30 at night.

"This has been great," Jane said, "but I have to go. I didn't even tell my assistant I would be out. I need to check my e-mails at least."

"Take it easy," Ansel said. "Everyone's gone home. Whatever it is will keep until tomorrow. I've got some cold cuts in the fridge. Sit right there and I'll fix you a sandwich." Before Jane could say no, he was gone, into the kitchen. And then he was back, with two cans of soda and balancing two plates, each with sliced corned beef on rye bread.

"You like your day job? The lawyer gig?" She practically lived in her office and Ted wanted her to live and breathe her work even more, taking up golf or other hobbies to bring in more clients at the upper levels. And here was Ansel calling it a day job, as if its proper place was to support something creative, like gigs at the Thin Dime or something like that. He just assumed that a job in a big law firm was to support something she loved better. Was he right? And if he was, what did she love better? Her songs? Roy? The baby that was on the way?

Jane looked at Ansel. He had such an easy manner. Always so welcoming where Jane was concerned. Did it come from having a good balance of work and creativity in his life? Or was he just one of those people who could put other people at ease without even trying? It probably made him a good drummer, able to put the lead singer or guitarist at ease and then follow them seamlessly. And a good paramedic, staying calm and helping others to avoid panic, even in an emergency.

Ansel didn't say 'earth to Jane' or 'are you still there' as Jane sat thinking and looking at him. He did smile a little, but she didn't notice.

"Yeah, on the good days I do," Jane said. "On the good days I feel proud that I'm helping people protect their families and preserve their family businesses. I'm making sure that good, solid advice on complicated tax and other laws gets to the little people and not just the big dogs in the big cities. I feel like I make a positive difference at a reasonable price in a lot of people's lives."

"And the bad days?"

"On the bad days," Jane said, "I'm bored and I feel like I'm just spinning my wheels moving money around in useless ways for people who are difficult to deal with, ungrateful and demanding. And that I'm locked in this endless, useless and exhausting struggle to bill enough to stay ahead of the ever escalating costs of doing business, like the endless need for more money to pay for new computers and higher health insurance premiums for the support staff and so on. But the good days outnumber the bad days. And I do make a good living out of it. What about you? Do you like the work you do?"

"I love drumming. That's my real life. I love working with a band, writing and recording. And being a paramedic, that just started out as way to pay the bills when nothing was coming in with the music. I could pick up shifts here and there and pay my bills but still have time for the music. But the thing about the paramedic gig, is that I do like it. Like you said, I feel, on a good shift, that I've helped people and done something positive."

He took a bite of his sandwich, then a drink from his soda can. "The other thing I've realized about it, is that some of the same concentration I need for the music, I need even more with the paramedic work. Like when I'm up there on stage at the Thin Dime, maybe it looks really free-flowing, but it's not. I'm concentrating on staying with the singer or the lead guitarist, no matter where they go and I've got to remember every riff. It's a lot of discipline and concentration. Same with the paramedic shifts, but even ten times more sometimes. I've got to be focused, in the moment, every minute. If I put on my gloves and I'm thinking about something else, I can miss seeing a tear in them, and that could cost me my life. I've got to stay on, keep focused, just like in a tight band, but even more so. And I need to be aware of the other paramedics or EMT's in that ambulance. Everyone has to be together, in tune to each other, a lot like playing good music, and that much more in an emergency. I mean sometimes I get bored too, like you said, but on good days, I love drumming, and the paramedic gig is good too."

Jane nodded. So it just looked easy when Ansel was up on stage or with other people, but he was really concentrating and staying focused. That easy manner came somehow from his interior focus and concentration, while Jane wandered around in her mind and showed the world an uptight exterior. She looked at Ansel, seated on a folding chair with his plate resting on his knees. Maybe focusing on her songs could be good for her. She had been here for hours, after all, really concentrating on her songs and she wasn't tired at all. She was having a good time. They ate their sandwiches in companionable silence for a few moments.

"Did you grow up around here?" Ansel said.

"Yeah, in a suburb a lot like this one, not too far from here. You?"

"Buffalo, New York."

"Cold winters up there. I bet you don't miss that."

"Not now, I wouldn't want to deal with winters like that now, but those winters were great when I was a kid. My dad had a toboggan. Not a hat, but like a sled you could have a bunch of people sit on, in a row, and it had a curved front. The park near us had these towers with chutes on them and my sister and my parents and me would all climb up, dragging the toboggan and we'd pile on it and this park ranger would line it up at the top of the chute and then pull back this lever and we'd go flying down the chute and down this hill like a ski slope only for sleds and toboggans. My stomach would drop like it does riding on a roller coaster. The winters were a blast when I was a kid."

"So how did you land here?"

"My sister moved out here for a job. She died in a car wreck. Just like that. It didn't have to happen, but it did. She was working in the main office of this company, Integrated Products, right downtown, doing something for the top executives, at first, but then she got transferred to the company's plant in Westgate, and it's a two hour drive from here. We were never sure why she got transferred and my parents wanted her to quit. But she was never a quitter, not at anything. She always saw things through. Then driving home, on a stretch of road with lots of sharp turns and hills, she died in a bad wreck. Her car went off the road on a curve and down an embankment. The car was a total wreck. It was awful to see the pictures."

Oh no. Ansel's sister had been the young woman Oliver had harassed six years ago. And whose death in a car wreck Oliver had celebrated. Well, he didn't celebrate her death exactly, but it was her death that led to the harassment complaint getting dropped and that's why he had a big party. At least Jane had helped Adelaide take the eventual control of Integrated away from Oliver over it. But that wouldn't bring back Ansel's sister.

"I mean," Ansel said, "it's so hard not to think, why couldn't she have been in some other car on some other road on some other day? But that's useless. She was there and that's what happened. We lost her. And there's nothing to change it, no way to go back. We lost her just like that. My parents were hit the hardest. It's been six years, and I guess they're doing ok, but it's like something's gone inside of them."

"I'm so sorry."

"Thanks, I didn't mean to bring up anything so sad, but that's how I got here. My sister left me her house and I thought about selling it, but I couldn't decide. I didn't want to move here, but selling her house felt wrong. It was like that last piece left of her life. She had some company life insurance that she left to me and it was enough to pay off the mortgage. So I thought I'd move here, and live here a little while and then sell the house, once I was ready. But I found people who were doing some amazing music down here. I found my band. So I stayed."

"Was she your only sibling?"

"Yeah, and we were close. She was two years older and you'd expect a brother and sister that close in age maybe to fight a lot, you know, sibling rivalry, but we didn't. We did stuff together, like go to scary movies. She was the first person I smoked weed with. I miss her so much. You would have liked her. Her name was Dorothea. We all called her Thea. She was named for the famous photographer, Dorothea Lange. My parents were into photography so she was named Dorothea and I was named Ansel, like the photographer Ansel Adams."

"I'm sure I would have liked her."

"You have any brothers or sisters?"

"No. Only child."

"No more at home like you. One of a kind."

"If you don't mind my asking, were any of your parents or grandparents from India or Pakistan maybe? Or maybe you have some African American or Native American ancestry? I'm so pale I burn every summer even though I hardly get outdoors much and, again, I hope you don't mind my saying this, but your skin is such a great color. And your hair, where did you get that wonderful wavy hair of yours?" Telling Ansel she liked his looks could be counted, in some circles, as flirting. Was she flirting? She had just gotten engaged to Roy. No, she was just asking a simple question. Not flirting. "My hair is straight as a board."

"I have no idea, dear. My parents are Mort and Eleanor Kaminski, longtime residents of the Queen City, Buffalo, New York. I think their ancestry is maybe Polish or German or I don't know, something like that. But I was adopted. I don't know anything about my biological parents."

"You didn't want to find them?"

"I don't need to look to find my parents. I know some people do, but not me. My parents are always right there for me. Mort and Eleanor Kaminski. Best parents in the world."

"Was Thea adopted too?"

"No, but it was a difficult pregnancy. Mom has diabetes and kidney problems. They almost lost Mom and Thea both during the pregnancy, that's what I've been told. The doctors didn't think my mom should risk a second pregnancy. Mom didn't want to risk it, if it might mean she'd die and leave Dad alone to raise Thea. So they adopted me. But it's just the same, Thea and I are their children. They don't think of me as the one they adopted, I'm their son, period, and Thea was their daughter. And they're not my adoptive parents, they're my parents."

"I thought about adopting a child. When I was broken up with Roy, I heard my biological clock ticking and thought about adoption as a possibility for me."

"That's great. That you even thought about it. And now you've got Roy's baby coming along."

"Can I tell you something? I haven't told this to anyone, and I just need to tell somebody." Jane couldn't believe that she was about to tell Ansel about Jeff, Roy and her baby's uncertain paternity. She hadn't even told her mother or Sherri. But she wanted to tell Ansel. Of all the people she knew, Jane felt Ansel was the only one who would understand. Was that true? She hadn't known him for very long and really hadn't spent much time with him. So could that be true or was she just desperate to tell someone? Hard to tell. No, no, it wasn't. Jane knew, from deep inside, that it was easy to tell. Ansel would understand. Jane was certain of it.

"Sure."

"When Roy and I were broken up, I wanted a baby. That was when I thought about adoption. But I felt like I was really alone and not getting any younger. And I was afraid so I took a short cut. I did something really stupid. A week before Roy called and wanted to get back together, a week before I had any idea I'd ever even see Roy ever again, let alone get back together with him, I slept with my ex-husband, Jeff. Oh God, I can't believe it. Even sitting here saying it, it's so unbelievable that I did that. But it wasn't cheating, not on Roy anyway. We were broken up. But the thing of it is, I don't know if Roy is the father. This baby could be Jeff's baby. The timing makes it possible so that it could be either one of them. And I haven't told Roy. It's just eating me up not telling him, but every time I think I will, I think what if he hates the baby? What if he would have loved the baby if I hadn't told him, but I tell him and then he hates me and the baby? And besides that, if we did a paternity test, and Jeff was the father, I'm afraid Jeff would have rights, you know, visitation rights. Custodial rights. Especially if the baby is born before the wedding. I mean what if I told Roy and he wanted to put off the wedding until the baby was born and we could do the test? What a mess."

"You need to come clean with Roy. If he loves you, he'll love your baby no matter what. I would."

"You   wouldn't   care?"

"I would care if you cheated on me. Slept with another man while you were seeing me. But you didn't do that. The fool broke up with you."

"But you wouldn't care if you were raising a child that wasn't yours?"

"Raising the child would make him my child. Remember Mort and Eleanor Kaminski? Greatest parents in the world? They're my parents. I'm their child. But you need to come clean with Roy. Every day you let pass and don't tell him what's going on with you, that's like another lie between you two. You can't build your castle on lies, Lady Jane."

Roy was back in town and back in Jane's house a few days later. There were opportunities for her to come clean and tell him about the paternity issues that weighed on her mind. She could have told him as they sat at dinner together, night after night. She could have told him on the day he finished the railing, completing the deck. He was so happy to tell her the railing was up, sturdy and secure. She could have told him as they drove home from Anita's house after a wonderful family Thanksgiving. But she didn't. She let all her chances to come clean, just pass right by.

CHAPTER FOURTEEN

*J*ane walked over to the offices of Jerris and Langer in mid-December for the mediation the court had ordered her to attend with Jeff. She wasn't feeling well. She thought the six block walk would do her good, but she felt cold, tired and more than a little nauseous. At least Jeff wouldn't know about the baby. She wasn't showing and Jeff didn't have contact with anyone who knew about her pregnancy. Jane's cell rang. It was Roy.

"Hi honey. What's up?"

"Since I've finished that big job, it's been a little slow. Can you knock off early? I'll come pick you up and we can go get a drink, well, I'll drink, you can have a soda, over at Fernanza's and then maybe we can have an early dinner somewhere and then who knows?"

"Sounds so good. But I'm on my way to that horrible mediation with Jeff. I'm walking over there now."

"When do you think you'll be done?"

"They said it won't go past five. If it looks like we're making progress, which I really don't think is possible, they'll schedule more time another day. But with or without an agreement, we'll be done for the day by five."

"How about if you call if you get done earlier than that, otherwise since you don't have your car, I'll just plan to get you at five. Where will you be?"

Jane gave him the address. She wished she could have a drink at Fernanza's. She had a feeling she was going to really want one after the mediation.

"I'm Jane Sidley," Jane said to the receptionist when she reached Jerris and Langer's offices. "I'm here for the mediation with Mike Jerris."

"Yes, Ms. Sidley. They're in the main conference room. It's through the door there and then just down the hall on your left."

"Is my lawyer Harvey Whitman here yet?"

"Yes. I just sent him back to the conference room."

If the receptionist had said that Harvey wasn't there yet, Jane was going to wait for him by the reception desk or even outside in the cold if she had to. No way she was going back there to the conference room without him. She knew enough not to go into any part of legal proceeding where she was a party, without someone to look out for her interests. Not only would she not do her own brain surgery, she wouldn't be foolish enough to do her own legal representation. Even professionals need professional help. And besides, she was dreading seeing Jeff again.

The door to the conference room was open and Jane saw Jeff, with a lawyer she hadn't met, sitting at the far end of the conference table, with Harvey sitting closer to the door. Jane walked through the conference room door and Harvey stood up.

"Ron," Harvey said, addressing the lawyer sitting with Jeff, "this is Jane Sidley. Jane, this is Ron Silver. He's here today representing Jeff Rogers."

Ron Silver stood up and held out his hand. Jane leaned over the table and shook it.

"Ron Silver."

"Jane Sidley."

"Hi there Jane," Jeff said. He did not get out of his seat.

"Hello Jeff."

"I hear congratulations are in order," Jeff said. "I hear you're getting married and you already have a bun in the oven. All the best with the new little family. What's his name, Roy Something, he must be a real proud papa. I know I would be."

Jeff's grin was ominous. How had he heard so much about her? Harvey looked like he wasn't sure if he needed to intervene. Jane's nausea was rapidly getting worse.

"Is there a ladies' room I could use?"

"I think I saw one out the door and to the left," Harvey said. "Just down the hall."

These days, Jane always felt better after she threw up. When she got back to the conference room, Mike Jerris had joined the group, sitting along one side of the long table, midway between the opposing camps.

"I'm Mike Jerris," he said to Jeff's lawyer.

"Ron Silver representing Jeff Rogers."

Mike turned to Harvey.

"Harvey Whitman representing Jane Sidley,"

"I'm glad each of you could attend this mediation today," Mike said. "Here we have a chance to take control of the process. To craft a result that meets with everyone's approval. If we can't reach agreement today, and that often happens, as no one is required to reach an agreement in mediation, then someone else will take control. An order will be entered by a judge and the terms of your property settlement won't be decided by you, but by a decision-maker in our court system." It already was. Decided by a decision-maker in our court system. Years ago. What on earth are we doing here?

"To start," Mike said, "I'd like to give each of the parties here today a chance to make a statement to the group. Tell me why you are here today and what you hope to accomplish. What you see as the most important points of conflict. How you feel they might be resolved. Give us, as a group here together, an idea of your feelings about the matters in contention today and what your priorities are. I don't want to get into an argument or discussion at this point. Just let's have each of the parties themselves, not counsel, make a statement. Then we'll move into separate conference rooms and I'll meet with one side and then the other and you can also confer with counsel in private. Then we'll meet back here together and discuss this together and hopefully reach some consensus on at least some issues. Then we'll repeat the process for any remaining issues and see if an agreement can be reached on all points. Jeff, as the petitioner here, why don't you start?"

"What we have here is your changed circumstances," Jeff said. "Jane got the house in the divorce, and an acquaintance I have in the real estate business tells me in this market, that place would sell for sure. People want to live in that neighborhood. I liked it. So that house is worth even more and I don't think we went over that, like we should of, when we did the property settlement. I didn't get a fair shake on that. And when I met Jane, she was just a law student, not a lawyer. And that's where she's making bigger money all the time. My alimony was just from her salary back then and it stopped. Well, I got a wife and baby to support and so there's still a need here. I'm still entitled. And she's got more now, a bigger cut at that firm of hers, and I'm gettin' none of it, even though we go back to when she was in law school and it's all coming from that degree she's got."

"Thank you Jeff," Mike said. "Jane?"

"I have no idea why I'm here," Jane said. "I don't owe Jeff anything. I paid him for half the house based on its value at the time of the divorce."

"But not for the upside," Jeff said. "You still owe me for that."

"Jeff," Mike said. "You need to let Jane make her statement without interruption."

"But she's wrong," Jeff said. "Sitting there like some kind of big deal. Don't forget I know all about you, Jane. More than that so-called fiancé of yours."

"Ron, you need to control your client," Harvey said.

"Jeff, calm down," Ron Silver said. "It's just an opening statement. Nothing's being decided. Let her have her say."

"And I gave him half my other assets," Jane said. "In the divorce he filed. Not me. Because he was having an affair. Also not me. Then I paid alimony until he remarried. I don't owe him anything."

"You owe me," Jeff said.

"Shut up, Jeff," Ron said.

"Hey, you're supposed to be on my side."

"So I'm telling you to shut up," Ron said. "So shut up and let her finish and we can get on with this."

"The only other thing I want to say is that I don't see any grounds whatsoever for reopening the property settlement here. It's done and over. From where I sit, I don't see any legal basis for this proceeding or this mediation. I don't see that we have anything   to   mediate   about   here   today."

"Ok, thank you both. Very good." Mike shuffled some papers and made some notes. "Now let's separate into conference rooms and I'll meet briefly with each side separately, then you can confer by yourselves and then we'll meet back here in twenty minutes or so."

Jane and Harvey sat in a small conference room while Mike met with Jeff and Ron. There was coffee and water. Jane poured herself some water. Harvey got a cup of coffee.

"Why are we even here Harvey?"

"Is that an existential question?"

"No, it's a legal one. This whole thing is ridiculous. I mean what are we supposed to be discussing right now? I'm not giving that leech another dime and even though I don't know much about family law, I can't think of any reason why I'd have to give him a red cent."

"I agree, I agree. But if we go through the motions here, and we can't agree, but in good faith, whatever that means, it'll be sent back to the courts and then maybe I can get the whole thing dismissed."

"Great. I'm going back to the ladies' room."

Jeff was in the hallway, coming back from the men's room.

"Cassie's sister knows the sister of that old guy you're marrying," Jeff said. "And I heard right away that you had that bun in the oven. Do the math, babe. If you don't want me talking to that old man of yours, or asking for a paternity test, you better play ball with me here today. You understand me?"

Jane had been afraid that Jeff would say something like this, but now that she heard it, she just felt blind anger. Rage. Absolute fury that anyone would threaten her with anything having to do with her baby.

"You trying to blackmail me? That's a felony, you SOB. I'll have you arrested. You're not getting one dime. You don't scare me."

Harvey, Ron and Mike came running into the hall.

"Ok, ok," Mike said. "I see we're airing the issues here. That can be helpful, but I think we need to take it down a notch." Mike managed to wedge himself between Jeff and Jane. "Let's all calm down and come together again back in the main conference room."

Three hours later they had reached no agreement. Jane held firm that there were no grounds for reopening the settlement. Jeff was adamant that he was owed something more. Mike said he would tell the court no agreement could be reached and that the case needed to proceed in the court system. As they passed through the door connecting the reception area with the hallway to the conference rooms, Jane saw Roy sitting in the chairs near the reception desk. She was really glad to see a friendly face after the ordeal of the mediation.

"Hi there." Jane said, smiling at him.

Roy stood up and gave her a kiss. "Ready to go?"

"You don't know the half of it."

"So this is the old guy," Jeff said. "I warned you Jane. Hey, old man, that bun she's got in the oven, you sure it's yours? That ass of hers was mine in October."

Roy looked confused for a few seconds and then he hit Jeff hard, knocking him back into the reception desk. Harvey grabbed Roy, trying to pin his arms behind him. Ron pulled Jeff up from the floor.

"Through here," Mike said, opening the door to the conference room hallway. "There's a back door at the end of the hall that leads out to the parking lot." Ron hustled Jeff through the door Mike was holding open. Mike closed it behind them.

"You open that door," Roy said. "I'm going to tear that asshole apart." Harvey was losing his grip on Roy's arms.

"Take it outside," Mike said. "If you want to rip him apart, you'll have to go around to the parking lot. Too late, there he goes." They saw Ron driving a car with Jeff in the passenger seat, speeding past the front window.

"Roy, let's get out of here," Jane said. She was pale. Jeff had really done it. He told Roy. She should have known he would make good on his threats.

"You ok?" Harvey said to Jane.

"Yes," Jane said. "I'll call you and we'll talk. I'm fine. Really."

Roy and Jane sat in Roy's truck where he'd parked it on the street near Mike's office. The light was gone. Roy didn't put the key in the ignition.

"What your ex said in there," Roy said. "About October and your ass. What was that about?"

"We were broken up," Jane said. "You said you didn't want to see me anymore and I wasn't dating anybody. Not you, not anybody. And I'm thirty-one, almost thirty-two. I always expected to be a mother by now. And there I was, wanting a baby, with no prospects."

"So you slept with Jeff?" Roy's face was all shadows in the

dim light from the streetlights and storefronts nearby. "It's true, then?"

"Wait, listen. Let me explain. I looked into adoption a little, I wanted a baby so badly. But it's a lot of paperwork. It takes years."

"You slept with him to avoid paperwork? Jesus. So what did you do, call him up and proposition him?"

"You and I were broken up. He came by the house to talk about this meeting we had scheduled with Gordon Wendell."

"You did it at our house?"

"It was just my house back then. We were broken up. I didn't know we'd get back together just a week later."

"A week? Just a week? So it really could be Jeff's baby. Or mine."

"I know I should have told you the baby might be his, but I was hoping it would just be yours, I mean no matter who the biological father is. I was afraid you wouldn't love the baby or me anymore. I know I should have told you. Ansel said I should have."

"Ansel? You told Ansel and not me? Did you sleep with him too? Is he in the running as a possible father of this baby?"

"No, no. It's just that Ansel said he was adopted, so I wanted to talk to him about it. I thought he might know something about loving a child even if there's no blood tie. His parents did that with him."

Roy didn't say anything for a few minutes. He just looked straight ahead, out through the windshield. Then he turned toward Jane. "I'm going to need some time to think about this. Not just about the baby, but about you not telling me. A marriage has to be built on trust. I'll drop you home and I think I need to stay at my apartment for a while."

Jane started to cry. "Do you want the ring back?"

"No, I'm not calling off the wedding. I still love you, I just need some time to think. I'll take you home. But I can't stay with you in that house tonight."

Roy dropped Jane off and drove away. She sat down at the piano. She played a few random keys. Then a few more. Tears dropped down onto the keys. But then Jane dried her eyes and when to get a pencil and paper. She started writing down lyrics.

She went back to the keyboard and felt her grief pouring out as she played her new song. About love and loss. About wind and rain and tears and darkness. She called her land line with her cell phone and sang into her voicemail so she wouldn't forget any of it. She jotted down the basic chords. She couldn't believe she'd written a new song. Her first since high school. Maybe someday she could even sing it to her baby. Her baby. However things turned out with Roy, she had her heart's desire.

Ansel Kaminski. There was his name the next day on her caller id at work.

"Jane Sidley."

"This is your partner in musical crime. Calling to see if we could work a little more on your old songs. I'm thinking if we work up an arrangement for guitar and keyboards, I could see if my band could do one or two of them at the Thin Dime. They're not dance tunes, but when it gets really late, sometimes we can do some more serious, acoustic folky stuff."

"I wrote a new one," Jane said. "Last night I wrote a new song."

"Hey, the lady reigns supreme. Way to go, Jane. Love to hear it. When can you come by?"

Jane felt a pang of guilt about taking another afternoon off. Her personal life was having an effect on her hourly productivity numbers at the law firm. She'd missed her weekly billables target several weeks in a row. Time off for the mediation, time with Ansel, it was starting to add up. And she'd need time off to work on the wedding, wouldn't she? If there still was a wedding. .

"How about Wednesday afternoon?"

"See you then Lady Jane."

By Wednesday, Jane had only heard twice from Roy. Two short, tense phone calls. He still he loved her but he couldn't come back home to her house just yet. And each time she pleaded for a chance to talk things out, he said he wasn't ready. He didn't want to talk about it. Not yet.

Jane drove over to Ansel's house. She could hear drumming coming from his garage. She went around to a side door that connected the garage to a small yard. She tapped on the glass panes in the door when Ansel paused in his drumming. He came right to the door and gave her a hug.

"So glad you're here. I can't wait to hear your new tune, sweetheart."

Jane thought, for an instant, that coming to a single man's house, especially one who had just given her a hug and called her sweetheart, was not the best idea if she was hoping to patch things up with Roy. She was still hoping he would forgive her and they could get on with the wedding plans, right? She pulled the paper with the lyrics and the chords out of her pocket. Ansel looked it over and picked up his guitar.

"Something like this?" He strummed some of the chords she had on the paper.

Jane sat down at the keyboards. "More like this." Jane put some fat piano chords underneath a melody. She started singing the lyrics from memory. When she finished Ansel was staring at her.

"That was so incredible. So beautiful. What made you write it? I mean, it's great, but so much sorrow."

"Oh. Yeah. It is sad. But that's what's going on with me right now." Jane was determined not to cry. "Roy found out about the possibility of Jeff being the father of our baby. He's staying at his apartment for a while. Says he needs time to think."

"Are you guys still getting married?"

"Roy said he just needed time to think. That he wasn't calling off the wedding. But I've hardly heard from him, so I don't know." She couldn't help it. She started to cry.

"Hey, hey there." Ansel sat down on keyboard bench beside Jane, put his arm around her shoulder and handed her a roll of toilet paper from an open pack on a shelf in the garage. "Don't cry. It'll be alright. He'll get over it. Things will work out. You'll be Jane Adams, wow, Jane Adams, really, in no time."

"That's part of why I'm crying. It's not just Roy. Now I'm not sure I want to marry him." There. She'd said it. She hadn't even really admitted it to herself, but now she was telling Ansel. And she knew he would understand, even if she didn't really understand herself. He always did. She looked down at the ring. "He didn't want me to give the ring back but now I'm thinking I want to send it back. I just don't know anymore."

"Could be the baby hormones messing with your mind. Get

some rest. Let it sit for a while. Nobody's chasing you. You'll figure things out."

Jane looked at Ansel. She was always questioning her own instincts, her ability to know her own mind. But Ansel never wavered. He knew she could write again and now he knew she'd figure out what she really wanted. It was like he could see and speak to a part of her that she'd lost touch with somewhere along the way. As if she was disconnected, in pieces somehow, and he kept speaking to her as if she was whole again. And if he could see it, maybe she could too. Maybe that was what St. Paul meant about hope. That thinking something was possible, and acting as if it really was possible, that somehow, it changed things. Made things better.

A few days later Anita invited both Roy and Jane to come see her son's swim meet. It was the last one before his school's Christmas break would start at the end of the week. Anita thought seeing each other might bring them closer to getting over this hurdle and back on track for a wedding. In Anita's opinion, the sooner the better in terms of the wedding date as Jane would be starting to show in January or February at the latest. These two absolutely needed to patch it up and get married before the baby was born, Anita was sure of that. A baby took precedence over everything.

Even if Jeff turned out to be the biological father, Roy needed to step up and be the real father, making a home with Jane and the baby. He needed to get over himself and forgive Jane for the sake of the baby. Which might be Roy's baby after all, and if Roy didn't quit pouting, he'd lose Jane for good and then Anita would be lucky if she saw her new niece or nephew once or twice before the child was off to college. And Anita's parents would have to fight for grandparents' visitation rights. Anita had seen people talk on television about how heartbreaking that could be. Anita didn't want her parents to have to go through anything like that.

While seeing Jane might have helped Roy, it didn't help Jane. That is, it didn't help in terms of making wedding bells ring. Seeing Roy sitting there on the tiered metal benches by the side of the pool, so obviously disinterested in his nephew's swim meet, Jane reflected on how many times that same disinterest had come between them. To be fair, her reasons for marrying him were more practical than passionate. This could work out. Over the long haul. That's what she'd been thinking. Was it just a reaction to her huge mistake in marrying Jeff that she was doing something so deliberate, almost plodding along into marriage instead of being anything like swept off her feet?

"Can we go outside and talk?" Jane said. "Maybe take a walk around the parking lot? I know it's cold out, but not too bad."

The air in the parking lot felt cold on her skin after the heat and humidity of sitting inside by the pool.

"Are you ok walking out here?" Roy said. "We could sit in my truck and run the heater."

"No, I'm good." Jane pulled the big solitaire diamond ring off her finger. "I want to give you this ring back. I just don't think this is working out for us."

Roy didn't take the ring. "I just need a little time to sort things out. This is a big deal finding out not just that the baby might be Jeff's, but that you weren't going to tell me. You can understand my needing a little time to think about things. But I don't want to break it off with you."

"But I want to break it off. I'm sorry, but that's how I feel. And it's not that you needed time to think. Sure you did. This is my fault here. But I just don't see a future for us anymore. I just don't." She put the ring in his hand and pressed it closed into a fist.

"That baby might still be mine. I'm going to want a paternity test and then visitation if the baby's mine."

There it was. That was the problem. If he had said he wanted visitation without any test, no matter what, she'd have married him. She'd have begged to marry him. But he didn't say that. He only wanted visitation if the baby was made with his sperm. She knew she'd made the right decision. Just like Ansel predicted. She would figure it out. And she had.

"Sure," Jane said. "We'll do the test as soon as we can. If it comes up heads, you win visitation."

Chapter Fifteen

*T*he next day in the office Corinne Eberly stopped Jane in the hall. "Hold up, I need a pow wow with you."

"What's up?"

"New case," Corinne said. "Huge. I mean huge. Defense work as local counsel for Regents Mark Life. Complicated mess. Criminal indictments, SEC complaints, state insurance commissioner problems, plus plaintiffs' lawyers swarming and the possibility of an enormous class action suit. We might need your help."

"I'm not much on litigation defense," Jane said. "And I'm up to my eyeballs with wills and trusts right now. I can't seem to get any associates interested in helping with it. They all want to be trial lawyers in case you haven't noticed."

"No, that's the thing," Corinne said. "This case involves your kind of estate planning stuff. Something called 'SOLI.' It stands for 'Stranger Owned Life Insurance.' Where somebody is maybe dying and a company buys their life insurance at a discount so the dying person has cash before they die and the company then collects on the policy, making a profit when the person does die. The sooner they die, the bigger the profit. And while that's legit, here the lawsuits and the indictments are over allegations that Regents Mark Life Insurance and Life's End, the SOLI company, were allegedly doing something under the table with splitting commissions with attorneys to get the attorneys to steer dying clients with Regents Mark policies to Life's End. Life's End buys the insurance policies at a discount from the dying people and then Regents Mark was taking a cut of the fees for packaging and selling shares in the policies as derivatives or in some kind of mutual fund. And the worst allegations are that Regents Mark and Life's End got together on some phony projections on life expectancy. To fool people into paying more for the derivative shares in the policies. I don't understand it all yet, but that's why we need you on this. You understand these things and the tax rules and all that. And you won't believe who got indicted here in town. The Trusts and Estates partners at Fembrick Latterly and Richmond, Ellis and Watts. And this insurance guy Gordon Wendell. And your ex, Jane, Jeff Rogers. He's under indictment too."

"Jeff is under indictment," Jane said, "along with Gordon Wendell and Carl Dennison of Fembrick Latterly and Annette McHenry of Richmond, Ellis and Watts?"

"That's right."

"Gordon Wendell and Jeff I can see getting indicted," Jane said. "It was inevitable with those two, my ex especially. But Carl and Annette, I just can't believe it. Carl and Annette are the last people on earth I could imagine getting mixed up in something like this."

"I guess you never know. Actually the last person I'd expect to get mixed up in something like this is you. So I'm assuming we don't have any exposure on this here at the firm. Right?"

"I do have clients with Regents Mark life insurance policies. But I never split commissions with Wendell or any agent in exchange for steering business to Regents Mark. Wendell asked me to, on the phone and once in a meeting with my ex, where they also discussed the SOLI products and Life's End selling some kind of derivatives or mutual fund shares in policies they bought from dying people. But I wouldn't bite. No way was I getting involved in any of it. I turned them down flat. I didn't think the existing law on it was entirely clear at the time, but it didn't just didn't sound right to me."

"So your ex is an agent for Life's End?"

"Last I heard he wanted to be an agent for Life's End, working the system every step of the way. He'd seek out people who had life insurance policies and who needed cash, and offer to have Life's End buy their policies at a discount and he'd get a commission for that. Then he'd work somehow with brokers to sell the shares in the pools of policies after Life's End bought them up, and get a cut of the fees from that. He wanted to associate with Wendell's agency so it would give him more credibility. So he wouldn't look like some guy selling magazines or something out of his car, I think he said. But I thought Wendell said no to taking Jeff on as an agent, but maybe he changed his mind, I don't know. I absolutely didn't know there was anything going on in terms of playing with the figures on life expectancy for the people cashing in their policies, to get the price up on the derivatives, but it wouldn't surprise me."

"This mess is having a huge impact on Regents Mark. They have their fingers in a lot of pies worldwide and this thing is shaking the markets as everyone starts to lose confidence in Regents Mark. So they're willing to throw a ton of money at defense costs. We should be able to keep at least half of our litigation associates busy with discovery on this for at least a year or two, maybe ten. Who knows? This is huge, huge. I'm going to tell the associates to come to you if they have technical questions about how SOLI and all this works. Ok?"

"I guess. I mean I'm not kidding about being already up to my eyeballs in work. But who else is there? I suppose they'll have to come to me. Wow, I just can't get over it about Carl Dennison and Annette McHenry getting indicted. That could have been me. Wendell asked me I don't know how many times to take part of his commissions under the table in exchange for steering business his way. Do you ever feel like even doing your best, even trying to be as careful and honest as you can, that you're still walking through a minefield with bullets whistling past your head?"

"No, I never feel like bullets are whistling past my head. If you're having feelings like that, or hearing things, we do have the firm Employee Confidential Counseling Program. You could talk to someone. I mean if you felt you needed to."

"I meant that as a figure of speech. I'm not actually hearing bullets."

"It's completely confidential. I'm on the Well Employees Committee and while we do get a report on how many people use the program, there's no names."

"Thanks," Jane said. "Good to know."

Jane knew Corinne would be making a bee line straight to Ted's office to drop hints that Jane was having emotional problems, possibly involving mental health. She wouldn't mention the bullets whistling specifically, because he might recognize that as a stock phrase and call bullshit on Corinne. No, she would say Jane said some things, just things, nothing specific, that might signal underlying mental health status issues. Vague, yes, but it would stick. It would be added forever to the list of reasons why Jane should not make junior equity partner any time soon. And why Jane's compensation as even senior non-equity partner should be set slightly below the average attorney at her level. Jane's terrific, they'd say, but a little unstable. Didn't they hear that somewhere, they'd say, when her pay came before the Compensation Committee for discussion. Corinne would leave her gossipy whispers in Ted's ear, and just a little more here and there. It would spread like wildfire through the firm. Probably hit the firm's satellite offices by noon.

Those idiot consultants the firm hired, they told her what to do about garbage like this. How Jane wouldn't be so vulnerable to office politics and maneuvering, like these rumors today, if Jane spent more time with her colleagues at the firm. Jane didn't think she could stomach another lunch with Corinne but the idiot consultants were probably right. More time with Corinne and attorneys at the firm like her would reduce offensive maneuvers and allow Jane to successfully play defensive office politics. And four hours a week playing golf with any attorney who sat on the firm's Compensation Committee would give Jane a better chance of higher pay than ten more hours a week working at her desk.

But the work was there, undone, with clients yelling at her to get their work done faster. Who had these extra hours to spend on a golf course or go to long lunches and schmooze other attorneys in the firm? Jane managed to take just a little time off for the mediation and to see Ansel and now she was behind on her hours and her clients were howling about unfinished work.

How did Corinne find the time this morning to head to Ted's office to spread rumors about Jane? Would Corinne bill that time to the Regents Mark litigation defense file? Is that how it's done? Jane wanted no part of that. But even so, even if Corinne is padding her hours with time spent on office politics, there's still the actual work that isn't getting done while she's going office to office to talk trash. How do the Corinnes of the world manage to keep up with their actual workload? Jane had no idea. And hadn't Jane heard that Corinne's five year old son was

ADD or maybe ADHD? Imagine keeping up with that and having an affair and still staying on top of office gossip and actual legal work. Amazing. Unless Corinne was swiping some of her kid's medications? Could Corinne's amazing ability to speed through her day come from prescription speed? Jane heard her phone ringing and went into her office.

Thank goodness. I'm running poor Corinne down for wasting time spreading rumors and here I am standing around wasting even more time not even spreading them, just running them around in my head. And when I'm behind on my billables, no less. Better get back to something productive. She reached across her desk and grabbed the receiver.

"Jane Sidley."

"Jane, it's Harvey. I have some bad news on the motion to dismiss I filed. They didn't go ahead and dismiss Jeff's petition to reopen the property settlement in your divorce. Instead they set it up for hearing on the motion to dismiss. I know you're going to be unhappy about having to go to another hearing and see Jeff, especially after how badly the mediation turned out for you, but I'm really confident, well pretty confident anyway, that this will be the end of it. If you can just go to this one last hearing, I think we'll have this thing beat."

"A hearing?" No way. Not a hearing. "I have to see that weasel again?"

"I think it will be the end of it, really. I'm asking for dismissal with prejudice. It'll make it really hard for Jeff to try to reopen this again down the road."

"Are you serious? He can do this again?"

"Guess that wasn't the best time to mention that. But let's stay in the moment, and not worry about things that might never happen. Let's just deal with this hearing."

"Ok, ok. You're right. One more hearing. I can deal with it, really I can. Send the notice to me. I'll meet you outside the courtroom a few minutes before the hearing."

Jane sat down in her desk chair and put her head in her hands. Another hearing? She knew how slow the legal system could be, but couldn't Harvey just get this dismissed without another hearing? For heaven's sake, she'd only been married to Jeff for four years, and he got half her assets plus alimony. She swiveled around in her chair to look out the window. The winter sunshine was brilliant, but showed every streak. The window washers wouldn't be back for months. At least Jane didn't have to work like that, up there with ropes at heights like that. How did people manage up so high with so little to protect them? Her office was nine floors up. At least she didn't have to risk her life cleaning windows on skyscrapers, but could make a living inside at a nice desk in a fancy law firm. And if she wanted to keep it that way, she needed to get some actual work done.

Jane pulled into her driveway after work just in time to get her cell phone out of her purse and answer it before it stopped ringing.

"Lady Jane, it's Ansel."

"Hi."

"Listen, dear, I hate to do this, but I have to ask you a favor. Could you look after my two cats? They're not much trouble, and good natured, but the thing is I'm going to be out of town until March or maybe April."

"What's going on? I mean, I love cats, and I'm glad to look after your two, but when are you leaving?"

"Already gone. I'm calling from a cab in Miami. East End got this great gig. Steady work for months on a cruise ship. Some band canceled last minute and Donny got a call late last night. The only flight we could get to Miami in time to meet the ship was out of Atlanta, so we got in Donny's van and drove most of the night. Caught a 6 a.m. flight from Atlanta to Miami. I hate it but I'll be using a drum set they already have on board. Hope it doesn't suck."

"You're in Miami?"

"Yeah, getting on the ship as soon as we get to the dock. Can you take care of Bugsy and Annabelle? I hate to ask, especially since it's for months. Donny let me get online on his smartphone to forward my mail to my parents, but that still leaves the cats. There's a bag of cat chow in the pantry next to the kitchen and a big bag of litter in the basement next to their box. Let me know if you run low and I'll send you some cash for more. I left a key for you under a flower pot by the back door."

A key? Roy hadn't coughed up a key to his place even when they were engaged. "Sure, I'll look after them. Cats are easy.

Oh, wait, except for the litter box. I'm pregnant and I can't change the litter box. But I'll handle the food and water. And I can ask Sherri about the litter box. If she can't do it, I'm paying my cleaning service extra to take care of the litter box for my cats while I'm expecting, and maybe I could arrange for them to come to your house to clean the box for yours. And I'll either leave Annabelle and Bugsy at your house or take them to my place."

"Great, if you pay your cleaning service to help out, let me know and I'll send a check. I knew the lady would come through. Hey, I kind of think this goes without saying, but use the recording equipment in my garage anytime. Send me any tracks you put down. I think I'll be pretty limited in terms of internet while I'm on the ship, they charge a fortune and staff doesn't get free internet, but we're stopping somewhere in the Caribbean or in Cancun and or back in Miami every four or five days and I may be able to get to an internet café. So I can hear what the Lady writes."

"Thanks. I think I can figure it out from what we worked on last time. I'll see what I can do. But the cats are covered. I know it's for work, but wow, Cancun and the Caribbean, pretty nice."

"I'm not complaining. And thanks so much dear. Let me know if you change your mind or when you go out of town on your honeymoon and need me to get a sub for the kitties. I don't know anyone I'd trust as much as you, but I've got some friends whose arms I can twist."

"No honeymoon to worry about. Roy and I aren't getting married. You were right when you said I'd figure out what I wanted and it's not getting married to Roy."

"I'm not sorry. I mean I don't want you to be sad, but I can't say I'm sorry to hear it. Except I'm sorry we couldn't talk before I left town. You gonna be ok?"

"I'm ok. Not just ok, I'm good."

"That's good. Oh crap, I gotta go. They're saying I need to shut off this phone to go through the security for the ship. Jane, I don't know about cell phone reception on the ship, but I'll try to call and you can try to reach me anytime. I wish I could do more for you, sweetheart. If you get sad, lean on your music. And send it. Let me know what's in that heart of gold of yours, ok?

"Ok, I'll send you some tracks that'll blow you away. You be safe. Bye."

Since Ansel was going to be gone so long, Jane thought she would take his cats to her house to see if they could get along with her own cats. But when she got to his house a few days later after work, they seemed to be fine where they were. If she came by every few days to look in on them, pat their heads, check their food and water and got Sherri or her cleaning service to change the litter box, they should be ok. The recording equipment would be a tempting distraction, especially if she was stopping by so often for the cats, and she was already behind on her billables at work. But she could limit the time she allowed herself to noodle around putting down tracks for her songs. She could maybe work on a song or two for a little while once a week, not every time she came by to check on the cats, right?

It helped that the house was chilly. Warm enough for the cats but with the thermostat still set fairly low so Ansel didn't go broke heating an empty house while he was gone. The garage was even colder, even though it was attached to the house and heated, at least it was supposed to be heated, but it wasn't heated much, that was for sure. Even if Jane kept her coat on, along with a hat and a pair of gloves with the fingers cut off, she still didn't think she could stay out in the garage working on her songs for very long.

Jane sat down at the keyboards. She turned on an amp and one of the mikes Ansel had handing from the ceiling. After some trial and error, trying to remember how he turned music on the keyboard into computer files, and using some instructions from notes Ansel left taped to various pieces of his recording equipment, she got a few tracks recorded from the keyboard to computer files she could send to Ansel. She also had a small video camera in her purse and she balanced it on a speaker so she could shoot a video of herself singing and playing keyboards. She looked less than elegant in her winter hat, but she thought a video would be the best way to give Ansel the emotional content of some of her songs, something that might be lost if she just sent him a computer file attached to an e-mail with the lyrics typed up.

She looked at her watch. Four hours had gone by. How did

that happen? It was ten at night already. She realized she was freezing and really shouldn't be skipping meals in her condition. But before she left, she wanted to take a look around the rest of Ansel's house.

There was a grouping of pictures on a wall in the hallway between the kitchen and the living room. Ansel with his parents and a slim, smiling blonde young woman that Jane assumed was Thea. There was even a framed picture of Thea with a large group of co-workers posed in front of the headquarters of Integrated Products. Oliver was in the picture, looking serious and patrician. Jane wished she could explain to Ansel how ironic and sad that picture really was, but client confidentiality would keep her from ever saying anything to Ansel about his sister's unfair treatment at Integrated.

Walking through the rest of the house, Jane could see that Ansel had made some efforts in the past six years to make the house his own. The living room furniture was masculine, something with chrome and dark colors. Ansel's bedroom was also simple and dark, but the other bedroom in the house was frilly with gingham and colonial blue stencils on the walls. Thea must have done that. The bathroom was pink. At least Ansel had put in mini blinds and a shower curtain that looked like his taste, but Thea's influence was still apparent. Jane thought that was something she and Ansel had in common. They both lived in houses they hadn't quite made their own. The rooms at each of their houses showed that they were each still in the process of moving on from the past.

Jane felt she might be further along with the process than Ansel. She had finished the deck after all. And there were no longer any of Jeff's clothes in her closets, while Jane found boxes of Thea's clothes still shoved in the back of one of Ansel's closets. But then again, Ansel had apparently replaced the living room furniture, which Jane hadn't done yet. And her bed was still the bed she'd used with Jeff. But Jane had picked out that bed, so maybe it didn't count as a relic from her marriage. Maybe it was just hers. Anyway, it wasn't a contest. There were no prizes awarded for getting on with one's life, except the living itself.

Jane stood looking at one of the large framed collages hanging in the frilly bedroom that she assumed must have been Thea's. The collages included strikingly beautiful photos and of nature scenes and plants, mixed in with pieces of fabric and even drawings. Maybe the photography was done by one or both of Ansel's parents? Ansel said his parents were so into photography that Ansel and his sister were named for famous photographers. But Jane saw that the collages had the initials "T.A.K." in bottom corner, so they must have been put together by Thea. Had Thea taken some of her parents' photographs and put them in collages or was Thea a photographer in her own right? If they were collaborations, with Thea building on her parents' creative work, they must be so heartbreaking for Ansel's parents to see. No wonder Ansel couldn't take these back to Buffalo, New York, to his parents, but had them here suspended on these walls. And in a way Ansel was suspended with them. Jane understood that too. She checked the cats' food and water bowls, locked up and headed for home.

Ron Silver, Jeff's attorney, kept asking the court for continuances, postponing the date for the hearing the court had set on the motion to dismiss Jeff's petition to reopen the property settlement in their divorce. Harvey figured Ron was busy trying to keep Jeff out of jail in the Life's End mess and just didn't have time to focus on fighting to keep Jeff's petition to reopen the property settlement from getting dismissed. Harvey's advice was to keep agreeing to the continuances because if Jeff did get a nice long prison sentence in the Life's End case, maybe the divorce petition would just go away. The most recent continuance was until late March.

Jane found herself driving over to Ansel's house pretty often. One afternoon in mid-January, she meant to just stop by on her lunch hour, but at 3:00 she was still sitting at the keyboards in Ansel's garage, with his cats curled up in an old chair nearby. Jane had her coat and hat on, and she could see her breath in the marginally heated garage. The keys of the keyboard felt like ice on her fingertips. She knew she shouldn't stay too long in the cold like this, and she really needed to get back to the office, but she had this new song in her head.

"Hope is all we ever had." Jane leaned close to a microphone and cranked up the amp. "Even so, my heart is glad. I see you in memory. Happy end may never be. But it's alright. Yeah it's alright. And I'm alright." Her cell rang. It was Ansel.

"Hey, dear lady," Ansel said. "How's life in the frozen but good old USA?"

"Cold," Jane said. "Especially in your garage. But listen, I'll put the phone by the speaker on your amp. See if you can hear if I sing."

She sang as much as she had so far of her new song.

"Wow, not the best acoustics, but it's great, sweetheart. What would you think about a little brass in there? Could be I'm hearing too many Mariachis with the stops at the resorts on the coast of Mexico, but I'm hearing trumpets playing just a lick or two with the 'it's alright.' You know what I mean? You sing 'it's alright' and the trumpets then go, 'da dut dut dah,' kind of like an echo, and then after the last 'and I'm alright' they go up a fourth or so on the last note 'da dut dut deeeee' and you roll into the next verse."

"I like it" Jane said. "I really like it."

"You got to get down here and get all the music they have here into your head. It would be such a boost for you. It would infuse your writing, even if you just came down here for a few days. There are so many musicians to hear and jam with. We're docking in Cancun in the middle of February and some time off. You could fly down. It would be a great time. I really miss you."

"I'll see what I can do. Give me the exact dates and I'll check my calendar. I'll need to check with my doctor about whether I can still fly. I don't know if I can, but maybe. I miss you too."

If Ansel was trying to start a romance, and Jane wasn't sure if he was, now wasn't the best time, when she was about three months pregnant. Still, she missed Ansel, more and more as the weeks passed and they managed as best they could to work on their songs together by phone and internet. If she was honest about it, she was thinking about him and missing him a lot. Could she be falling in love with someone over the phone? Or was she just in love with songwriting and having something creative in her life for the first time in a long time?

And it was scary thinking about having a baby alone. Was that it? Was she grasping at attention from a handsome man, even just over the phone, because she was scared? He was handsome. And probably getting even more handsome out in the sun, with his olive skin getting even darker and all that wavy dark hair he had. But flying to Mexico to see him? Even if her doctor said it was still ok to fly in February, she wouldn't know for sure. What about changes in cabin pressure? What kind of studies had really been done? They couldn't put a bunch of pregnant women on a plane and have it climb and fall, changing altitude up and down as a test to see if it caused any problems with the pregnancies. No way. It was making her sick just thinking about it. And if even she got there ok, what about the water? What if she got some intestinal thing? That couldn't be good for her baby.

All that worrying turned out to be for nothing when Corinne stopped by her office with a deposition notice. Frederick, Corinne's lover and a plaintiffs' attorney, represented the plaintiffs in the class action suit against Regents Mark. He'd served notice that the plaintiffs wanted to take Jane's deposition. As a witness in the class action suit. And that was very bad news because if they could show that she was a necessary witness in the case, it could jeopardize Regents Mark's ability to use Jane's firm for its defense. The notice set the date for Jane's deposition on the day after the date Ansel wanted her to meet him in Cancun in February. So Jane was unhappy about being deposed, but pretty happy about having an excuse not to get on a plane to Mexico.

"They want to depose me as a witness?" Jane said. "They can't mean as an expert. Not if we're Regents Marks' defense firm. So do they mean as a fact witness? What facts?"

"They're alleging," Corrine said, "that you have some kind of crucial testimony to give about what Wendell and your ex did that was out of line as agents of Regents Mark and Life's End."

"I don't. I don't know anything about what they did. I mean they did show me some brochures and a computer presentation. But it was basic promotional material, not any sort of inside information. It's like seeing a company brochure and being called to testify about accounting fraud at the company. It's ridiculous. They showed me public, promotional materials and I said I didn't want anything to do with SILO or splitting commissions.

How does that make me an essential fact witness?"

"I suppose, and I'm just playing devil's advocate, if the commission splitting business were the key issue here they might have a point. Since you were asked, even if you said no, to take some of the commission money on the side. But the real issue here is the games they played with the figures for the life expectancies on the dying people who sold their Regents Mark insurance policies to Life's End. Know anything about that?"

"Only what I've heard from you and I think that's privileged because I heard it in discussions with you as counsel for Regents Mark. So they won't be able to get me to say anything about that."

"Right. But that's exactly what's at stake here, Jane. Whether or not you have information, factual information, about events that took place relevant to the case, and not as anyone's counsel, but just from events in your life, that are material to the case. If you do have that kind of information and if they can show you are an essential material witness, it could interfere with our ability to continue as Regents Mark's counsel. So we need to beat this. Otherwise the associates won't be able to bill to the skies on this and Ted will have my hide. The big shots around here have trophy wives and second homes to pay for. We need to win this round or else. So if there's anything else you know or saw, outside of discussions as counsel for Regents Mark, anything Wendell or your ex told you or showed you besides those brochures and the computer presentation, especially anything about cooking the books on the life expectancies they used to push the derivatives, you need to tell me."

"There's nothing here, Corinne. The only thing I know, other than what you told me, is from publicly available materials. We're solid on this."

Ansel was able to send an e-mail from the ship the next day, again encouraging her to come to Cancun in February. Jane remembered how Roy had sulked after she had to leave their beach vacation for a work meeting. Would Ansel react badly to the news that she was choosing to go to a deposition, even if she was the person being deposed, instead of seeing him? But she and Ansel weren't dating, were they? They weren't together, so he was just inviting her as a friend. So no big deal, right?

"Ansel," Jane wrote in her reply to his e-mail, "I'm so sorry but I can't come to Cancun. I have to stay here for a very important deposition in a big case that means a lot for the firm. I could try to reschedule, but honestly I'm nervous about travel and the drinking water in Mexico since I'm expecting. Even if my doctor said I could still travel I would still be too worried. I hope you understand. Yours with best wishes, Jane."

"Lady Jane," Ansel wrote back, "your wish is my command. I would love if you could play here in the sun, but work is work. And being careful about baby, that's just you, being you. Beautiful."

The day of the deposition, Corinne wanted to talk to Jane in a small conference room before they went into the larger room where the other parties were waiting. "Ok, ok, ok. Are you with me? This is important, really important. You have to know this." Was Corinne's suit jacket buttoned wrong? "You must, absolutely you must, look at me before you answer anything. Anything. No answering without looking at me. At me. So if you're asked a question, what do you do?"

"I look at you. Is that a mailing label stuck to the bottom of your shoe?"

"At me. At me." Corinne was leaning toward Jane, looking Jane directly in the eyes and pointing to herself. "And nobody rushes you. You set the pace. At a pace that is good for you. If they ask questions fast, you go slow. Slow them down. Answer at your pace. Yours."

"I think you've got your jacket buttoned wrong. One button off."

"Ok, pace, we covered pace. And don't get nervous. And if you don't recall, say that. And answer what's asked. Don't add anything. Answer in a complete way, but don't offer up extra. If you don't understand a question say that. But first look at me. Look at me. That's crucial. Remember that. Only answer what's asked."

"I get it. Ok. Calm down. It's me being deposed, not you." Was there something funny about the size of Corinne's pupils? Like after an eye exam?

"That's right, it's you being deposed. So let's take a deep breath here. Deep breath. Deep breath. Ok. Ok. Let's go. We need to go." They headed into the larger conference room. Jane sat down with Corinne next to her.

"Frederick Harrigan of Harrigan and Lester, LLC, appearing for the plaintiffs."

"Ronald Silver, of The Silver Law Firm, appearing on behalf of defendant Jeffrey Rogers."

"Laura Anderson of Bagley, Jamison and Lind, appearing on behalf of defendants Gordon Wendell and The Wendell Agency."

"Sean Hirshfeld, of Meyer and Edelman, LC, appearing on behalf of defendant Carl Dennison."

"Janet Haynes, of Janet Haynes Associates, appearing of behalf of defendant Annette McHenry."

"Corinne Eberly, of Hantler Vintberg, PLLC, appearing on behalf of defendant Regents Mark and deponent Jane Sidley."

"I don't think you can represent both," Frederick said.

Corinne slapped the pen she was holding down on the table. "Until the court rules on your motion to include her as a material witness, she's part of the defense team for Regents Mark, Frederick. So unless you want her listed on the record as counsel for Regents Mark you'd better back off on this one. Oh sure, I'll list her as co-counsel if that's what you want. You'll be asking a lot fewer questions this morning because we'll be done here and dealing with that question in court. Don't think I'm bluffing here. All these nice people can just go home if you don't want me representing Regents Mark and Jane here today. We can fight about this in court and then come back here and start over. Go ahead. Try it. Make my day."

"Objection reserved for the record," Frederick said.

Jane was sworn in by the court reporter.

Frederick turned to the notes he had on a yellow legal pad. "Please state your name for the record."

Jane opened her mouth to answer and Corinne cleared her throat. Oh right, Jane was supposed to look over at Corinne before answering. To make sure there was no objection from Corinne before Jane said anything. But he'd only asked for her name. Jane looked over at Corinne. What was she doing? Was she trying to pick lint off her suit jacket? Now?

"Jane Sidley."

"Your full name please," Frederick said.

"Jane Anne Sidley."

"You are under oath, Ms. Sidley."

"That's my full legal name," Jane said.

"Isn't it a fact that your name is Jane Anne Sidley Rogers?" Frederick said.

"No—"

"Objection." Corinne was on her feet. "Not relevant. No foundation. What are you going to ask next, what else her name isn't?"

"This is a deposition," Frederick said. "We're not in court here. You don't need to object to everything. You'll get to challenge all of it later. This is just a discovery deposition."

"You started it," Corinne said.

"And I reserved my objection for the record," Frederick said. "You can do that too, and we can get on with this. I'm just asking her legal name, for Pete's sake."

"Asked and answered," Corinne said.

"She hasn't answered in terms of her basis for saying why she thinks her name isn't Jane Sidley Rogers," Frederick said.

"And I said not relevant," Corinne said. "And no foundation. Are you going to ask her to explain why her name isn't Jane Smith or Jane Doe or Jane Green or Jane Blue or Jane Purple?"

Jane thought Corinne's affair with Frederick was probably all that was keeping him from threatening to ask for court sanctions against Corinne if she didn't calm down and stop holding up the deposition over something this stupid.

Frederick looked at Jane.

Jane glanced at Corinne. She was now picking invisible lint from her skirt. At least she was back in her chair. "The court order in my divorce from Jeffrey Rogers," Jane said, "allowed me to go back to use of the name Jane Anne Sidley. It is, as I said, my legal name."

Frederick asked about her address, education, work history and law license. Jane recited her home address and the names of her college and law school, along with dates of attendance and graduation. She gave her start date with Hantler Vintberg and said that her work with her firm began right after law school and continued to the present time. Jane stated that she was admitted to the state bar and the federal district court that included their city.

"We need your complete work history," Frederick said.

"That's it," Jane said. "This is the only job I've had since I graduated from law school."

"Is it your testimony that you did not hold a summer job in the legal department at Hampstead Insurance during the summers while you were in law school?" Frederick said.

"Objection." Corinne was on her feet again. "Are we going to include babysitting jobs here? Maybe household chores if she got her allowance for doing them? How about volunteer work?" She put a hand on Jane's shoulder. "Is this going to be a fishing expedition? I'm not standing for a fishing expedition. You've got another thing coming if that's what you're after." Corinne looked down at Jane and with the hand she'd put on Jane's shoulder, she started to pick at the fabric of Jane's lapel.

"Could we take a short break here?" Jane said. "I need to confer with my counsel."

Jane steered Corinne back into the small conference room across the hall.

"Great move," Corinne said. "Asking for a sidebar with me. This will throw them off completely. Let's do this at least once every half hour."

"What's with objecting about my name and then about my summer jobs? I mean who cares about that stuff? They could probably find out absolutely everything they've asked me about so far with a two minute internet search, so why object?"

"Don't you see it?" Corinne said. "You don't see it? It's plain to see. Plain, Jane. But you don't see it, do you? Every question they're asking, they're trying to connect you to Jeff Rogers."

"Well that's easy enough. I was married to him."

"And you met him at an insurance agency and you're trying to hide it. Get it? And you're trying to hide something having to do with Jeff Rogers and the name change. They're trying to connect the dots."

"I'm not hiding anything. I did get my name changed back to Sidley. I was going to say so right away, but you objected. And I didn't think they were asking about summer employment or I would have mentioned my summers with Hampstead Insurance. I wasn't hiding that either. And when Frederick asked the follow up question about summer jobs, I was going to answer it, but you objected again. And what dots? Just what on earth do you think these dots, that they're supposedly connecting, add up to anyway?"

"Conspiracy. If you're more than a witness even, but a co-conspirator, in this with Jeff and trying to hide it, our firm is toast with Regents Mark's defense. And I'm toast with this firm. Ted Willingham will fry me. He'll fry me."

"I don't think you're toast and I don't think Ted will fry you. And the conspiracy thing is just ridiculous. They're going to put together a conspiracy theory because I met the guy at a summer job, married him, then he divorced me and I took my name back? That's just crazy."

"Well it doesn't help that you might be carrying his baby."

If Corinne knew the baby might be Jeff's, then everyone in town must know. It might as well be on the front page of the paper. But even that didn't matter here, in terms of the Regents Mark case. Stupidly having sex with one's ex is not evidence of conspiracy to commit insurance fraud. It's evidence of really bad judgment, but there was not a shred of evidence that Jane was involved in anything under the table with Regents Mark or Life's End. Even if Jeff perjured himself, and said she was involved, there was nothing to back it up. Corinne was just running wild with this conspiracy nonsense. All they'd asked was her name and her employment history, for heaven's sake. Corinne was straightening the set of volumes of the State Code on the bookshelf in back of the small conference room.

"Corinne," Jane said, "are you on something right now?"

"On something? What do you mean?"

"Drugs. Maybe prescription?"

"No. I mean yes. I mean no, of course not. But I have allergies, I may have taken something for that. An antihistamine. Sometimes they can have an effect. That does happen."

"That Employee Confidential Counseling Program you mentioned to me a few weeks ago, you might want to think about seeing somebody."

"We need to get back in there. We can't take too long with

these sidebars. They're a good idea and all, but we don't want to overdo it."

"I'm not going back in there without taking someone else from our litigation department in there with us. Anthony Listerman does mostly domestic cases, but he's good and he'll keep his mouth shut even if you continue to behave like a lunatic this morning. I want him in there with us."

"No way. You're just jealous because I make more money than you."

Ted must tell everybody they're ahead of everyone else on the same level of partnership at the firm. He told Jane she was making more than Corinne, and then told Corinne she was making more than Jane. Way to go, Ted. Hope it doesn't come around and bite you in the ass too often.

"Either I call Anthony, right now, or I call Ted. Your choice, but I'm calling one of them. Right now."

"You bitch. You used to be such a mouse. Old nose to the grindstone meek and mousy Jane. Now you got that baby on board and all of sudden you're playing hardball with everybody."

Jane picked up the receiver on the conference room phone.

"Wait," Corinne said, "ok, ok, call Anthony."

CHAPTER SIXTEEN

*J*ane thought she'd hear from Corinne pretty soon after the deposition was over. Maybe in a day or two, when Corinne wasn't still flying around on whatever it was she was taking. But Jane didn't see or hear from Corinne for weeks. Not until she saw her in the hallway in early March.

"Could we talk for a minute?" Corrine said.

"Sure."

"Not out here in the hallway." They went into an empty conference room and shut the door.

"I wanted to give you an update on the fallout from your deposition in the Regents Mark case," Corinne said. The deposition, aside from Corinne's antics, had been incredibly dull. Ten hours of nothing. Jane answered endless questions about her business meeting with Jeff and Wendell at Wendell's office. Frederick Harrigan grilled her about each slide in the computer presentation they'd shown her about Life's End. And how many times could she tell them? Her reason for looking at the computer presentation was pity. Pity for her down and out ex-husband, that's why she politely listened to their pitch and just as politely, turned them down. That's all there was. And here was Corinne, ready to discuss the fallout, like the deposition was some kind of international incident or nuclear attack.

"Ok," Jane said. "Fire away."

"The deposition got them nowhere," Corinne said. "Nothing they can use. Not against you or Regents Mark. We consider it a complete victory on that front. I don't have to tell you the CEO at Regents Mark is pretty pleased with me as a result. This could be big for me. I mean for the firm too of course."

Anthony was who Regents Mark should be pleased with. Corinne had been a train wreck that day. But Corinne probably didn't even mention Anthony's name when she reported to the client about the deposition. Sure, Anthony's name was there, starting on page thirty or so of the massive transcript of all ten hours of the deposition, and his name would be on a few of the reams of pages of invoices the firm would be sending to the client, but Corinne had the client contact on this one. She was the one with the ear of the anxious in-house counsel at Regents Mark. And it sounded like Corinne had even managed to set up a pipeline direct to the CEO's office.

Jane had certainly been on the losing end over the years in terms of men unfairly taking credit for her work. It was one of the reasons she now mostly worked alone, bringing in other attorneys on client matters, even young associates, with caution. She was sure other women experienced it all the time. The woman puts in the long hours, diligently getting the work done, and the man takes the credit, bending the client's ear in the locker room or at some men's club meeting. So was she pleased to see Corinne do the same to Anthony?

Corinne was able to pull it off because the chief in-house counsel at Regents Mark, Cathy Inglewait, was a brilliant attorney who would be managing partner at a big firm if she were a man. Instead she was parked as chief in-house counsel at a big, but not top flight, insurance company. Without even a chance of moving up to the executive suite, not in this lifetime. In-house counsel, even chief in-house counsel, was a popular parking spot, just below the glass ceiling, for bright women who got sidelined because, how had Ted put it, they brought in lots of business and did great work, but didn't have the 'intangibles needed for the upper levels' at a major law firm. Cathy Inglewait was probably instrumental in helping Corinne get the ear of the CEO at Regents Mark. So Corinne could take credit for a successful deposition, when that credit was due to Anthony.

But Jane wasn't happy to see the shoe on the other foot. To see a woman steal credit for good work from a man, even when it was almost always the other way around. Because it didn't matter if it was a woman or a man taking credit for someone else's work. It was still wrong and just made things needlessly competitive for everyone at the firm and in the entire profession. That was bad no matter who was doing the stealing.

"So," Jane said, "are you and Anthony thinking that I'm no longer a target in all this?" Jane mentioned Anthony mostly just to irritate Corinne. And to let her know Jane hadn't forgotten about Corinne's erratic behavior at the deposition. "No more worries about allegations that I was in some kind of conspiracy with Life's End or Regents Mark?"

"They have no evidence of it," Corinne said. "The deposition revealed nothing. And both sides have been going over a warehouse full of documents. E-mails, memos, receipts. We've deposed many of the people who sold policies to Life's End, those who haven't died yet anyway. And your name never comes up. Not on paper and not with any of the other witnesses."

"So I can forget about it? Have I been dropped off the plaintiffs' witness list?"

"Well, that's the thing," Corinne said. "That's kind of why I wanted to talk to you. They won't take you off the list. We're going to have to go to the judge on this. She's asked for briefs. Frederick keeps hinting that he has some information from Ron Silver that Jeff might give testimony that implicates you. Even if he did, it would just be his word with no back up from any of the discovery documents or other witnesses like the policyholders or the people who bought the shares in the derivatives or mutual funds with the SILO policies. But would he do that? Would your ex-husband perjure himself to implicate you? I know your divorce was messy, but perjury seems like an extreme step to take to get back at a former spouse, especially this long after the divorce."

"It would be a new low even for him," Jane said. "But it's possible. Jeff will do just about anything if he feels cornered."

"If he does lie about you, can we count on your help to fight him? I mean to really go to war, no holding back. I know you've felt sorry for him in the past, but if he's going to lie about this we need to bury him. Completely. No chance you'd be reluctant to hit back with everything we've got because you're hoping he'll pay child support or something like that, is there?"

Jane laughed. "Hoping he'll pay child support? Not a chance. Anyway, the baby might not even be his. But even if the baby is Jeff's, there's no way he'll ever pay a dime of child support. What they say about how you can't get blood from a turnip, they're not just making that up. It really is true."

"Ok, we'll notice Jeff Rogers for deposition. We'll put him under oath and see what he has to say. That way at least we'll know if he intends to implicate you or not. And if he does, then we crush him."

What was that nursery rhyme? Jane ran through it in her mind as Corinne hurried off to send the notice for Jeff's deposition. And when she was good she was very very good. And when she was bad she was horrid.

Next Sunday Jane met her mother at Church. Jane's social life, with Sherri busy bonding with Hauser's kids, Ansel on a ship in the Caribbean and Roy out of the picture, was pretty much non-existent. Next to sitting at her desk, she probably spent the most time with cats, her own and Ansel's. But she didn't feel lonely. No, she felt more connected and surrounded by love than she had in a very long time. She could feel little movements from the baby, at first like bubbles breaking, but more definite little kicks and pushes lately. She carried the ultrasound pictures with her all the time. The baby was a boy. A perfect little guy.

The sermon was about gratitude. Jane felt lots of that. She couldn't believe she had her heart's desire, a baby on the way. Sure, it would be nice to be getting married again. She wished sometimes things had been different, or Roy had been different or she had been different. She thought about how nice a wedding at the Eden Glade Inn would have been, maybe in April or May on a pretty spring day. With fresh bright green leaves on the trees. And tulips, that's what she would have carried for a Spring wedding. A bouquet of tulips.

But none of that mattered. Jane's baby was who mattered. And here he was, safe and snug, right here with her. Waiting to be born. So she could love him, care for him and God willing, someday launch a fine young man into the world. Leaving it a better place. Jane felt that not only her belly, but her soul itself was expanding with the pregnancy. People mentioned she was braver and tougher. But it was more than that. Becoming a parent made her more vulnerable, and somehow that left her feeling more open, less closed in. What was the word Jesus used when He was healing a man's hearing problems? Ephphatha. Jane felt her soul was doing that. Opening up.

The following Monday, her office phone showed Harvey's firm and direct dial number on the caller id.

"Jane Sidley."

"Jane, Harvey here. You been poking any hornets' nests with a stick lately?"

"My specialty. Any particular hornets' nest you have in mind?"

"All these months Ron Silver has been asking for continuances for the hearing on my motion to dismiss. Now all of a sudden he's withdrawn his latest request for a continuance and filed a motion demanding to move up the hearing, on Jeff's petition to reopen the property settlement in your divorce, to next week. Nothing's changed from where I sit, so I was wondering if you did something. You do anything lately to tick off your ex?"

"Actually, yes. But it involves a case here at the firm so I can't talk about it. Wow, I didn't think he'd retaliate this fast. Is there any way you can just make this go away? I mean I'm almost five months pregnant. Do I really have to waddle into court for a hearing on my divorce? How depressing is that?"

"On the bright side, no judge is going to give Jeff an increase in his share of the divorce settlement if it means taking money from a pregnant woman. In fact, and I hope you don't mind me saying this, but I heard Jeff might be the father, so I just wanted to mention that if you bring up Jeff's possible paternity at the hearing, the judge might order Jeff to pay, instead of you. At least child support, if he is the father. Whether or not you'd ever collect, that's another story."

"No thanks. This is embarrassing to admit, but it's true that I'm not entirely sure about my baby's paternity. And I'd like to keep it that way. If I can avoid having to do a paternity test, and don't put anyone down as father on the birth certificate, I figure that gives me my best shot at never having to share custody or even visitation with either of the two contenders for fatherhood here, Jeff and my former fiancé, Roy Adams."

"It's your decision and I understand your reasons. But if you change your mind, let me know. Might be something worth bringing up as long as we're in court. I'll send the notice over. It's set for hearing in Judge Miller's court at 10 a.m. next Friday, the 15th. Meet me in the hallway about 9:45 and we'll go over things. And don't worry, I think it's a pretty sure bet the judge will grant our motion to dismiss. This was a fair property settlement at the time, and it still is. We should be out of there with our dismissal order in no time."

March 15 felt unseasonably warm. Jane enjoyed the two block walk to the courthouse. The past few days had been really cold, with freezing rain and snow, but the 15th was pretty. Jane liked the bright, warm sunshine. She looked up at the big, clear blue sky with just a few wisps of clouds. She could still feel winter in the air, but there was enough warmth and light that its grip felt loosened. It could snow again, but no storm would last. The spell was broken.

The purse slung over her shoulder was still overstuffed even though she'd unloaded a few items into her desk drawer back at the office. The purse, along with the briefcase she carried, would have to pass through security at the courthouse. So no pepper spray or Swiss army knife today. In her briefcase, Jane had an assortment of papers that might prove relevant to the motion to dismiss Jeff's petition. She had a certified copy of the divorce decree, with the property settlement attached as an exhibit. Three years of her tax returns, including copies of last year's schedule K-1, showing her income as a junior non-equity partner and the W-2's from the two years before when she was still an associate at the firm. She had copies of each of her bank and brokerage statements from the past two years. She didn't know quite what to expect, and Harvey said she wouldn't need any records, as this should be open and shut. But Jane liked to be prepared. She'd also grabbed a few files from her desk. If there was a lot of waiting around, maybe she could get a little work done.

Security was tight. Even though Jane's purse and briefcase went through an x-ray, a guard still opened each of them and looked through. The guard also checked each for bomb residue. Then each person entering the courthouse, including Jane, not only walked through a metal detector, but went over to yet another guard who checked each person, even if the metal detector didn't signal that there was any metal, with a hand held wand. Jane was glad she left a little extra time because the line was moving slowly.

The elevator seemed to stop at every floor. It stopped at 2 to let some people out. Then 3, and a woman with a stroller had trouble squeezing in, Then 4, 5 and 6 and several people had to get off and then back on in order to let some people in the back of the elevator out on 7. Then 8, then 9 and finally, the elevator reached the tenth floor, the top floor of the building, where Jane could find Judge Miller's courtroom. Jane looked for Harvey as she walked down the crowded corridor on 10, but didn't see him. There were so many people in the crowded hallway, most of them bunched at the end of the hallway by Judge Miller's courtroom, that maybe she just hadn't spotted Harvey yet.

Jane did catch sight of Jeff, straight ahead, seated on a heavy wooden backless bench, bolted to the floor and set along the outside wall at the very end of the corridor, near Judge Miller's courtroom. Sunlight streamed in behind him, through a wide plate glass window that had its bottom edge at the height of the bench and stretched up almost to the ceiling. All that sunlight made it hard to look directly at the people packed together on the bench, but Jane could clearly make out Jeff's familiar frame, compact, strong and tense, among the others on the bench. The light spilling in from the large window made the people near him seem to be in shadow, but not Jeff. The little weasel looks almost angelic, like he has a halo, Jane thought. Go figure. She knew she shouldn't say anything to Jeff without Harvey and Ron, their lawyers, being present, but she still pushed through the crowd, down the hallway, and squeezed in between him and the next person on the bench. They were pressed shoulder to shoulder sitting on the crowded bench, and it was like being on a crowded bus, with people standing and milling around right in front of them. As much as she was continually angry with him, especially today, she still liked feeling the electric energy that never seemed to stop radiating out of him.

"I hope you're happy," Jane said. "Dragging me in here for this hearing when I'm getting close to five months pregnant. The judge isn't going to give you another dime."

"Nice to see you too, Janey baby," Jeff said. "And it's nothing personal. Cassie got laid off and I can't get anything with this indictment over the Life's End sales hanging over my head. Tell you what, you get that firm of yours to help Ron get the Regents Mark and Life's End charges against me to go away, and I'll drop this. How about it, Janey? You do that for me and this goes away. Forever, babe, I promise."

"I can't discuss Regents Mark or Life's End with you without your counsel present," Jane said.

"Always a bitch," Jeff said. "But you know Janey, even though you were always on me, and never could give me a break, I am sorry about how things turned out, you know, with us."

"But not so sorry that you couldn't stop yourself from trying to bleed me for more money?"

"Nothing personal."

"Nothing personal? What does that mean? How is it not personal if you serve me personally, me, Jeff, not someone else, with a summons and haul me into a court of law to reopen a settlement that you wanted in a divorce that you wanted, from me, a divorce from me personally? How is that not personal?"

"I know you're sore about my ruining things for you with that old guy, but if you play ball with me and help me out in the Life's End thing, or cut me a break in court today, maybe I can help to patch things up. I could tell him I was delusional or something. That I made it up about us sleeping together because I was mad at you. He'd believe that. Anybody would."

"No thanks. Actually I ended up breaking it off with him. It just wasn't going to work out."

"Once you've had the best, babe," Jeff said, "there's no settling for anything less." He was grinning that grin of his that she would never forget. Even if she could get rid of him, she would never forget that grin. That cat who ate the canary grin.

"Jane! Jane!" Jeff grabbed her, pulled her from the bench and pushed her toward the floor.

Jane tried to pull away from him. "What are you doing? Stop grabbing me. Get off of me. Are you crazy?"

Jeff pushed Jane under the bench. "There's a tall guy, just down the hall, and he's got a bomb strapped up on his chest."

People started screaming and trying to run, but the man with the bomb was between them and the stairwells and elevators. The bomber was pushing through the crowd toward the door to Judge Miller's courtroom. Some people tried to run into Judge

Miller's courtroom but then someone yelled that the bomber was headed for the courtroom. Then people were trying to run out into the hallway, pushing and shoving the people behind them who were still trying to get into the courtroom. People were shoving and trying to run in every direction.

Jeff straightened up and turned toward the bomber in time to see a bailiff pull out his gun. The bailiff was pushing through the crowd toward the bomber, trying to get close enough to take aim. But the bomber was too far away for the bailiff to get a clear shot. The bomber was headed down the corridor just a few steps from where Jeff stood near the bench and the doors to Judge Miller's courtroom.

Under the bench Jane closed her eyes and curled into a ball. She was on her side, scooted as far as she could get under the bench, facing the back wall under the plate glass window at the end of the corridor. She had her knees tucked up right against the wall, trying to protect her belly.

Jeff stretched out his arm between the two people nearest him and managed to catch and pull the sleeve of the bomber's shirt, slowing the bomber just enough to let the bailiff get his gun up against the bomber's head. The bailiff pulled the trigger as the bomber pressed the detonator.

The blast slammed Jane into the wall below the bottom of the plate glass window. Her head hit the wall hard. She heard the explosion and the sound of breaking glass for just an instant. Then silence and darkness.

Chapter Seventeen

*J*ane was brought into the hospital about an hour later. A nurse found one of Jane's business cards in her pocket and called her office. Helene called her mother. When Jane's mother arrived at the hospital they'd already cleaned and bandaged the shrapnel wounds where nails and metal from the bomb, along with bits of the courthouse's granite flooring and other debris, had torn through Jane's trench coat, suit jacket and blouse and cut into her back. They'd already done a CT scan of Jane's head and an ultrasound to check on her baby. The baby was moving well, they said, and appeared to be uninjured. Jane had a bad bruise on her forehead, and a concussion, but no fractured skull or bleeding in her brain showed on the CT scan.

Both eardrums were ruptured.

Jane was unconscious for three days until Sunday morning. Jane's mother had called Sherri. Ansel had called Jane's cell Friday afternoon and evening several times, getting no answer, and while that wasn't all that unusual, he had a funny feeling about it and he decided to call Sherri late Friday night. Ansel's ship was still docked in Cancun and he was able to get a flight from Cancun to Miami and then home. He arrived late Saturday afternoon at the hospital.

When Jane woke up, she saw her mother, Sherri and Ansel in chairs near her bed. Aside from careful hugs, due to Jane's injuries, and lots of tears, communication was difficult because Jane had so much ringing in her ears and sounds were muffled and garbled. If someone looked directly at her and spoke at nearly a shout, she could understand, more or less.

Jane's eardrums, the doctors thought, were likely to heal in about a month. With luck, the ringing would stop and she might get most, though probably not all, of her hearing back. The doctors wanted to have a neurologist examine Jane once she was awake, to check for signs of impairment or brain damage from the concussion. Aside from her badly bruised forehead, most of Jane's wounds were from the shrapnel in her back. The bomber was tall enough and close enough that the bench shielded most of her, except some of her back, from the flying pieces of debris.

Jeff had not survived. The force of the blast blew him out the large plate glass window. It was unclear if he died from the blast or the fall, but probably he was gone before he even started to fall.

One of the cable news stations reported that the bomber might have been connected to international terrorism, or possibly supremacists or separatists of some kind. The main networks thought he was upset about his divorce, which involved several hearings before Judge Miller. The extra tight security that day at the courthouse was because of threats she'd received in the mail throughout the winter.

The bomber had been a window washer. March 15 had been the first day warm enough to have the window washer crew work on the outside courthouse windows. They thought the bomber used scaffolding to go up the side of the building until he reached a place where he could get in through some vents that led to the tenth floor. That seemed the most likely explanation of how he got a bomb into the building without getting caught at security. And how he got to the tenth floor after strapping on the bomb, without being seen by people in the hallways or in the elevators until he was spotted in the tenth floor corridor.

There were a lot of interviews and news stories with people who knew the bomber at various points in his life. His ex-wife said he had a bad temper and maybe got into something on the internet, she wasn't sure. His supervisor at the window washing company gave an interview at first, saying the bomber was a good employee who never missed work. But then there were questions about failure to check the tool kits and window washing equipment for anything unusual, like bomb making tools or supplies, and then no one at the window washing company was giving interviews. There were government hearings on the window washing bidding process, and it looked like there might be a scandal and some reform legislation, but it was all about payments and kickbacks, not safety issues or the bombing itself. A talk show got an exclusive interview with one of the bomber's grown children, but if Jane was hoping for an explanation of why his father had done such a terrible thing, it wasn't coming from him. All he wanted to talk about were vitamins he was selling.

Jane's mom stayed at her bedside pretty much all the time, with a few breaks from Sherri and Ansel. She was the easiest for Jane to understand, as she always remembered to lean in close and speak loudly.

"How are you feeling today, honey?"

Jane wasn't sure with the ringing in her ears if she was answering at a normal volume. "Better, I guess. The pain meds have kicked in pretty well this morning. What day is it?"

"Monday. The doctors think you can go home tomorrow."

"Tomorrow?"

"Yes, tomorrow."

"We'll never know why, will we, Mom? I'd like to know why he did it. For some terrorist plot or because he hated Judge Miller. It wouldn't bring back Jeff or any of the people who died in that hallway, but at least we'd know why."

"It's beyond reason, honey. There's no why to it. It's just senseless."

"I know, you're right. The funny thing is, I've been wondering if maybe I've seen the bomber before. Or even spoken to him. The pictures on the news looked kind of familiar. One time this man in a cleaning van startled me at night in a parking lot. And I saw him again talking to our pastor once in the parking lot at Church. I think he might have been homeless, living in his van."

"Jane dear, don't upset yourself. Just rest."

"But Mom, is this the kind of world I'm bringing my baby into? So much anger and despair and ugliness and violence?"

"I'm so happy you and the baby are alive, I can't be upset about anything bad. Maybe that's selfish, but I'm so grateful, honey, I just am."

"I know, Mom, me too. It's a crazy world but I'm happy too that I'm alive and so grateful the baby is alive and ok. That I even still have the chance to bring this baby into the world, crazy or not, that's a miracle and so much to be thankful for, you're absolutely right."

When Jane got out of the hospital on Tuesday morning, she insisted that her mother drive her to see Cassie. Jane still had bandages on the wounds on her back and her obstetrician wanted her on complete bed rest for at least another week, but Jane wouldn't rest until she'd seen Cassie. Jane had despised Cassie for having an affair with Jeff and for having his baby, but none of that mattered anymore.

Jane knocked on Cassie's door wondering if Cassie would even open it, if she could see that it was Jane, but Cassie did open her front door and immediately reached out to hug Jane.

"Easy there, easy, she's got bruises," Jane mother said.

"Come on in. I'll get J.J. out of his playpen."

For Jeff Junior. Jane had wondered what they'd named him. Jane and her mother sat down on a well-worn couch in the living room.

"I'm so sorry," Jane said. "How are you doing?"

"Some days I'm ok, some not so good. Did you just get out of the hospital?"

Jane looked confused and her mother leaned next to one ear. "She asked if you just got out of the hospital."

"Yes," Jane said. "It's my ears. The explosion ruptured both ear drums and I have trouble with my hearing. Lots of ringing and everything sounds jumbled and muffled. J.J. is adorable."

"Thanks."

"Jeff saved my life and my baby. I wanted you and J.J. to know he was a hero. My baby and I would be dead if he hadn't pushed me under a bench."

"I'll make sure J.J. knows when he's old enough. And I heard they're saying he helped stop the bomber from reaching the courtroom too. That more people had run in there and more would of died. I'll make sure J.J. knows his daddy was a hero." Cassie started to cry.

Jane's mother took J.J. from Cassie and handed her a packet of tissues she pulled from her purse. J.J. was squirming to get down so Jane's mother put him back in his playpen.

"He's still in the morgue." Cassie was sobbing now. "I don't have money for a funeral or anything."

Jane looked at her mother. She sat back down on the couch and leaned over toward Jane. "She says Jeff's body is in the morgue. She needs money to bury him."

"I owe him my life and my baby's life," Jane said. "Let me arrange the funeral. I'll pay for everything. I owe him at least that much."

"Oh thank you, honey, bless you. I didn't know what I would do. It's just me and J.J. now," Cassie said.

"We better be going," Jane's mother said. "I'm sure you need to rest and I need to get Jane home."

The memorial service was held Thursday morning at Jane's Church and was attended mostly by Cassie and her family. Jeff's father was in jail in Texas. Jeff's mother didn't make the trip from the West Coast, apparently too devastated by grief to travel. Jane was there, with her mother, Sherri and Ansel.

Anita came up to Jane by the guest book. "I'm so sorry Jane, but thank goodness you and the baby are ok."

"I'm sorry, burst eardrums, I can't hear in crowds," Jane said.

Anita leaned close to one ear. "Glad you and baby are ok. If you need help, or a sitter once the baby comes, call me. I'm here for you."

"Thanks. I'm a little short on family, and I'd welcome an Auntie in my baby's life if you're interested."

"I'm in, Jane. Auntie Anita."

With the ringing in her ears and everything still sounding garbled and muffled, Jane couldn't understand any of the eulogies. But the insert to the programs handed out for the memorial service had the Scripture readings printed in them. When Jane read Jesus' words about a man having no greater love than he lay down his life for his friends, the tears came. Ansel, gently and carefully, mindful of the injuries on her back, put an arm around her and Jane, just as carefully, leaned on him and sobbed.

Jane's mother stayed with Jane for a week after she got out of the hospital. Jane needed help keeping the wounds on her back clean and her mother was worried about Jane driving while her hearing was still not very good.

Ansel came to visit every day. Jane was sleeping most of the time so Ansel talked with her mother. They talked about Jane's childhood, her father and even about Jane's mother's childhood.

Ansel told Jane's mother about his parents and how much he missed his sister Thea. He told her about his band, and stories about people he'd met on the cruise ship over the winter.

Two weeks after the bombing Jane was much better, even thinking of going back to work. Her hearing was improved, although she still had the ringing. If just one person was talking to her, she could understand pretty well, but voices were still too garbled to understand over the phone or if two people were talking at once. Her mother filled Jane's fridge and then left to move back to her own house, after making Jane promise she wouldn't go into her office for another week. Her mother didn't believe her, but made her promise anyway.

Later Jane would wonder if he was hidden somewhere, watching for her mother to leave. Within minutes of her mother's car pulling out of the driveway, Ansel was at Jane's door. It could have been that he was just arriving for his daily visit, but Jane wondered if he had some kind of radar that could detect when her mother had moved out and the coast was clear.

He stood in the open doorway and they just looked at each other. Jane smiled. Ansel's light brown eyes were filled with the kindness and concern she'd seen in them from the moment she'd opened her own back in her hospital bed. With Jeff and Roy everything was a negotiation, stay or go, give or take, with someone always winning or losing. But with Ansel, once he stepped over the threshold, they both knew they wouldn't be competing, they wouldn't be negotiating, they would just be a part of each other.

Ansel reached for Jane and held her close, gently. "I'm so grateful I can hold you. Every day, every minute, I think how close I came to losing you. I love you so much."

Jane pulled him through the doorway and shut the door. "I love you too."

"I almost lost you. Before I even could tell you how much I love you. When I think of losing you it's like looking into an abyss. I can't believe how much I love you." He walked Jane toward the living room and started to take off the shirt she was wearing.

"My back. It's still a mess. It's ugly, Ansel."

"No, nothing is ugly about you, my Lady Jane. Never." They took each other's clothes off until they were both standing together naked, holding each other, in Jane's living room. Still holding her, Ansel pushed aside the coffee table and pulled blankets Jane had on her couch onto the area rug in front of the couch. The curled up together on them, on their sides, like spoons. Ansel looked at each of the scars on Jane's back. He was careful to avoid touching the wounds that were still bandaged, running his fingers around the bandages but touching, slowly, gently and lovingly, each of the scars in the places on her back that were completely healed. He reached around from where he was curled behind her and gently ran his palm over her pregnant belly. He kissed the back of Jane's neck and her shoulders. He kissed the edge of her ear. Then he shifted her position on the blankets and Jane felt him enter her so very slowly. He was almost rocking her, barely moving inside her. Jane felt so much emotion, with all the love and loss and grief of the past weeks coursing through her in the safety of Ansel's rocking, pushing forward and yet holding her back, keeping up his pace, channeling everything into a long aching ascent, to a peak of helpless release. They slept for hours curled together on the floor, with some of the blankets pulled over them, not waking until evening.

Later they padded around the kitchen. Ansel pulled a carton of eggs out of the fridge. "How about an omelet? Looks like your mother left a package of mushrooms, and there's scallions and some roma tomatoes. You sit down and I'll have it ready in no time."

"Wow. That's sounds great. I'm starving."

Jane took out a screw top bottle of sweet Italian wine. "Not everybody will drink this, but I think it's all I have. Can I pour you a glass?"

"That looks truly terrible. But sure."

Jane poured herself some orange juice and handed a glass of the sweet wine to Ansel. She put silverware and napkins for two on the kitchen table and sat down to watch Ansel cook.

Ansel had his back to Jane by the stove, but he was careful to turn around and face her when he spoke. He knew she was still having trouble with her hearing. "I was already falling for you when we were at the beach," Ansel said. "Not just literally, off the porch, but really falling for you."

"I liked you right away, but I'm sorry, I didn't think about love or anything like that back then. I was with Roy and wasn't looking around."

"Understood. I was drunk off my ass and acting like an idiot that week anyway. But when you came to see me at the Thin Dime that night in November, by then I was so crazy about you. It was like a stab wound to the heart when you asked me to give you away to Roy. And then when you came to see me with your songs. Talk about going out of my mind." Ansel brought the plates with the omelets to the table and sat down beside Jane. "But the absolute worst was when I was in Cancun and thought I'd lost you." He took her hand. "I hate it that I was so far away when you were hurt. I just hate it."

"It's ok. You were there when I woke up at the hospital. I really don't even remember anything before that. Just the terrible blast and then waking up in the hospital. I don't remember the ambulance or even how they got me out of the building. I was out cold."

Ansel reached into his back pocket and pulled out a ring and a marriage license application. He handed them to Jane. The ring was a gold band with three tiny diamond chips, more like diamond flakes really, set in the slender gold. "I wanted one with three diamonds. One ring with three, because that's how we are. You, the baby and me. Three of us, but one family."

Jane looked at the ring and the marriage license application. Ansel said he loved her, and she loved him, but she hadn't been thinking marriage.

The ring wasn't like the one Jeff had given her. It was paid for. No string of unpaid installments like she'd had with Jeff. And it was a ring that didn't come with an apology, like Roy's ring had.

She looked at Ansel. He spoke as if they already made a family, all three together. That was Ansel, seeing the possible. Seeing her as part of something bigger than herself. He always saw her connected to something beyond her, something larger and always good. Like music and creativity and now a family. His family. His family of three. Not two, like Jeff who didn't want a baby and only had one when Cassie accidentally got pregnant. And without conditions like Roy wanted, asking for a paternity test before he could decide if he would accept her baby. She scanned the marriage license application. "You know I love you, don't you? You know I'm going to sign this."

"We'll have to wait three days after I turn it in tomorrow," Ansel said. "But not a minute longer, ok?"

"You want to get married on Monday?"

"I almost lost you. Forever. Life is too precious to wait around."

What had her mother said about her father's courtship? Two dates, they got married, then a lifetime together. Simple. And it was simple with Ansel. Like what he said about writers. That writers write. Just like breathing. That's what it was being together with Ansel. Like breathing.

"I'll call my mom to let her know. And I'm still nervous about driving with my hearing not up to par. So can you drop by to give me a ride on Monday or should I ask Mom to drive me to the courthouse?" At the word courthouse Jane shuddered. Would she have to go back there? Would it even be open this soon after the bombing? She knew she would end up back at the courthouse in the probate courtroom sooner or later with a client, but just three days from now? Could she do that?

Ansel put his arm around her and pulled her close. He spoke directly into her ear. "I'll still be here Monday morning. I won't need to drop by to pick you up. I put my house on the market the day you left the hospital. I've got my best drum set, in pieces, out in my car. If you said no, I was going to stop by my house to get Annabelle and Bugsy and then leave town. Move back to Buffalo and let a realtor deal with my house. But I was hoping you would say yes and I could set up the drums in your garage."

"Our garage. But put the drum set in the bonus room by the piano, not in the garage."

Ansel's parents managed to get a flight from Buffalo on Sunday, the day before the wedding, and they stayed at Ansel's house. Jane was worried they might be upset by staying in a house with so many reminders of Thea, but they weren't. They were glad Ansel had her collages on the walls. Ansel's parents, although they looked nothing like Ansel, were just like him. Artistic and warm. Jane got along with them immediately. Just like breathing.

When they got to the courthouse on Monday morning, Jane

held back tears as they went through security at the entrance to the courthouse. The lower floors had been checked by building inspectors and reopened to the public a week after the bombing. No one was allowed past the fifth floor. The courtroom was on the second floor but it had a plate glass window and a bench at the end of the corridor just like the tenth floor had on that awful day, and Jane's knees buckled when she saw it. Ansel caught her and asked if she was well enough for the ceremony, or if she wanted to postpone.

"No, I'm ok," Jane said. "It was just seeing that bench and that window. No, really, I'm ok. And Mom is here and Sherri too, and your parents, so let's do this. But I mean, Ansel, you do know that it doesn't matter to me if we do or don't because I love you so much, nothing changes that, it just is. No matter what the judge says or if we just walk away now and live our lives together without a license. You do know that, right?"

"I know, my beautiful Lady Jane, I do know. But if you're ok, let's get in there and get married to each other, for forever, ok?"

Jane needed a little prompting to say "I do" because the ringing was louder when she was nervous or excited and she had trouble understanding the judge. But then the judge pronounced them man and wife and Ansel kissed his bride.

Buried in the law books in the judge's chambers, there was a section of the State Code Jane learned back when she was first studying for the bar. A Code section that had been on her mind a lot when she was agonizing over the difficulties in her relationship with Roy. And even though she didn't think of it that day, it was still there. As the judge pronounced them man and wife, turning Jane into Jane Anne Sidley Kaminski, that particular section of the State Code, on page 241 of volume three of the row of books on the top shelf of the bookshelves nearest the door in the judge's chambers, gave Ansel an easy route to a legal presumption. The legal presumption of fatherhood. He would be legally presumed to be the father of any child born during the marriage. All Ansel needed to do was stay married to Jane until the baby was born and any rights Jeff's relatives might have, if any of them had cared to assert them, which they did not, regarding Jane's unborn child, and any rights Roy might have, would take a back seat to Ansel's presumptive fatherhood.

The ringing stopped, pretty much anyway, after about a month and Jane's hearing gradually improved. She went back to work, with an understanding that she wouldn't be putting in the same long hours, and would spend more time working from home. Helene had trouble not crying every time she saw Jane. And there was a general sense among the support staff that Jane had won a great victory for everyone, as if she'd won an Olympic medal they could all be proud of, just by beating the odds and surviving, when that lunatic bomber had tried to end her life.

Even if they usually wrote songs separately, just making suggestions about each other's songs, living under the same roof was a real boost to Ansel and Jane's songwriting. Ansel put all his feelings, about his days of longing for Jane and not being able to speak up, and then those terrible days after the bombing when he was afraid he'd lose her forever, into his music. But he didn't write flowery love songs. Instead, Ansel put all that emotion into some incredibly powerful dance tunes, recorded with multiple pounding, booming tracks from drum machines. Jane thought the songs were astonishing. They had the mindless, feel-good, big sound any club would want, but they had deeper levels too, that kind of snuck up on the heart strings. Just like Ansel.

Jane had a lot to say in her songs too. About all the fear and pain involved in healing from her injuries and sorrow. After her divorce, Jane felt she was never going to get back to being the person she was before the marriage, and now, even with her injuries healed and her happy life with Ansel, Jane felt she would never be the same as she was before the bomb blast. As frightening as the experience had been, she was actually less fearful as a person now. She had been through the whirlwind and survived. And even when she was under that bench, she hadn't felt alone or lost. She'd been terrified, but God had been with her and her baby every second, she was sure of that. She knew, in a way she hadn't known before, that while things could be pretty scary, even terrifying, there really was no reason to be afraid.

Jane wrote a song 'No Reason to Fear.' She wrote the lyrics so it sounded as if she was writing about two people falling in love, but she knew it was really about trusting God. When she sang it for Ansel, his drums gave it structure. Jane felt she could put her heart into the song without holding anything back and his drums would stay right with her, holding her up even if her heart was breaking from the memories behind the song.

East End recorded some of her songs and Ansel's new dance tunes. They were starting to get a little more buzz about their music, mostly local but some through releasing their music on the internet.

CHAPTER EIGHTEEN

*T*he baby was born in July. A healthy, chubby baby boy. Walker William Kaminski. His middle name was Jane's father's name. How her father would have loved this baby. The baby's first name was after Walker Evans, the American Depression-era photographer. When the nurse asked for the baby's father's name, Jane said Ansel Richard Kaminski.

Ansel stayed with Jane in the delivery room until Sherri and Jane's mother could get to the hospital. Then he gave Jane a kiss and went to the waiting room with her mother, leaving Sherri as the designated coach. Jane had offered Ansel the job of coach, but he was old school about men not being in the delivery room.

The delivery went so quickly that Sherri hardly had a chance to try out all the coaching skills she'd learned. Before they knew it, the baby was crowning. Then he was born. Jane's dream come true. A perfect red faced little baby boy. After a little yelling and cleaning, he settled in to nurse right away. Jane was so tired and so happy. And so grateful to be alive.

Sherri went to get Ansel from the waiting room. Sherri and Jane's mother went out into the hall to make phone calls on their cell phones to everyone they could think to call. Jane, Ansel and their baby were together in the delivery room. Their baby. Not Roy's, not Jeff's. Theirs. The legal presumption settled on Ansel's shoulders the minute Walker entered the world. But legal presumption or not, as Ansel had said back in his garage so many months ago, time spent raising the child was what mattered as a parent. And both Jane and Ansel were overjoyed at the prospect of raising Walker. Walker, their little baby Walker.

Ansel sat on the edge of the bed right next to Jane. The baby was nursing and peace settled over all three of them. He put his arm around her and kissed the top of her head. He kissed the top of the baby's head too.

"You're so amazing," Ansel said. "Look at what you did

today. You brought this beautiful little guy into the world. I am in awe. So amazing, Jane, so amazing, is what you are. I love you so much."

"I love you too." She leaned into Ansel's embrace.

Anita stopped by with flowers. They had security in the maternity wing and wouldn't let Anita go into Jane's room, but she was able to send in the flowers with a note that she couldn't wait to see the baby. Jane appreciated that, and made a mental note to give Anita a call as soon as she was home with the baby. If Anita wanted to be an aunt to the baby, Jane would let her, not because Anita was Roy's sister, but because she was Jane's friend.

Jane had three months of maternity leave with her firm and she wanted to enjoy every minute with her beautiful baby. She was negotiating with her firm to make the part-time schedule she had after the bomb blast, with the understanding that she'd often work from home, into a permanent arrangement. All of the firm files were stored in the computer, and using her cell phone, she didn't think it was necessary to work in the office all the time anyway. Except for client meetings, what difference did it make if she was there or home? Other people were making it work. With the firm's progressive use of technology to unchain their attorneys from their desks, Jane could make it work too.

Sherri was still living with Hauser in her very cramped apartment until he could get through his divorce and recover enough financially to get a bigger place. Hauser's daughters, Meredith and Lindsay, couldn't wait to see the baby. When Walker was two weeks old, Jane invited them over for lunch on a Saturday afternoon.

It was a beautiful summer day, so they had lunch on the deck. Jane didn't worry if Meredith and Lindsay leaned on the railing, as long as they didn't climb on it or lean out too far. Walker was in a baby carrier, dressed in a blue terrycloth onesie, with a light blanket over his legs. Jane had peanut butter and jelly sandwiches for the girls along with a fruit salad, green salad, rye bread and cold cuts. She'd made herbal iced tea and had a six pack of beer in a cooler. Ansel made a run to a nearby grocery store and returned with a chocolate cake and ice cream.

The day was warm but not too hot and the deck was a mix of

sunny spots and shade from the overhanging trees. Jane's hearing was pretty good these days and the ringing was completely gone. Other than some trouble hearing conversations in restaurants, crowds and places where there was a lot of background noise, she didn't even think about it anymore. Her shrapnel wounds had completely healed, without infection, despite the filthy nails and other bits of metal the bomber put in the explosives. She still had scars on her back, but they would fade if she avoided getting too much sun on them this summer.

"Walker has quite a head of dark hair," Sherri said. Ansel had taken the girls down to the yard to get butterfly nets he'd bought for them.

"If you're hinting about the paternity test," Jane said, "I haven't done it. I'm not going to do it unless Roy calls and insists on it. And I haven't heard from him. Not when I was in the hospital after the bomb blast and not since Walker was born. Anita has been over several times to see the baby. I think she wants to be a part of Walker's life. That's fine with me because other than you, Auntie Sherri, Walker doesn't have any aunts since I don't have any siblings and Ansel's sister passed away years ago. But no word from Roy. Not even one phone call. Anita hasn't said anything about him and I'm sure not going to ask."

"Are you sorry if he doesn't want to be in Walker's life?"

"No, glad really," Jane said. "Walker has parents. Two of them who love him. Right here. If Roy insisted on the test, and turned out to be the biological father, I'd let him have visitation rights. In fact, if he said he wanted visitation without the test, I'd say ok. And I know Ansel would understand. But if not, if he just doesn't want any part of this, that's ok too. Even better, really."

"Are you going to tell Walker someday that Ansel is not his biological father?"

"Yeah, when he's older. Then it'll be his choice if he wants to see if he's related to Roy, or even J.J."

"Oh yeah, J.J. could be his half brother. I forgot about that. Complicated."

"Is it? Is it complicated for you with Meredith and Lindsay?"

"It was at first, but it gets simpler and better every day. Time, it's the time I spend with them that makes it simpler. Every day it's easier. I know them and they know me. Being with them is getting to be just like breathing, I guess."

"Can we have the cake and ice cream now?" Meredith was shouting from the yard.

"Ok with you?" Sherri said

"Yeah, sure," Jane said, "I could use a little cake and ice cream."

Ansel and the girls came back out on the deck. Ansel went over to Walker in his baby carrier.

"He's a little drummer boy," Ansel said. "That's what we've got here. My son is a little drummer boy. I can tell. He'll grow up to be just like me."

Jane reached for Ansel's hand.

OTHER ANAPHORA LITERARY PRESS TITLES

British Literature
Pennsylvania Literary Journal
Summer 2010
Edited by: Anna Faktorovich
1-4563-0432-1; paperback; 208 pp.

New and Old Historical Perspectives on Literature
Pennsylvania Literary Journal
Winter 2010
Edited by: Anna Faktorovich
1-4505-8358-X; paperback; 272 pp.

http://sites.google.com/site/pennsylvaniajournal
Submissions Welcome: pennsylvaniajournal@gmail.com
Director: Anna Faktorovich

8064073R0